Igniting the Ice

A Flaming Rogues Novel

Igniting the Ice

Alexa Whitewolf

To Mom, for teaching me that good things are worth waiting for, and bad things don't have to keep you down.

Glossary

Yeps, again with the Romanian "how the hell do I say this word" :)

Legătură, or the binding - leh-guh-tuh-rah
Împerechere, or the pairing - ihm-peh-reh-ke-re
Frate, or brother - frah-teh
Da/nu, or yes/no - dah/nuh
Zmeu/zmei, or Romanian dragon shifters - zh-mehu
Balaur, another type of shifter - bah-lah-uhr
Sânziene, or lady's bedstraw flowers - sunh-zee-eh-neh
Draga mea, or my dear/darling - drah-gah meh-ah
Mama, or Mom - mah-mah
Tuică, or... Romanian alcohol you don't want to try unless you have a strong stomach (I happen to like it!) - tsh-uh-y-kah
Trădător, or traitor - trah-duh-tor
Ileana and *Făt Frumos*, or Prince Charming* - E-lya-nah and Fuh-th
*They're heroes of lore in Romanian folklore :)

Happy readings, Alexa

"What strange creatures brothers are!"
~Jane Austen~

Prologue

Tytus

Long ago, two brothers were born, heirs to an obsolete legacy. They were strong, they were grand, and meant to do many beautiful things.

But somewhere along the line, they lost their way. Some say it was due to a prophecy that tainted their sibling bond, and caused one to be Light, and the other Dark. Others say it was because of their rivalry, period.

That is nowhere near the accurate story. The truth, as always, lies somewhere in between.

Declan and I *were* meant to be great. To

bring our kin into the future, to lead the way to a new beginning for the zmei. Until we lost our way, and each other. Until we turned against one another, and our only focus became vengeance.

My story was told, and in it, I found my one and only. My truest mate. The love of my life, the half of my soul. Our journey was nowhere easy, not with Declan in the shadows, feeding on our sorrow. But we made it through.

And now, it is time to tell the other side… the darker side. And while it is dark, there is also light at the end of this particular tunnel.

I never thought I'd find my happily ever after. But I did. And despite what my brother has caused, I want to believe he can find his.

This is not my story, it is unequivocally Declan's. But we are as intrinsically intertwined by our fates as only two brothers can be.

Chapter 1

Sfârșit
"New beginnings are often disguised as painful <u>endings</u>."
-Lao Tzu-

Declan

What a fucking bore.

Humans love to speak of a lion pacing in a cage. Well, how about taking that lion, super-sizing it a few dozen times, tossing it in a cavern deep into the mountains, and seeing how well it does?

Da, not very well, as one may guess. Claustrophobic, more like.

My black diamond-shaped tail twitches from side to side of the cavern, swishing past the gold and treasure buried with me here. Ileana's idea of a joke–she's the immortal who imprisoned me. Her consort and my brother aided her, but that is beside the point.

The point is I'm stuck, imprisoned, and alone.

And my zmeu form has stopped being comforting, instead it only makes the area even more claustrophobic.

What a fucking life.

Da, one could argue I chose said life. Or, rather, that my choices led me to it, and this is my penance for those mistakes.

My massive head drops on the ground, and the soft puff of blue smoke escaping my nostrils reminds me of the power in my gut. Of roiling fire, blazing flames, and complete destruction. It is that same power that has brought me to where I am now.

Or was it the human I so stupidly fell in love with, in my youth?

Both, my zmeu chastises. He is not pleased with me lately.

It used to be we were one and the same.

But if I'm truthful to myself, it has been a long, long time since my zmeu and I have seen eye to eye. He is my impulsive, raw side, the primal part of me I cannot go without. And yet, lately, it seems my human side has lost its way, while the zmeu tries to tug us back into some semblance of a straight line.

Rather than listen to more berating from him, I let the change come over me. Flames encompass my zmeu form in all its dragon-sized mass, burning it until my human form steps from within, unharmed.

My body is completely naked, and I run a hand through my hair. It's shorter now–I cropped it after landing here, while I still had a modicum of magic at my disposal. Boredom at its utmost. I wish now I'd used those moments for other things... like scheming.

Still, as my wrists rise with the movement, the manacles around them draw my attention. And scowl.

They look like the gaudy golden bangles humans love, or the ones placed around a genie. Only, it wasn't so much a master as a mistress who placed them on me, ensuring I cannot touch the primordial magic deep within me. Not while I'm here.

Instead, I'm meant to simply... exist.

I would have escaped, had it not been for my brother Tytus and his newfound mate. And the plan they ruined for me, the one I'd had all figured out.

Igor, a balaur, was supposed to destroy Tytus, then help me open the gate to the Underworld. We would resurrect our fallen zmei brethren and storm Olympus, taking our rightful place as heirs of the skies–and the world.

Only thing is, I didn't count on Igor being a *trădător*–a damned traitor, even more crazy than the wolves I tried to control not long ago. I'd started this entire journey of vengeance thinking one witch's subservience to me, however coerced, would give me what I desired. And it did. Only, I made the mistake of choosing minions–wolf shifters–who were completely overrun by pack fights and inherited greediness. Not a pleasant mix, as far as the supernatural world goes.

When that went wrong, I had a back-up plan. Nestled deep in the Carpathian Mountains, in my ancestral home, it was meant to

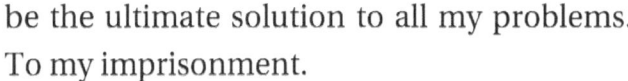

be the ultimate solution to all my problems. To my imprisonment.

It was not.

And in the end it had been Igor, not me, that led the charge. He had his own plan, and I was only a pawn.

Worse, though, I found out how much he had played me.

My hand clenches on air at the reminder. How I wish I could have wrought the final deadly blow on Igor, for all that he put me through, and all that he caused. I was in my brother Tytus' mind, connected with him, and we both worked together to win. But I still crave the satisfaction of his death by my hands.

And while on the subject of being played, my mind can't help drifting off to Alina. My ex-wife. The only human to ever have ensnared me, and ripped me apart more than anyone else ever had. Not even my brother's betrayal and condemnation hurt as much as hers.

I'm not proud of how I reacted when I found out. There had been many options, but only death won in my darkened heart. And only death and destruction has lived there, since.

Until lately. For the first time ever, my

thoughts have been focused on someone else. I helped my brother defeat Igor, and it has even led to his promise to get me out of here.

But he is mistaken if he thinks I did it for the sake of being a hero. My aid with Igor was only because of hate, because of a thirst for vengeance that overtook every impulse.

Did it make me miss the old times with Tytus? Da, it did. But I am not disillusioned enough that I believe we can go back to what once was.

With a sigh, I drop on a cot at the back of the room, and put on the pants Ileana so graciously gave me. In the past, I was able to conjure everything I needed, but that stubborn immortal has ensured such is not possible. No longer.

The ceiling zeroes in on me, or perhaps I zero in on it. Hard to say, with how long I have spent here. With no one to talk to, no one to bother, is it any wonder I've resulted to daydreams?

As if to spite me, the smell of violets permeates the air, and I close my eyes. She appears as consistently as ever, my very own goddess. And if she is all I am allowed here, I will gladly enjoy her.

A smirk replaces my bored look, and I open my arms wide as she runs into them.

"Declan!"

Her limber legs wrap around my waist, and I twirl us around. The fullness of her breasts, the tightness of her ass in my hands, it creates the usual response from me.

She pulls slightly away, glancing between us. "My, someone's glad to see me." Her twinkling blue gaze meets mine, and I nibble on those full lips, unable to resist any further.

Within hours of being imprisoned here, I started hearing laughter and voices. It drove me insane for days. And then, one night, *she* appeared in my dreams, as real as if I had conjured her. She took one look at me, and one thing led to another... The second time I saw her turned into a night that blew my mind, in more ways than one.

And in the morning I woke up yearning for more—only she vanished. I was forced to realize it had been a dream. Yet, two days later, it happened again. And again. Since I've been here, she has become a staple in my days and nights, making my fictional world much more appealing than reality.

I only know her as Connie. She is a fixation of my imagination, something my brain conjured to take my thoughts away from the past, from my loneliness.

But she is the perfect distraction. To touch her, to taste her, definitely makes me stop thinking of anything else. And a little pleasure, after all the hell and boredom I have endured for centuries on end, is exactly what I deserve.

As if to remind me I'm ignoring her, Connie wiggles in my arms and starts kissing down my throat, then my chest. A groan escapes me, and before long I've got her under me, teasing her to the ends of the universe and back... It's bound to be a gorgeous night, indeed.

Yet something changes in the air, pulling me out of my daydream. Unsure, yet intrigued, I lift my head off the bed and sniff around. Nothing.

Perhaps I was mistaken.

Incredibly bored, I sink back into the cot. Connie is gone, the fleeting image of her in my mind and the taste of her on my lips the only reminder she was ever there. It's crazy how real dreams can be, when you focus all your energy on them.

I remember the first time she'd shown up. It was smack in the middle of my plot against Tytus, and I'd been waiting for him to catch the bait and head off to the Carpathian Mountains. I was pacing the cave length from corner to corner, then decided on something that changed the course of my next weeks–I took a nap.

Within moments of closing my eyes, the scent of fresh mountains and violets hits me so strongly, I think I'm back home. And for a moment, I am. Not quite near the castle, but in a valley nearby, surrounded by snowy peaks and fields upon fields of grass and trees and nature.

I toss my head back, staring at the pure azure sky, picturing myself flying far, far into the clouds, and beyond. Not tethered to this world anymore.

And then the floral smell increases, and a voice tinkles on the wind.

"You look sad."

I turn around, surprised to be taken unawares, and my jaw nearly hits the ground. A gorgeous nymph stands facing me, her locks of blonde hair twirling in the breeze, her blue eyes an exact mirror of the sky. A full, pouty mouth extends in a smile, and she tilts her head to the side.

"Do you not speak?"

The utter delight in her tone snaps me out of my daze, and I clear my throat. "Da, of course I speak."

My voice comes out hoarser than intended, and my eyes trail up and down her body unashamedly. She's wearing a robe the color of her eyes, and it leaves no curve to the imagination.

"Hmm," she says and takes a step further, as if to leave.

I cannot allow that. *The thought is sudden, and I'm moving before I can change my mind. "Who are you?"*

Twinkling eyes meet mine. "Friends call me Connie."

My charm hits full force then, and I grin. "Shall I be counted among them?"

A tilt of the head, a coy look, and she graces

me with another smile. "We'll see."

🐗

I snap out of the memory. My human body is too wired, too eager now, and I let out a sigh, followed by an annoyed growl. I get off the bed and shift back to my zmeu form, letting the flames consume my body until it is no more, replaced instead by the beast.

As a zmeu, my head easily reaches the ceiling of my cell, and my black scales help me blend in with the darkness. Unlike Tytus, who blows regular flames, mine are blue, and spread a cooling fire. Our flames answer the primordial magic inside us, and despite Tytus being the calmer of us both, it is the color of passion that manifests for him, and that of ice for me.

Normally, the fire I can create destroys anything in my path, but no matter how many times I tried, it still has not helped me get out of this immortal prison.

One would imagine living permanently in my zmeu form would be comfortable, and offer heat, at least. And one would be correct.

Yet I also miss the human, and it is what

causes me to alternate, time and time again. See, as a Romanian dragon, I'm a shifter. Among many, *many* abilities, I can use primordial magic to the point of becoming a storm myself. Instead of achieving all I could, here I am, once more imprisoned by a witch's hand, all thanks to my dear, fucking brother.

Tytus.

Since I helped him, memories of our times as kids will not stop assailing me. It takes my every moment of being awake, my every will, to push them away. And still, much as I want to hate him, to hate he was not there for me when I needed him most, part of me cannot stop remembering.

Eons ago, we were brothers.

Eons ago, we were friends.

We would have done anything for one another... Back then, at least. And if I close my eyes, I can still see it...

❦

"Declan!"

I cringe at my brother's loud yell, ducking under the table in the kitchens. With a bit of luck, he'll pass by without thinking to look under the massive wooden table.

Alas, such is not my luck.

No sooner do his footsteps echo on the cold cement, that Tytus follows me underneath. His eyes narrow on my curled up form. Yet no matter how angry he tries to be, there is an answering mischievous glint in his glare.

"Where did you hide it?"

I gulp. "Hide what?"

He crawls across the stone floor, barely a few inches away. He's taller, the eldest by a few days only. And he makes sure to never let me forget it.

"You know what! Father's sword, Dec."

"Don't know what you're talking about." I tear my gaze from his and focus on the floor instead.

My mutters make no sense, nor do they push Tytus away. Instead, he laughs and tugs on my wrist until we're out from our hiding spot.

Once we straighten, he claps me on the back. "Lighten up, Dec! I thought you wanted to test its strength, no?"

I meet his gaze then, my own wide with anticipation. "Really?"

He nods, solemnly. "Da. It is what Father would have wanted. For us to know the art of true, honorable swordsmanship."

I'm already bouncing on my toes. "So you'll teach me?"

"Of course." He grins. "If you can catch me first!"

I take off running after him, my squeal of indignation drowned by his own laughter.

Those were easy times, back then. Too damn easy. Before it all went wrong, before...

A growl escapes me, reverberating in the cavern. *Patience. Soon enough, you'll get out of here.*

When I shift to a more comfortable position, the massive gold cuffs around my claws catch the dim light of the torches.

And then... It happens again. The air changes, and the scent of cinnamon permeates it fully. My eyes open once more, landing on my hated jailor–the immortal Ileana.

What now?

Constanza

"Connie, why are you blushing?"

I blink, my stare falling on the inky sky of the Underworld. The warmth in my cheeks is a telltale sign of my embarrassment. And darn, but my body is humming with the energy only Declan can instill.

"You have that look again."

I focus on my friend, pushing away some blonde waves out of my face. Persephone's violet eyes, a darker shade than mine, are twinkling with mirth and too much enjoyment. It's a reminder of the fun we always have, and the reason I'm spending more and more time here, versus the world above–the Living.

"What look?" I ask innocently.

She rolls her eyes, not fooled in the least. "You know which one, silly. Was it your nightly suitor again?"

I've never told Persephone his name, but she's caught me staring and blushing one too many times to hide the entire affair. Fantasy. Whichever.

The blush burns my cheeks now, and I

focus on the grass underneath me, pretending I'm picking marigolds. They feel too soft in my hands, almost unreally so.

"No suitor," I mutter. "And keep your voice low, would you? This place has many ears."

She glances around, noticing some wayward souls in the distance. They're easy to differentiate from the other creatures of the Underworld, what with their glowing forms.

What most people don't realize is each soul is, actually, different. Depending on the strength of their personality from their living days, some may have kept their memories, and others have become a shell of their former selves. The former have brighter glows and are almost corporeal–can be touched– versus the latter, who are more like the ghosts in human stories.

"You still think your parents are using them to spy on you?" Persephone asks.

The amusement in her tone makes my lip twitch. But truth be told. I'd seen a few too many of the dead pause by us, listening in to our conversations. My parents cannot enter the Underworld–something related to Hades and their past–but they do have influence.

Once upon a time, immortals used to protect the gods. But then they all retired, since humans were forgetting them, and now immortals are without a job. My parents have found new entertainment–I know Mom loves watching over a pack of wolves somewhere–but most of them simply, well, exist.

And I'm one of them. Yay, pointlessly eternal existence.

It's my turn to roll my eyes. "Have you met them? I don't think. I *know* they are."

Persephone goes back to the flower she's trying to use magic on. Unlike her husband, Hades, she possesses no godly powers other than the biggest heart I've come across. It's not unusual for some gods to have divine essence, yet no magic to speak of. Sometimes it's buried, waiting for the right moment–or the right incentive–to be coaxed out. And, sometimes, it just never manifests itself.

Still, Persephone tries, and her consort is always afraid she'll do something to hurt herself.

I don't blame him, knowing my clumsy friend. And too many times, I indulge her whims, even if they lead us in little escapades further into the land of the forbidden–the parts of the Underworld not sanctioned by Hades. My own magic is easily used, and our brief tutoring lessons give me a brilliant excuse to be down here.

My thoughts go back to Declan, and his hands on me. We'd been about to get into a very interesting part of the dream, but then it stopped. My mind probably got distracted with Persephone's incessant calling of my name and it shattered my concentration. *Sigh.*

I'm not sure what of my dreams is real, and what is not. The first few times, I thought for sure Declan was a figment of my imagination. But when I continued waking up more and more relaxed, as if I'd truly indulged in night-long sexy adventures with someone, I started wondering if maybe, just maybe, he might be real.

I still haven't figured it out. And, to be honest, it's probably better this way. If he is, it's uncomplicated. Our chemistry answers both our needs, our darkest desires. And lets us move on, free to do as we please. And if he's not real, well, my parents can't accuse me of tainting my innocence, can they?

Either way, I'll have to wait for tonight to continue, and see if I can tease him out of hiding again.

"Constanza!"

I cringe at the loud booming voice. Part of me wants to cower away, and the other part, well... I share a mischievous glance with my best friend. "Oops."

She rolls her violet eyes and stands from the grass. We'd been fooling around in the gardens near Lethe–again. It was my idea, even knowing Hades hates it when we linger here, on account of the dangers involved.

Lethe is one of five rivers in the Underworld, and one drink from its silvery depths will have any mortal forget their past lives, and be reincarnated in a new existence. It's a privilege only allowed to the purest of souls. As for immortals, well, that same drink would also affect us. It would make us lose our immortality and be reborn again–as mortals. Not that many know this.

One wonders why I'd be so close to it, given its dangers. But it's one of the quieter spots here, and it allowed for the perfect practice spot for Persephone, at least until I fell asleep... Plus, something about the silver river calls to me, and not in order to drink from it. It's just... pretty.

Still, given I'm Hades' long-standing guest, I really should pay more attention to his instructions. It's not like he's a control freak–much.

"Constanza!" He calls again, this time closer.

Persephone flicks a lock of her dark brown hair and winks at me. "I'll take care of this. But, um, perhaps go for a lengthy walk, yeah?"

With a grin and an air-blown kiss, I take off under some bushes. Hades' voice echoes behind me, followed by Persephone's softer murmur as she calms him down. She knows he's afraid of losing her to the depths of the Underworld, that is all. Which, in a way, is super romantic–the fact he loves her enough not to let go, not the other part.

I wish I had someone like that. It would make eternity less lonely, less boring.

The thought lingers, not unlike previous times. It's becoming more frequent lately. Mom and Dad leave me be, I mean after all

I'm immortal and have the rest of eternity ahead of me to find someone. No one's in a rush, and to some extent they prefer I'm spending my time with Persephone, rather than hunting for a consort.

Plus, immortals are known for being ice queens–or kings–and not giving in to emotions. Somehow, I think finding a soulmate would defy the purpose of emotional growth. It may have worked for my parents–by the grace of the gods, they've been together for millennia!–but who's to say it can for me?

Still, a girl has needs… And it's getting bad enough that my dreams are pulling me under. Sexy, sexy dreams of a blond god with eyes of molten gold. A god of pleasure, truly, because from the first touch he made me crazy. And he still does after all these times, to the point I'd even call it an addiction.

I lick my lips at the reminder, and suddenly, I'm wondering if it's too early for another nap.

If I'm lucky, I'll see Declan again. There's no harm in dreaming, right?

Chapter 2

Oportunități
"Victory comes from finding <u>opportunities</u> in problems."

Declan

One could say Ileana Cosânzeana is a peculiar immortal. With her flowing brown hair, eyes like the sun and garments made of flowers, she could be Spring personified. Yet there is a cold, calculating glint in her eyes when they settle on me.

In truth, our paths never should have crossed. Long ago, when the gods kicked us zmei out of the skies, and preferred immortals to be their champions, the paths of zmei and immortals split, never to converge again. Then there were the bloody wars between our kin, all of them leading to a horrid history of destruction.

Well, not so horrid, after all. I dare say I would have enjoyed beheading a few immortals–especially if her consort, Făt Frumos, was part of them. A snarkier being cannot have existed.

Yet ultimately, nothing should have put Ileana in my path. I did not foresee her, and I have been cursed with a Sight that is never wrong. Yet this immortal was never on my radar.

Until too late, that is. By the time I realized what was happening, I'd been left with only enough time to set the plan into motion, listen to Igor's advice, and let myself be captured.

Igor. Thoughts of that bastard leave an acidic taste in my mouth. How many centuries did I waste, consumed by hate for my brother, because of Igor's machinations? How many useless years did I guilt myself, over my inability to control my emotions and fall for the wrong woman? And how many times did I swear to myself, repeatedly, that I would never be in such a position again?

I force away the useless emotions, putting them back in their neat little box. For now, at least, they need to remain there, not churn and distract me. Instead, I watch the Romanian witch approach me.

"Would you morph to human for this conversation? It would make it much easier."

I snort and turn my head away. She waits a beat, two, then adds, "Please?"

If only because of my boredom, I humor her and shift forms, leaving my human one naked. Ileana is not fazed in the least, looking me up and down and arching an eyebrow.

"Is this supposed to intimidate me? Make me uncomfortable? Your childish games are tiring, Declan."

"Childish?" I pace to a wall and lean against it, crossing my legs at the ankles. "Do I look like a child?"

Ileana rolls her eyes. "Nu. You look like a Greek god, which I'm sure suits you. However, I'm not here to stroke your ego."

"I don't suppose your consort would like

if you stroked my *anything*," I purr, intent on baiting her until she loses her cool.

Her gaze widens, then lightning flashes in it. Ah, yes. Despite her impassable façade, I have pushed Ileana to the brink. These last few weeks, especially, as Igor drained her and Făt of their energies. Not that they didn't deserve it, the bastards.

"I will not tolerate your insolence," Ileana hisses, crossing closer to me.

She's a tiny thing, really. Her head barely reaches my shoulders, but her presence is something else. If I didn't have the damned cuffs around my wrists, we wouldn't have an issue. As it is, I'm not about to start a fight I cannot win.

"Yes, yes." I roll my eyes. "Heavens forbid I insult the immortals."

For a moment, I think she's about to hit me. Then she draws a deep breath and expels it harshly. "Are you done being an utter child? May I continue with my actual purpose here?"

"Do tell." My sarcasm fills the space between us.

"I have a proposition. One that might get you out of this place."

I arch an eyebrow. "And what's in it for me?"

"Do you not wish to hear the proposal first?"

The surprise in her tone is worth it. As if I'm a puppy desperate for anything she may throw my way? I think not.

"No. Tell me the reward."

She clenches her fists, blowing out an annoyed breath. "Very well. I–we–have need of you. Your zmeu abilities give you an edge, one that will be useful. In short, I need you to get something back for me, and in exchange your reward is freedom. Your own realm, if you so wish. Away from here."

Trepidation blooms through my chest, but I make it a point to keep my tone neutral. She doesn't need to know how bored I am, or how desperate for freedom. And there are one too many vague statements in the proposal for me to get too excited.

"Interesting. And where is it I'm supposed to wander off to?"

"The Underworld."

Hades' world? What in the hell would an immortal need from there?

A shiver of foreboding races up my spine, and I sense the hairs at my nape rising like a cat's, ready to hiss and claw. The Underworld–Igor had wanted access. To free our dead brethren, to capture Hades, and force our way into Olympus. Demand our rightful place.

I had never thought past the actual thing, past killing Tytus and following his soul to the Underworld... Now, it seems my past is about to catch up with me.

How very interesting, indeed.

I frown then, trying to see through Ileana's act. "If you want this thing so badly, why don't you go there yourself?"

"It's not a thing. It's a *person*. And I cannot go for reasons of my own." The way she looks away tells me more than she will out loud. "Are you, or aren't you, interested?"

"Hmm." I move past her, stretching and shrugging my shoulders as I pace the length of my cell.

Gold coins glitter under my feet, clinking with each step. I can feel her trepidation, and it makes the game that much more interesting.

"Go to the Underworld, retrieve a person

for you, and escort them out... Seems simple enough. Are they dead?"

Ileana shakes her head. "Nu. Very much alive."

It's my turn to be surprised. "What in hell would a living person be doing in the land of the dead?"

She pinches the bridge of her nose, letting out a frustrated groan. Just as quickly, she collects herself and stands tall and regal once more. "None of your business."

"It is, if you want me to go there. I need to know what I'm getting myself into."

A short laugh escapes her. "Do you not think it a tad late, to be worrying about becoming entangled in situations outside your control?"

Touché. Out loud, I say, "Not in the least, my darling immortal. Either answer my questions, or you can take your proposal out the door."

She stares at me, for all intents and purposes, like she'd rather throttle me. But in the end, she says, "This person, she is there on vacation."

"On *vacation*?"

Ileana taps her foot, annoyance oozing

from every pore. "Da, not all beings are as judgmental as you are, zmeu. This particular person has formed friendships down below. As for bringing her back up, it should be an easy feat."

"Hmm. So you keep saying. If she's there for leisure, why not wait until the *vacation* ends?"

Ileana narrows her eyes. "After what you did? I think not. Your brother and his witch may stick to their story that Igor only wanted to take over your minds, but on the off chance they are wrong... I will not wait any longer."

How touching. Tytus kept his mouth shut and didn't backstab me when he had the chance.

I'm being unfair. Truth be told, thanks to the witch Fiona, who is now his mate, I've recently found out how my hate had been unjustified. At least, partly. It still comes as a surprise that when given the chance, Tytus chose to actually stick up for me.

Ileana's words also remind of the balaur Igor's last words. *What we began, cannot be stopped.* I'd always thought he and I were in the scheming together. Since we weren't, and he had other plans, it's not such a crazy thought to believe his plan was bigger than even I knew. *Da, perhaps there is something here, after all.*

Ileana grows impatient with my silence and snaps. "Well? Do you accept?"

Rather than answer, I counter with another question. "After what I just did to you, you're willing to roll over and reward me?" Flashes of lightning fill her eyes. "Da, I thought as much. No, thank you."

I pace to the other end of my extended cell, averting my gaze from her so she gets the message and leaves.

"You can play hard to get, but I see through you. We both know this is an opportunity that will not present itself again."

"Perhaps." I turn to her. "But you're the one coming to me. *You* need this. I, on the other hand, do not."

"Ah. I understand." Ileana smiles then, but there is nothing warm about it. Odd, given she is supposed to be the white witch of the Carpathian Mountains, the ever-present *good* heroine.

"Still under the illusion you have control?"

Her features are rigid as a statue, and the next bit rolls off her tongue like the sweetest venom. "Let me make it clear. If you do not do this for me, I will make your eternity hell."

"More than it already is?"

"Extremely."

With one last incensed glare my way, she disappears in a flurry of flowers, and the cell door slams shut. Her minor threats don't bother me in the least. How bad could eternity be here, when I have such splendid company?

As I've done many times before, I push aside my annoyance and lack of control at my imprisonment, and instead focus on what I *can* control. Like the second time I'd seen Connie, something I vividly remember as I lean my head back and close my eyes.

I'm back in the field, this time not alone. Connie is dancing in the wind like a sprite, uncaring of anything and everyone. I envy that innocence— I want to possess it. It takes no genius to figure out why my mind created her… And who am I to fight my subconsciousness?

When she spins and sees me, she comes to an abrupt stop. Her lips part, and I don't hesitate. I was never a schoolboy, nor will I start now. In three strides I'm facing her, and I draw her against my body.

She gasps in surprise, and her body melts against mine. Head tilted back, she looks at me as if knowing exactly what's going through my mind.

"Thought I wouldn't see you again," she says.

"Oh, you'll be seeing much of me, darling."

Without giving her a chance to respond, I drop my mouth to hers in a kiss I meant cajoling.

Despite my best intentions, fire sings in our veins the moment our lips meet. With a pent-up desire I wasn't aware of, I savor her mouth, taste every recess, wanting to take it, to own something so beautiful, so innocent.

Connie is mine. She may be a dream, but this particular dream is mine.

And with that thought in mind, I let myself drop to my back, and she falls atop me, squealing and laughing. Her hair cascades all around me, and I cup both her cheeks, locking my gaze with hers.

"What do you say we make this interesting, darling?"

She smiles, and playfully turns to my palm, biting the padded flesh of a thumb. "It is a dream, after all... And I do love a game. What did you have in mind?"

One shift of my hips and her eyes widen, catching on to my meaning when my hardness is nestled between her thighs. The moment after she dips her mouth to mine, teasing my lips, before finally giving in to a kiss.

Our first joining is hard, and fast. Clothes moved out of the way, moans of passion, cries of ecstasy... It's a release that leaves us panting in each other's arms, our limbs still intertwined together.

A release that when I woke up, was still very much there... And has been ever since.

I open my eyes, staring at the ceiling. *Da, eternity with these dreams as company cannot be so bad, surely.*

Constanza

Hours after my near-run in with Hades, my

luck runs out. I'm sneaking back into his palace, intending to head straight to my room–quarters, as he calls them.

Hades' home is carved out of a mountain. The tallest mountain in the Underworld, to be precise. And it glints obsidian black under the waning artificial moon, a creation of the master himself. Half of the peak looks like they cut it off, and replaced it instead with half of a palace. Large, black towers, windows that reflect the same waning light, an utterly enchanting and gothic structure all at once. All manners of minerals and semi-precious stones decorate the inside. Black marble floors, granite walls in the bathrooms, chandeliers glinting with quartz or amethysts. Most of it is Persephone's work, I'm sure.

The other half of the castle is *in* the mountain itself, carved carefully and patiently through the structure. That is what houses Hades' quarters, while the guests, servants and guards are on the outer edge.

Each year I return here, I find fresh changes. This time around, they added a new library near the primary entrance, decorated in dark burgundy and furs. I've seen Hades have meetings there a few times, and today is no exception.

As I enter the palace, my feet bring me past it and I hear voices. Hades, and someone else.

"… impossible to ignore, now. Have you been able to connect with Cerberus?"

My footsteps falter, and before I realize it, I find myself eavesdropping on a private conversation.

"No, sire. When my men tried, he attacked."

"Then I wish to speak with Charon directly."

An awkward pause, and I peek past the open door. Hades is tense, facing a massive fireplace. His clenched fist on the dark marble seems close to breaking it. Beside him, on bended knee, is a satyr.

Part human, part goat, these creatures are about a head shorter than most humans and run everywhere around the Underworld. Most of them are alive, but shunned by the outside worlds. Hades granted them refuge here eons ago, and they have served him ever since. Some prepare meals, others are in charge of security, and some, like this one, spy for Hades. Their hooved feet can be heard a mile away, and their horned goat-like heads have more than once acted in good defense.

This particular satyr, I've seen before, but I can't recall his name. He's definitely one of Hades' favorite errand boys, though.

So what is he doing here?

I focus back on the conversation. There's an uncomfortable silence as the satyr tries to figure out a way to answer Hades' request without angering him.

Charon, the one they mentioned, is the guy with the boat who protects the entrance of the Underworld. I run into him every time I come here, and each time he freaks me out more than the last.

"Sire, I tried," the satyr finally says and bows his head. "Charon refused."

"You, or me?" There is an ominous undertone in Hades' voice. I've heard him annoyed before, but this is more than that. It's threatening.

The satyr seems to pick up on it, as he cowers further into his slouch. "I... can try again, sire."

"Do not bother. Capture him and drag him on his knees before me. I will handle it."

My eyes widen. This new, darker tone Hades uses is one I've never heard. He's been on the verge of angry previously, but there was always some control that kept him from lashing out. He is seen as kind and generous by the souls and satyrs here. Persephone herself has more than once described him as a big bear with a heart of gold.

This, however, is not a side of him I would ever intend to cross.

"As you wish." The satyr interrupts my thoughts and gets up. "What of Persephone, sire? Should I warn her?"

"No, there is no need to worry her just yet. Soon... but not yet."

As the satyr moves to the exit, I'm not fast enough. He catches sight of me, and freezes. Hades doesn't even look my way, only sighs.

"Come in, Constanza."

Once the satyr leaves and closes the door behind us, we're alone. I hesitate to approach him, sensing his mood nearing an explosion.

"How much did you hear?"

"The end part only." I should keep quiet, say nothing more, but my mouth runs off without me. "Something's wrong, isn't it?"

"Yes. A little *too* wrong."

I think back to what the satyr said. "And it's connected to Charon?"

"It is, yes." Hades' eyes meet mine, for a flicker of a second. It's too fast for me to figure out the depth of his current mood, but enough to realize this is serious.

"Why not tell Persephone?"

His hold on the fireplace mantle tightens. "When you love someone as I love her, you try to protect them. Make their days happy. I will fix this, and if I fail, I alone will speak to her. In the meantime, please do not share what you have heard with her."

It's his use of *please* that makes me agree. I've never seen him so dejected, or at the end of his wits. This is the lord of the Underworld, sibling to Zeus. *Dejected* is simply not a word that one would associate with him.

I turn to leave, intending to allow him some privacy, but he calls out to me again.

"Earlier, I was looking for you."

I cringe like a child caught in a destructive act. "Right, about that, I–"

Before I can continue, his next words stun me. "Your mother entered my realm. Did you have anything to do with it?"

"What? No! I didn't even see her."

Mom was here? And didn't even drop by to say hi? Her antics shouldn't hurt me, but somehow, they do. Last time I'd asked, she admitted being unable to enter the Underworld anymore, saying something was blocking her. Obviously, that's not true.

Hades rubs his jaw, as perplexed by my answer as I am, it seems. "Very well. Thank you, you may leave now."

I rush out before he can change his mind, and run up the marble stairs, not stopping until I'm panting at the doors of my chambers. I push on the dark wood and step inside, inhaling deeply. A bouquet winks at me from the center table. One of the servants must have left fresh lilacs in here.

They are my favorite flower, and their scent soothes me more often than not. Even as I go about taking off my clothes, and leaning on the side of the massive tub by the balcony, my mind is downstairs, with Hades and what just happened.

My eyes take in the lightly decorated room, in off-violet tones and darker furs.

Persephone made sure it was comfortable, yet luxurious, and it's part of yet another set of reasons I feel more at home here than... elsewhere.

With a touch of my hand, the water in the tub boils. I open a small jar of cream and pour it in the water, knowing it'll create the bubbles I so love. Then I sink into the warm depths, soaking in pure bliss. Wouldn't it be nice if the entire world solved its own problems?

Yet my thoughts keep churning. Unlike me, really. I grew up in times of peace, and thus I have been sheltered. Even spoiled. I take no shame in it, or in the fact I always see the world through rose-colored glasses. I much prefer this way of life to being dragged down by negativity all day long.

And yet, tonight, my mood is very unlike my usual self. Not even the bath relaxes me, and by the time I get out and dry off, then lie on my satin-covered bed, my muscles are very much still tense.

Perhaps Declan will visit me again tonight....

Declan

Hands stir my hair, then move down my skin, tracing it lightly. The sun hits me, adding to the warmth already spreading through me. None as much as the tempting touches causing my body to tighten.

When the hands move lower, I steal a glance through half-lidded eyes. Blonde hair tumbles all around me, pouty lips trail a fiery path down my chest, then lower, and lower.

My hand fists in her hair, and I stop her progress with a gentle tug. "Mm, good evening to you, too."

Connie peers at me, not moving from her precarious position. Her blue eyes shine, darkened by lust and desire. The same echoes within me. My turbulent emotions of the day don't matter. Not when she's here, my little fictive vixen that blows my mind every time.

"Unless you have an excellent reason to stop me..." She grins. "Unhand me."

With a groan, I let go, and she drops her mouth on me. My gaze moves to the blue, blue sky, even as the wet heat around my member drives me to oblivion and beyond.

Before she can finish what she started, I shift positions and pull her atop me, driving inside her even wetter heat, burying myself to the hilt.

Connie shifts her robe around and then she's riding me, head thrown back. And this may be a fantasy, a conjuration of my mind, but damn it feels like heaven and hell rolled into one.

When I awake, my body is as spent as if it was real. I hover on the edge of consciousness, close to sleeping, yet not quite there. And on that edge, another memory hits me… much less pleasant.

I rub my eyes, tip toeing to the library in our castle. "Tytus?"

He's always here reading in the middle of the night, and I'm hoping this time is no different. For a young zmeu, he may be serious, but it's his rocklike reassurance I need right now.

His head of ebony hair pokes from behind a sofa, and he waves me over. "What's wrong, Dec?"

"Nasty dream," I mutter as my feet pitter patter on the floor.

I climb on the couch, curling up next to him and the massive book he's holding.

"What's that about?"

Tytus ruffles my hair, and points to the title of the current chapter. "Some war fought long ago. Want me to read it to you?"

"No…"

"Do you want to talk about your dream, then?"

"No…"

He sighs, and wraps his arm around my shoulders, squeezing. "It'll be alright, Dec. You'll see."

I say nothing, dozing off instead in his reassuring hold. But then murmurs reach us, and the library doors open. Tytus freezes and I look up at him, but he's pressing an index to his lips. Be quiet.

I nod, even as the whispers grow to a full conversation. It sounds like a few of the elders from our zmeu Council, but I do not understand what they're up to so late at night.

"The princes would not take kindly to us invading the library in their absence."

"Perhaps… But we must know, once and for all."

Footsteps grow closer, but they must not see us yet. We hear shuffling by the bookshelves closest to the door, and a small exclamation as they find whatever it is they're looking for.

Pages are rifled through, and a third voice says, "There is no mention of that prophecy in here."

"Then it cannot be true."

The first voice who had spoken says, "It is true. It is too similar, too close to reality to be a fluke."

"Two princes born under a full moon, one Light and one Dark? That could be anyone!"

"No," the original speaker says again. "You know as well as I do, that there are similarities."

The third person intervenes. "Does it really matter, in the end? They are our princes."

There's the sound of a book being closed, and their voices grow further, as if they're exiting. "Not yet, it does not matter. But soon, it may become the only thing that truly matters."

We wait in silence, holding our breaths, until we hear the door to our castle close. Tytus then jumps off the sofa, and runs to the bookshelf. He frowns when he notices the missing book, and turns to me.

"Was that… were they talking about us, Ty?"

He pauses, then a weak smile stretches his lips. "Probably not. Old fools, the lot of them."

That night was the first time my brother lied to me. But it would not be the last.

Chapter 3

Declan

My eyes open in the darkness. The last vestiges of the memory linger, then return to whence they came. Unlike before, my mind is clear, oddly so. I was always meant to be the Dark one, even then.

Sure, I have since learned that Igor had come up with that entire prophecy, and it was yet another of his machinations. But was it really a lie, given how I turned out? And what is the point of fighting my true nature, when giving in is so much easier?

I don't bother rehashing my intentions any further. Instead, I look at the ceiling and mutter, "Very well, Ileana. I'll do it."

It doesn't take long for the witch to manifest herself. And her consort is right there with her. His cool blue eyes settle on me, his demeanor not pleasant by any expectation.

"Brought reinforcements this time?"

Ileana snorts and takes a step closer to me. "Glad you have seen reason, zmeu. And as we cannot afford for you to mess up, we will remove your bindings."

"And what stops me from running away?"

"A different type of bind." Ileana smiles coolly. "You have one week from the moment I remove these to bring her back."

"Her, who?"

"The name is Constanza. That is all you need to know."

I nod. Probably another immortal.

"Very well. And what happens if I take longer than a week?"

"You cannot. The Underworld is precarious, and they dislike the Living down there. As one of us–only because you use primordial magic–you will enter with your body, not just your soul. Which means all wounds you receive there, will carry through. The longer you stay, the more you risk never returning."

My eyes narrow on her. "Shouldn't you be helping out, given there is a god down there?"

"Absolutely not."

"Right. I forgot immortals and gods don't mix anymore." I raise my wrists and shackles. "Let's get on with it, then."

When she touches the manacles holding my magic captive, a jolt of pure fire runs through me, and I have to grit my teeth so I don't scream.

Constanza

When I wake up the next morning, it's with a scowl on my face and my body aching all over. And not for the right reasons. After the first round, Declan didn't show again, and I'd really needed something more to take my mind off the conversation with Hades.

It took forever to fall asleep, and when I

finally did, I'd had the weirdest dreams. But none that I wanted, no matter how much I tried to think of Declan before falling asleep. Instead, I dreamt of the damned Underworld being in danger, of what Charon might do, and of Hades' expression. I also dreamt of my friend kicking me out when she found out I'd been less than honest.

Deceitfulness has no business in mine and Persephone's friendship, never has. Since we met, we'd been open with each other. It's why she's the only one who knows about my infatuation with a fantasy. So keeping something from her feels... shady.

And why in hell is Hades doing that, too? Why can't he be honest with his consort, with his soulmate? I understand his need to protect her, but surely this isn't right? Or perhaps it's that I don't understand the depth of their love, of their bond.

With a sigh, I go about getting ready. An outfit is laid out for me on the bed, and my bath water from last night was changed. I put on the pale red dress with flared sleeves, braid my hair, and head to the dining room.

Persephone is already seated, munching

on a breakfast of fruits–piled high with the grapefruit she loves. We could easily have a party in here, given the length of the table and the amount of food on it. Still, the master of the castle is inconspicuous with his absence.

I sit a couple places down from Persephone, not wanting to be too close lest she see what I'm trying to hide.

Turns out my efforts are wasted. After a few moments of silence, Persephone calls me out on my silence. "What's going on?"

"Nothing," I mutter, bringing to my lips some raspberries. They taste like ash, so I drop them back on my plate. My gaze can't settle on anything. "What did, um, Hades want yesterday with me?"

She tilts her head, studying me. "The usual, to yell at you for letting me get so close to Lethe."

"Oh."

Why in hell did her consort have to tell me, of all people, what's going on? I cannot lie to save my life!

"Connie... Talk to me."

I sigh. At a loss for anything else to say, and not wanting to betray Hades' confidence,

I mutter the only other truth that's on my mind. "My guy didn't show up last night."

A brief silence answers me, followed by what sounds like a carefully worded sentence. "As in, you didn't dream of him?"

"That's what I just said."

"Not quite."

I turn her way, noticing her frown. "What do you mean?"

"You said he didn't *show up*. Like he's real. Not a fantasy."

I roll my eyes and stuff a piece of roll in my mouth. "You know what I mean."

"Do I?" She stands from the table and heads to me, sitting right next to me. "Connie... sometimes you worry me."

"There's nothing to be worried about. You didn't have an issue with my dreams until today!"

"That's because I kept hoping you'd see past these fantasies."

"What the hell's that supposed to mean?"

Persephone sighs. "Only that perhaps you're using these dreams and latching onto something you can never have."

I lean back in my chair. "And why would I do that?"

She looks away.

"No, really. Tell me everything. Don't hold back."

Her expression shifts at the bite in my tone and she straightens in her chair, a perfect picture of the Queen of the Underworld she is. "Fine. I think you're avoiding searching for the genuine thing out there, because you're afraid of commitment."

"What?" I scoff. "That's the stupidest thing I've ever heard. My parents are so in love it makes me sick. Why would I fear commitment, when I know how good it can be?"

"Because you're frightened it'll never match what they have."

I scowl at her. "So, let me get this straight. You think I'm an immature child hiding within dreams with a hot guy so I can avoid acting like the adult I am and finding a real immortal to bang. Wow. Thanks. Great to hear it."

I push my chair back and it scrapes against the floor angrily. My napkin falls off my lap and I don't even bother picking it up. Instead I stomp off, ignoring Persephone calling out after me.

Declan

"You don't have to babysit me, you know?"

Făt ignores me, stomping ahead of me in our ever lengthy quest of finding the entrance to the Underworld. After they both removed the cuffs around my wrist, Făt was quick to take me away from his consort, straight through a portal, and another, and another.

Ileana never followed. Which is fine. She may be an ice queen, but I'm sure if I push the right buttons, I can get a rise out of him, and find out exactly what I've got to play with. Immortals are known for their ability to be less impulsive, but they've still got feelings. I just need to figure out which to turn to my advantage.

Because if they think I'm fool enough to believe they'll set me free, they have another thing coming.

I also won't be letting them imprison me, ever again.

As if on cue, a tug at the edge of my consciousness turns my attention inwards. *Where are you?*

Tytus. Since I saved his ass, he's been

trying to make amends. *This isn't the best moment, frate.*

I don't care. Where are you, if not in your cell?

Suspicion rifles through me. *How do you know that?*

I can almost sense his sigh in my head. *Because it woke me from a dream, when they took off your cuffs.*

Hmm.

Declan….

I hesitate. How much should I tell him? Until recently, I thought he'd fucked my wife, and taken everything from me. Until recently, I also assumed he'd been behind a Council of zmei who chose my first imprisonment. Finally, I knew for a fact he'd orchestrated my second imprisonment, with the immortals.

But only a week ago, everything came to a standstill. Through his witch, his soul mate, I saw proof that not only Tytus never betrayed me with my wife, but rather he'd been trying to protect me. And as Ileana had said, he had not been the driving force behind my first imprisonment.

As for the second… Well, if I'd been in his

shoes, knowing what I thought my brother did, perhaps I would have done the same.

Does that make us best friends? Not in the least. But he is no longer someone on my list of people to kill, that much is sure.

Declan!

Da, frate. The immortals offered me a chance to be free, if only I do a minor task for them.

Task? What task?

Escort someone out of the Underworld.

A jab of worry flashes through me, and it takes me a moment to separate it from my own emotions. Though we are able to still get in each other's heads with ease, it seems we also cannot control the flow of emotions from one psyche to another. Ever the elder brother, Tytus is concerned. How... quaint.

I have one week to return to the world of the Living. Quickly, I run him through my promises to the immortals. By the time I'm done, I sense his stupefaction.

What in all hells are you playing at, Declan?

What else? My freedom.

We may no longer be at each other's

throats, but I am still wary of his intentions. And, there is no need for him to know what mine are, and how they fit with the less-than-stellar image he's had of me for centuries.

Before Tytus can say anything else, I kick the connection closed and focus on the immortal ahead of me. *Right. Let's get back on track.*

"Didn't your consort give you a map to where I'm going? I hear she's pretty cozy with the guy who runs the place." Or so my Sight showed, once Ileana became more than a blip on my radar.

Făt mutters something under his breath, but it's too low for me to hear it. I don't let up, desperately wanting to see his control snap. Immortals are cool and calculating, da. But if I rile him up enough, I may be able to dig into his mind without him noticing, and find out a little more about this quest.

"You sure we're going the right way? We wouldn't want to tire you. Especially after you've only just recovered."

Făt stops, takes a deep breath, and tosses over a shoulder, "Keep pushing me, zmeu. Keep fucking pushing."

I let silence descend on us for a few more moments, then I deliver one last jab.

"This Constanza I'm supposed to get, why's she so important? Unless she's your, what is it humans call it... side piece?"

Făt whirls on me and before I know it, his fist is in my face. Despite his lankier build, the strength of it is enough to knock me off balance, and send me stumbling back. He delivers another punch, and the surprise has me lose my footing completely, and drop on my ass. Next, his sword is at my throat, materialized out of nowhere.

I freeze, feeling the tip of the steel way too close to breaking skin than I would like. I know this sword–it's a zmeu killer, and its blade is made of an ancient art, that of Damascus steel. It catches the light of the sun, glinting even more dangerously.

Nostrils flaring, Făt's clenching and unclenching his other hand. "Now I understand the human satisfaction that comes out of a brawl. That felt good." His glare sets on me. "Are we done here?"

I wipe my lip, tasting blood, and stand taking care not to let the tip of that sword get too close. *Well, that answered my question. Whoever she is, this Constanza means something to them. To both of them.* It takes mastery of my every facial muscle to avoid grinning like a fool. I may not have broken through his mental barriers, but I learned enough.

"You should take care. Your consort made it clear you both need me. Last thing you want is for me to change my mind."

Făt pushes the sword closer to my neck. "Keep testing me, and that won't matter. You have one task, and one alone. Get Constanza back up here, unharmed and in perfect condition. Then you'll get your due."

At the reminder of the freedom promised, I tell myself to be patient. My plan may have failed, Tytus may have won, but I can still get out of here. And once I'm out, I'll be truly free, by any means necessary. Perhaps I was never meant to be Dark–but it is who I have become. And while Tytus is feeling guilty now and trying to help out, it won't last. Especially when he learns the true purpose of my quest here.

Being alone is all I have known, yet one

good thing has come out of my isolation. I am not afraid to do what needs to be done, and burn whoever I have to, in order to get there. Soon, I won't be wasting my time with this world. Instead, I'll be seeking another just for myself.

And if the immortals don't give me what I want, then at least I'll have a hostage. *Should make negotiations easier.*

Făt steps back, and lowers his sword from my throat. Without another word, he starts walking again. I follow behind, biting back a grin and trying not to skip ahead.

Another few moments of blind trekking, and we both end up at the entrance of a cave. Hidden by weeds and moss, it's barely more than a crack in a mountain side.

He gestures for me to head in. "Off you go."

I look beyond. "One week, yeah?"

"Da." His expression doesn't change from a glower. "And not a minute more."

"Anything else I should know?"

His jaw clenches. "Don't trust Hades."

"Interesting thing to say about a god. Care to elaborate?" When his glare grows more ferocious, I add, "For the sake of me succeeding, and all."

He purses his lips, then nods, tightly. "Very well. When you enter the Underworld, you'll run first into Charon, the ferryman of the souls. You may see Cerberus, as well, the three-headed dog that guards the entrance." He narrows his eyes on me. "*Try* not to antagonize him. He's one of the original monsters from the Old World."

I nod to his sword. "How about I borrow that, then?"

Făt scoffs. "Not likely. Second, you'll want to make sure Charon leads you on the path to the Elysian Fields. Hades' lair is past it. Make sure he doesn't bring you somewhere else."

"And, he would?"

"Da, well, Charon doesn't take kindly to the Living entering. Last time it happened, eons ago, Hades imprisoned him in Tartarus for a year, for allowing a Living soul inside."

"Right." I rub my chin, the sting of his blow still annoying me. "What's Tartarus, exactly?"

"Are you purposefully trying to waste time, zmeu?"

I scowl at him. "No."

"Then get the fuck into the cavern, and bring Constanza back here."

Something about the blaze in his eyes warns me not to push it this time, so I don't.

"Got it. I'll be back with your prize. You just keep your promise," I mutter as I pass him, "and I will keep mine."

Then I pass through the portal, the sound of his cussing the last I hear. When I'm through, I find myself on the banks of a river.

Constanza

I've run as far out of the palace as I could, which is to say, not far enough. Out of breath, I plop down on the grass, resting my head on my knees.

Persephone's wrong, I know she is. And what's wrong with enjoying some fun, even if it's not real? Flashes of my times with Declan run through my head, helping to dissipate the anger running through my veins. I focus on that one particular time...

I don't immediately hit the world of dreams, this time. My thoughts have been all over the

place today, and I fear I won't be able to control them enough to conjure Declan.

But then he's there, in my bedroom, on my bed... and naked except for a sheet that covers the best part.

I fake a grin and jump next to him, squealing when the soft mattress sends me bouncing against him. He catches me by the waist, holding me steady against him.

Golden eyes search mine, and his question surprises me. "What's wrong?"

"Nothing," I mutter, looking away. "Stupid things."

"If they put a frown on your pretty face, surely they cannot be that stupid."

I force another grin. "How about you distract me?"

He grins. "That, darling, will be my pleasure."

Before I can realize what he's doing, he's tossed me on my back, and moves between my legs, massaging from ankle to thigh in a slow, maddening pace. By the time he reaches the top of one thigh, my right leg is putty at his touch. He smirks, kissing the side of my knee—and ignoring my gasp—then moving to the other.

"Dec—" His name ends on a long moan as

he finishes the second massage, but instead of removing his hands, one moves closer to my core, and he pushes a finger inside me gently.

My eyes lock onto his, and I shift my hips, trying to set a pace. The moment I do, he removes his hand, and I hit the bedsheets in frustration. A full belly laugh escapes him and he moves on me, kissing me with breathless abandon.

By the time he stops, I'm ready to have him satisfy all *needs. But Declan was only getting started... And that night, he drives me to the brink of insanity, until we finally topple into ecstasy together.*

Needless to say, my woes of the day were long forgotten.

I blink, staring at the inky sky above me. Time and time again, he'd done that for me–a glorious distraction, yes. Now, looking back with Persephone's words clear in my mind... Could it be there's some truth to them?

Introspection has never been my strong suit. And though I stare and stare and stare, the sky delivers no answers.

Hours later, Persephone finds me outside, my gaze still glued to the dark ceiling. Hades must have really missed the outside world, for he recreated the evening sky here, only there are no stars. Just an odd illumination that sifts through the clouds like a snake, alternating between deep purple and deep red.

"Can I sit?" Persephone asks me.

"It's your Underworld."

She sighs heavily, then lowers herself next to me. "I'm sorry. I didn't mean to hurt you with my words."

"Why did you, then?"

"Because I care."

I look at her. There is no malice in those eyes of hers. At the reminder I've been hiding things from her, things her consort confided in me, guilt overtakes my anger, and it evaporates.

In truth, it had only been there because, in some way, I do believe she might be right. I may not want it to be so, but it is nonetheless… a possibility. And while immortals may be cool and collected by nature, I find myself to be meeting less and less of those assumptions.

"I know you do. It's just hard to hear." I force a deep breath in my lungs. "Do you really think that's why I'm latching on to my guy?"

"I think only you know that."

Silence descends on us. "Maybe you're right. It's just.... so amazing with him. So easy."

Her voice is soft, not accusing. "Because it's a dream. It's bound to be the way you want it to be."

"And you're saying reality is not the same."

Persephone chuckles. "No. It's a tad different, and takes compromise. It takes work. And sometimes you find someone who's so unequivocally complicated, he makes you crazy, happy, and everything at once. Then, it's worth it."

"Was it, for you?"

"Yes." She intertwines our fingers, squeezing mine. "And when the time is right, I have no doubt you will also find it."

"Thank you. For caring enough to tell me the hard truths."

"Always."

Hand in hand, we keep our gazes on the

angry sky above us, illuminated by millions of souls floating around. And I wonder, not for the first time, how much of what she said is true.

Have I been running, and hiding, all along?

Tytus

Declan breaks our connection with such force, it knocks me back a step, and my head slams in the headboard. Fiona lifts her head off my chest, frowning at me.

"What happened?"

"He wouldn't talk about it."

"But if it woke you from a deep slumber…"

I run a hand over my face. When will my brother's antics finally cease, for once?

"He said the immortals removed his bindings, and released him."

Fiona freezes in my arms, and I read the wariness in her eyes. She may hate my brother less, but the thought of him roaming around free still leaves her on edge.

"They sent him to the Underworld."

"The Underworld? But that's where Igor…"

I nod. "Da, precisely my point."

"You think Declan plans to pick up the plan from where he left it?"

"No, I didn't sense that intent. But he is scheming again, that much is true."

And knowing my brother, it's likely something that will land him in trouble. Again.

Fiona sighs and lowers her head back on my chest. "Try again. He's family. Eventually, he has to open up."

I say nothing, busy frowning at the ceiling instead. Is Declan still the monster I thought all these centuries, these millennia? Can I trust he will do the right thing, whatever Ileana and Făt want with him? Or will he use this as an opportunity to get what he has always wanted–vengeance?

No matter how I search for the truth in my heart, I cannot find it.

Chapter 4

Decepție
"The art of pleasing is the art of deceiving."
-Luc de Clapiers-

Declan

The eerie silence surrounding me is odd.

Long ago, when I grew up with Tytus, we took pleasure in keeping up to date with the world. Despite our elders' efforts to keep us away from human folklore and mythological literature, we found solace in it. Perhaps because it was something forbidden we did, together.

Whatever the cause, I have distinct images

in my mind of what the Underworld should look like. And this... Is too quiet. There are no souls floating around. No boat waiting for me. And definitely no Charon, the ferryman.

Without Făt driving me insane, or Tytus pestering me, these new surroundings are even odder.

I thought once the immortals would free me I would feel something. Or at least, something more than this emptiness inside me. Instead, the silence only presses down on me, reminding me of one increasingly impossible fact to ignore. That I am alone, and always will be.

Eons ago, I had my few moments of joy and a woman who loved me–or so I thought. Had the support of my brother–or so I thought. Had a purpose–once. It was all smoke and mirrors, of course. But it was good while it lasted.

My jaw clenches as I drive the thoughts away, refusing to think of the past. Of *her*. Of a time that should be as far removed from me as the immortals now on the other side of this barrier.

Focus. My zmeu grumbles, reminding me

of our purpose here. Of the fact we are no longer restrained, rather in full control of our powers.

I throw my head back, glancing at the midnight sky above me. Everywhere I turn, there is only darkness. *Then let us make some light.*

One hand rises in front of my face, and I clench my fist. At the same time, I reach deep within for my well of primordial magic, tugging on the surrounding elements, on what I *can* affect. Sparks flicker across the ceiling, falling over me in a curtain of light.

Da, being free has its perks.

I stop the magic as quickly as I started it and let my eyes adjust to the darkness once more.

Behind me, I cannot even see the portal any more. Ahead of me is only darkness, and a sky of red above. The glinting mass of the river Styx winks at me, implying I should not be attempting to swim its length.

"Guess I'll be flying, then."

I step back and let the change shift over me. The Underworld isn't a cave. It's another fucking world. And if I had time, I might consider exploring its entirety. As it is, I only keep the zmeu form until I reach the other side.

Or, I intended to.

But once I land, whimpers in the distance draw my attention. I hold on to the change just in case and get closer, peering at the shadows. It's useless, so I shoot a ball of fire to my right. Rather than orange, it comes out with a bluish hue.

The flames illuminate a monster in a corner, licking his wounds. Its hulking mass is curled up, the muted gray of his fur, mixed with brown, providing a natural camouflage. One of his three heads looks up at me, floppy ears pushed backwards, massive canines bared, while the others continue licking at a fast bleeding wound.

Isn't this the feared creature meant to guard the Underworld?

I roll my head around, surveying the surroundings, but there is no sign of its master, nor whomever caused those wounds. It's not pity that draws me closer, though something about seeing such a big, clumsy monster on his knees makes me aware of the mortality of even massive creatures.

No, rather, an odd feeling creeps on me. Like what predates a vision, only this time it's settled in my gut, warning me to get the hell away from here, as fast as I can.

Leave, my zmeu rumbles, and I am tempted to agree.

Tentatively, I reach out to the beast with my mind. *What happened?*

He doesn't react to the question in Romanian, so I try in old Latin, and old Greek.

The head tilts to the side, and he answers back. It's a dialect even older than the one I know, but I can understand it.

I was attacked.

By whom?

You speak many languages, the other head says instead, its voice a tad different.

I have been around for many eons.

Not longer than us.

I take a step closer, inclining my head as if in agreement. A hissing makes me look down. The dog's tail has slithered my way.

Do not step any closer, the original head warns.

I can help.

How?

By cauterizing the wound.

Two of its heads share a glance, then their attention is back on me. *And what makes you think we believe that, when you could use flames to char us to death instead?*

Why would I kill you, Cerberus?

You know of us?

Another head warns, *He cannot be allowed to pass. He is Living!*

I focus on the calm head. *Da, I know of you. And it would be a shame for one such as you, with so much knowledge, to perish because of one fight. And, I need information. You can help me get it.*

I'm not lying, not really. My bleeding heart and ability to care at a drop of a hat died along with Alina and her cries of pain. But I am in uncharted territory, with little information since the immortals do not trust me. I need as many allies as I can get.

The heads stare at one another in silent communication. Finally, one nods. *Very well.*

I move closer and blow just enough fire to cauterize the wound. The blue flames roll over the bleeding gash in controlled wisps. Even as Cerberus is focused on the pain, I nudge into his mind–and the Sight rolls into me with a vengeance.

Roars that deafen the ears, caves that shatter from impact. Cerberus is fighting another creature—another shifter! The mane of a lion, and another head, a goat, in a massive body. It's a chimera—fully grown, and meant to be extinct. And he is fighting like the Furies themselves are after him, all to protect.

Cerberus is protecting, too. Charon is on the side, watching the fight unfold, and some humans are near him, more Living. They fade out of sight as Cerberus' entire being focuses on the chimera—and the battle he will lose.

I shake my head, returning to the present. Damned visions always pick the worst moment, as if I truly needed to see any of that. What's it to me, if a monster lost to another monster? Survival of the fittest is the only rule I've ever known.

Cerberus groans in pain but by the time the flames ebb away, he is healed.

Now, will you tell me what happened?

Sure.... One head says.

The moment after, the enormous lump of dog is up and lunging at me. We go rolling on my back, and three heads attempt to bite me.

What the fuck. I saved you!

And we thank you for that. But one shifter already hurt us. We will not allow another.

I can't believe my damn luck. Even when I try to do something good, it backfires. But what else is new? Holding back my anger won't work, so I give it free rein instead. Only, I'm fighting three instead of one. Four, if you count that damned snaked tail.

My talons manage to scratch him some, but it's hard to gain full control of my body while on the ground. Cerberus reaches for one of my wings, its massive paw coming inches away from tearing it. I push off, elevating enough that my own tail smacks his head, drawing another howl.

Panting, I fly higher still, leaving him below me. Then I pull deep inside me for the blue fire and burn the area under me–and hopefully the fucking monster with it.

I'm not so lucky, I realize once the smoke clears off. Cerberus is very much alive, and all three heads are staring in my direction.

You cannot enter my domain, the dog growls.

I may have my myths crossed, but I do believe this is Hades' spot, not yours, mutt.

Not for long.

Considering I've more than had my share of information, it's time to fly away. Through the wall of fire, I watch Cerberus roar and try to follow. He cannot.

As soon as I'm far enough, I shift back to human. If Cerberus has friends nearby, at least I can confound myself with the rest of the souls... somewhere. So I head deeper into the Underworld, wishing I had a fucking map.

A few hours later, I still haven't found a single soul. It's starting to be eerie–then, in the distance, a faint glow. *A soul, finally!*

"Hey!"

It's an old man, dressed in rags and looking like he's seen better days. The glow around his body is faint, like I'm seeing him through blurry eyes.

He freezes at the sound of my voice, then tries to run. Chasing a dead person is a first for me, but I've always loved challenges. Plus, being younger and stronger, I easily catch up with him and block his path.

He won't meet my gaze, acting shifty and rubbing his hands back and forth.

"Where is everyone?"

"E-everyone w-who?" he stammers.

If I didn't know better, I'd swear he is on something. When I was originally imprisoned, I tried many times to find a mind to connect with. Sadly, that meant hitting a lot of impressionable human folk, and most of those were pitiful drug addicts. That is who this guy reminds me of.

Perhaps blinded by that judgment, I don't immediately figure out he is petrified, not high.

"The souls, old man!" I cast my arms wide. "Does it not strike you as weird that we alone are here?"

"Know nothing. K-know n-nothing."

He tries to move past me, but I grab his arm instead and stop him. I shouldn't be able to, my hand should go straight through his, but nope...

My shocked gaze meets his. "What the fuck?"

He seems to calm down, an eerie smile on

his face. "If you can touch, the Fates must have something in store for you. Something more than Tartarus' depths of misery."

"Huh?"

He shakes his head again, and again, and again. Like he can't focus, or like bees are swarming around him.

"If the Fates have interest in me, then you had best tell me what you know, old man."

His gaze widens, this time with even more fear. "C-Charon. He wants the dead out on the surface."

"The surface?"

"In the Living world."

"That's impossible. Only one can open the Underworld, and that's Hades."

"Charon will do it. C-Charon will d-do it."

"How do you mean?"

In a flash of utter human freak-out, he jerks and bites my hand, his teeth sinking into me with enough force to break skin. I yank it out of his grip and shove him away. He scrambles away, still muttering about Charon. Not about to be deterred, I catch up to him one more time, keeping my distance this time.

"Where is Hades' palace?"

He hesitates.

"Please." I'm gritting my teeth, but I have no time to waste here.

"If I help a Living, it's my neck on the line."

"Then won't it also be your neck if you're seen being followed around by one?"

My logic seems to break through, as he finally points where I need him to. I don't bother with a thank you, instead I take off on a run towards it. My cargo should be there, and once I get her, I'm out of here before shit hits the fan.

I'm no fool. I've been around long enough to see kingdoms fall, and kings are the first ones to be killed. Hades has lost control of his spot, and I don't want to be here any longer than I have to.

If Charon is trying some coup, then I best get what I need and get the fuck out of here before all hell gets loose. No pun intended.

Constanza

Commotion draws both me and Persephone's attention from our luncheon on the grass. We've gotten over our little minor spat and spent the rest of the afternoon reminiscing. Until the loud noises, that is.

She stands first, then takes off towards the palace. By the time I catch up, the entrance is almost packed with a mix of satyrs, souls and other creatures.

I follow Persephone's lead and push through, ending up in the large hall. They call it the audience hall, and it's something straight out of an old monarch mansion. Massive ceilings supported by white columns, torches hanging and casting dim glows, a checkered marble floor… And in the middle, the center of it all, is Hades's throne. A masterpiece of bones, layered one upon another to form a perfect seat.

I've seen Hades here many times as he goes about his lordy business, listening to souls and grievances. Who knew humans had so many demands after death?

Either way, it comes as no surprise that Hades is already there, Persephone whispering to him. She usually assists him, given she has a softer touch with the humans What does surprise me is the man kneeling in front of him. Or, what's left of him.

He's old, with a long, dirty beard peppered with dirt, and dressed all in black. The ratty cloak obscures his features, but as he moves his beard shakes and out fall minor pieces of bones. In his hand he holds a staff, grimy as well, and from the way he's leaning on it one would think it's where his strength lies. That without it, he'd be weak. I know better, of course.

I've seen him before, every time I've come here. It's Charon, the ferryman of souls. And though he pretends to be blind, yet moves with uncanny accuracy, *weak* is not something I would associate with his person. Some say he lost his sight while protecting the Underworld, and others whisper he uses it as a ruse to get souls to trust him. Whatever the case, the guy has always given me the creeps.

Even so, his beat-up state cannot be good news.

"Silence!" Hades yells, and everyone goes quiet. Persephone included.

I watch as she steps behind Hades' throne this time, as if to blend in with the shadows. Her face is impassable, but I notice a flicker of hurt in her eyes. What did Hades say to her?

"Charon, do you know why you are here?"

Hades' tone draws my attention back to the scene playing out in front of my eyes. We're surrounded by souls, but also soldiers. Dead ones, but dangerous ones nonetheless— and new to here. I've never seen them around, but their dark clothing is enough to put me off, even more than the vacant looks in their eyes, visible through masks that resemble human motorcycle helmets.

Where did Hades find these guys? And why?

"No, sire," Charon says in a sweetly voice, answering his master's question after a lengthy pause.

I'm reminded of the previous night, and what I overhead. Hades had been worried the ferryman was doing things on his own, letting certain people enter that shouldn't... Could those worries be founded? And if they are, what do they mean for me?

Hades shifts on his throne, and I notice one of his hands clenches the sidearm. "Why did you refuse my direct orders for an audience?"

"I never received them, sire."

"Bullshit!" Hades yells, surprising us all. He rarely uses human colloquialisms. "You did it on purpose, to defy me. The question is, why?"

Hades stands then, and circles Charon. That same energy I felt off him last night is even more emphasized now. In his dark, silk clothing, scowling as he is with his eyes shooting daggers, he acts every bit the master. He is imposing, a true king to this place, and it only makes Charon appear feeble next to him.

Especially when he bows his head, hands lifted as if in a prayer of mercy. "I am your humble servant, sire."

"Lies," Hades hisses. "You attacked the wolf I gave my blessing to."

"He was breaking the rules, coming in here as a Living."

That's news to me. A wolf, like a shifter? In the Underworld?

My eyes meet Persephone's, and she gives a slight shake of the head. Hmm... As far as I know, Hades never let a Living enter. Immortals, that's not an uncommon thing, and even so he blocked us eventually. Tired of our meddling. But a human?

Must be someone pretty damn special.

"He was not breaking any rules," Hades says to Charon. "You wanted what he represented. A way to keep the Underworld open at all times. And if you had a chimera under your command, just like Cerberus, you would have full control of that power. Is that not true?"

"Never, sire."

A chimera? My father fought those monsters, and others. They were long thought to be helping the Titans wage war against the Olympians. But what would one do here, in the Underworld? Sure, they were always tied to death, much like Cerberus himself, but... I almost open my mouth to say something, but bite my tongue just in time.

Hades' mask drops for a moment. "You are my oldest servant. Why would you betray me?"

"I have not, sire!" Charon lifts his head a bit, and from my vantage point I catch sight of his smirk. "But perhaps the immortals you associate yourself with have addled your mind, blinded you to your real allies."

Hades clenches his jaw. "Whom my wife keeps as friends is not your business."

"No, sire, never. But these immortals are always cunning, and have designs. There is a reason the veritable masters, yourself and the Olympus gods, disposed of them too, in the end."

"That is old history, Charon. Why bring it up now?"

I know the minute Hades realizes he walked right into a trap, because his gaze shoots into the crowd, seeking mine. Meanwhile, Charon does his best to still appear the ever-worried servant.

"Old history, sire, but not forgotten. After all, it is one of them immortals who gave free passage to the wolf shifter, the same chimera you accuse me of coveting. He fought Cerberus. Injured him. Yet he was allowed to leave. I remember a time not so long ago when allowing entrance to a Living here was punishable... I paid the price, in Tartarus, if you recall."

Hades frowns. "You are reshaping the events to your liking. Why?"

But I can already see why. The surrounding faces grow wary, going back and forth from Hades to Charon. The little slimy weasel wants Hades' throne, he must be! I don't know why, or how he intends to get it, but it's apparent he won't stop until he has it.

Hades turns to Persephone and in that moment, Charon rises from the ground like a cobra prepared to strike. Or, he would have. But I'm not about to let him hurt my best friend, or her consort.

Without thinking, I raise my hand and let the anger manifest as a jet of light, shooting towards the ferryman. At the same time, a sword appears, blocking Charon's staff from striking. My blast tosses the old man into a wall, and gasps echo everywhere.

Then someone shouts, "Intruder!"

Another person yells something else. But I'm not paying attention to any of them. Instead, my eyes are glued to the man wielding the sword. Because it's not Hades... and it's not a random soul, or satyr. He's got eyes the color of molten gold, and blond hair I've run my fingers through many, many times. And that body...

"Declan?" I whisper out loud.

When our eyes collide across the distance, I swear I see his jaw slacken. "Fuck me."

Chapter 5

Deteriorare
"Truth never damages a cause that is just."
-Gandhi-

Declan

I nearly drop the sword when my eyes land on *her.* The same goddess from my dreams, only she's here. In flesh and blood, and staring at me like I've personally offended her by walking out of her dreams and into her reality.

Well, fucking hell.

After the old soul pointed me in the direction of the palace, I made haste. I have one goal here and the sooner I get what I'm here for, the earlier I can get back to the surface and my freedom.

Despite my desire for a smooth process, of course more shit had to happen. I should've realized the moment I ran into the monster that it wouldn't be the last. After all, every bad thing comes in threes, right? Cerberus. The crazy old man. And now her. My three perfect fucking curses.

Good thing Ileana took off those damned shackles, and I was able to use my primordial magic on the fire of the torches around here to get a sword. Creating something out of nothing is an art, one that I thankfully still remember.

My gaze shifts to the lord of this place, whom I just helped save. Hades is younger than I thought he would be, with piercing gray eyes and dark hair streaked with silver. We're the same height and it appears I'm about to be fighting for my life, judging by the way he's looming closer.

And to think all I did was act out of pure instinct, and stop what looked like a rat from causing havoc! Speaking of...

I chance a glance away from Hades, searching for the other guy. "Where did your prisoner disappear to?"

That seems to stop the big guy in his tracks. He snaps his fingers to some satyrs, pointing to the back. My eyes follow them, just in time to catch sight of–

No, surely I cannot be in for more surprises. I must be wrong. Many knights wear black cloaks, and act like perfect robots. Surely?

Movement in my periphery draws my gaze back to Hades. *I'll worry about his guards some other time.* He's moving on me now, barely held back by another gal I'm very familiar with. One I didn't see at first, hidden as she was by his bulk.

I flash a smile her way and let the sword vanish from my hands as I hold them up in a peaceful gesture. "Well, isn't this cozy? Long time no see, Sephora."

She blinks at me, and Hades freezes in his attempt to throttle me.

"Sephora?" He turns to her.

"I can explain," she whispers. "But not with everyone here."

As if only then realizing we have an audience, Hades dismisses everyone. The same satyrs usher the souls out–but not before I notice a few too many glares aimed my way, and some disgusted looks towards Hades. Hmm. Whatever did I stumble into?

"Explain," Hades grunts to Sephora.

"Yeah, please do," Connie says, only her gaze is on me.

I've looked into those eyes so many times, but in completely different situations. Namely, horizontally. While I was balls-deep in her, and enjoying some damn pleasurable distractions.

How the hell did I not realize she was real? Surely my mind couldn't conjure something this perfect!

I drag my eyes from Connie and mutter to Sephora instead. "Should I?"

"No!" Sephora says and starts speaking a little too fast. "I have known Declan since I was a young, more foolish goddess. My mother forbade me to go to the mortal realm, but I didn't listen. Unfortunately, I chose the Carpathian mountains to try out."

I smirk. "More than try out."

Out of my periphery, I catch a flash of hurt over Connie's face, but that's not my problem. Why didn't the little witch tell me she was real, and an immortal? I would've thought twice before getting tangled up with her.

No, you wouldn't have, a snappy voice answers inside me. I ignore it.

"So you two were lovers?"

"No! Constanza, you have to believe me–"

I freeze at the name and my gaze fully turns to her. "Constanza? Your real name is *Constanza*?"

Fuck me sideways. Is this what the old man meant with the Fates having an interest in me? 'Cause I could do without that, at this rate.

"And?" Connie asks, completely cool and collected. This is not how I knew her, that's for sure.

The tilt of her head, the power she'd shown... It finally all fits together. "Holy fuck, you're her daughter, aren't you?"

"Whose daughter?"

"Ileana's."

Connie–Constanza–crosses her arms and

lifts her chin in the air. "And if I am?"

Well, hell. I shouldn't be surprised by now that yet another female manipulated me. Really, it seems to have been written in my stars the moment I was born. Yet there's something increasingly wrong here...

And I wonder if Ileana knew just who I'd been banging. Did she send me here on purpose? Is that what made her so sure I would return? Because if she thinks a few tumbles in bed made me care for her daughter, she's got another thing coming.

"Your mother sent me to get you." I throw a look around. "Said things are getting dicey in the Underworld and it's about time I escort you out."

The oddest look comes across Connie's face as she glances between Sephora and me. "I don't believe that."

"Darling, it doesn't matter if you believe me or not. You're coming with me, 'cause my ass is on the line."

As she glares my way, Sephora says, "Is that really true?"

I hold back a growl, barely. "Not your business, Sephora."

"Enough with this Sephora bullshit, shifter!" Hades thunders. "You've got the wrong woman, and you had best watch the way you talk to my consort."

I take a step back when the room darkens alongside his anger. *Consort?*

Hades' eyes narrow on me. even as the rest of the realization falls over me like a cold shower. "Sepho... *Persephone.* Another lie, then?" I should be asking for compensation at this point.

Her violet eyes flash at me, no longer filled with youthful insouciance. "And good thing I did. If you'd known who I was from the beginning, you would've used me for your own gain even more. It was bad enough you realized I was a goddess."

I shake my head, holding my hands up. "Fine, whatever. Let me take Constanza, and we'll be out of your hair. Let you two settle this."

"I do not think so," Hades threatens. "You have stirred up enough shit for one night."

"Uh, you mean the old guy with the bones falling out of his beard?" I laugh. "Buddy, you had that coming a mile away."

Hades takes a step closer, eyes narrowed

on me. "What do *you* know about what is taking place in my Underworld?"

I should learn to keep my mouth shut, every once in a while. But with both Constanza and Persephone watching us, I'm not about to cower from Hades. *This is the most fun I've had in ages!*

"Only the barest minimum, oh sire," I grin mockingly and bow. "Ran into a pal called Cerberus who was a mess, and some poor soul who's seen better days, muttering about Charon doing this and that."

My grin widens, especially as Hades seems two steps away from punching me. To my utter surprise–and disappointment–he doesn't. Instead, he jabs a finger in my direction.

"Then you will remain here as a guest until you help me fix it."

"Is that an order?"

"Consider it one."

He jerks his head to the shadows, and another satyr shows up. He barely reaches my shoulder, and I could easily dispose of him. Instead, I allow him to escort me out. I've stirred the pot enough, and I need a moment to come to terms with my next course of action. Because Olympian or not, I take orders from no one.

Still, as I leave the audience room, I glance behind one more time, my gaze settling on Constanza. She's avoiding me purposefully, and it's just as well. No need for her to see my shit-eating grin.

If she's truly Ileana's daughter, then someone must be looking out for me because I just hit the jackpot. With her, I'll get everything I want–and more.

Constanza

I'm still reeling from the implications of their little banter. Declan–*my* Declan–is also known to my best friend in the universe. *How the hell…? And here I was worried about what I was keeping from her!*

I can't wrap my head around it. Declan was in my dreams, and now he's here. Sent by my mother. How? Why? And how could I have connected with him? Is this a setup, from my mom, to make sure I find someone worthy?

Yet something about his demeanor, the coldness in his glare… It's unlike the man I gave my body to, in my wildest fantasies.

"Will you please explain?" I fight back tears of confusion as I face Persephone. "I think Hades and I deserve to know what happened. How do you know Declan?"

"It's not what you two think." Persephone wipes at her eyes.

Hades says nothing. From his stance, the distance he's put between us, he already decided what he'll believe. I want to give Persephone a chance, but this is damning.

Not to mention–Declan! Of all people.

After a deep breath, Persephone says, "As I mentioned, I went to the mountains. I was stupid, young. Ran into a pack of strigoi–vampires. They love special blood, and I must've smelled sweet to them. Unfortunately, while my birth gives me power, it does not make me immune to these low lives. Immortals are immune, but gods are more like humans than not. In either case, Declan swooped down and saved me."

Declan. At least he told me his real name, and it's as hot and exotic as him. Even more so in real life. *Stop it,* I tell myself. *This is not the time.*

Persephone gulps, her hand going to her throat. "I stayed for a few days, charmed by him and his brother, Tytus. Declan wined and dined me, but we never slept together."

"You kissed, though? Had intimate relations?" Petty jealousy courses through me, but Persephone blushes and lowers her head.

"Yes. I was enamored. A fool. When I tried to leave, Declan wouldn't let me."

A growl tears from Hades, and something about his features tells me he's seeing more than either of us realize. I recall the other night and how he knew I was there, even before the satyr had seen me. And how he could finish my thoughts...

Let it go. You have enough on your plate for now. With a monumental effort of will, I focus on Persephone.

"He didn't harm me," she hurries to say, "but he spoke about wanting to see my mother. Talk to her. It was only later I figured he needed a bit of influence with members of his zmeu council to escape trouble."

"Zmeu?"

"Dragon shifters."

I glance back at the closed door. I'm aware of our history, of course. Daddy drilled it into me enough times, about how they're impulsive and dangerous, and holders of primordial magic. I just never thought I'd meet one, let alone...

"Wow." The word escapes me in a whisper, not that anyone notices. Least of all Persephone, who's talking the fastest I've ever heard her, as if desperate to get the words out.

"My mom came. She made it clear she wouldn't be blackmailed, and took me away. I learned the true nature of the zmeu–that they'd been guardians to the gods, once upon a time, until we cast them out of the skies. And Declan was only trying to play on old wounds. And then, half a century later, I met you," she says to Hades, "and that was it. Please believe me."

He nods. "I do."

When she moves to go into his arms, Hades holds up a hand to stop her. "But I need a minute, please. I'll come see you."

I wish I wasn't there to see the shell-shocked expression on her face. Biting back tears, Persephone runs out. I almost follow, but something tells me to stay behind. And within a few moments, I'm rewarded with Hades' question.

"Did you know your mother would send him down?"

It catches me unawares. When I'm down here, I lose track with the Living, and my own parents. Occasionally they send me a message with a new soul or something, but mostly I'm cut off. Not that I'm complaining.

"No. I would have told you. I'm aware of the rules of the Underworld regarding the Living being in here, and I would not have broken them."

His angry glare aimed my way speaks volumes. "You break plenty of other directives from me."

"And I apologize for that. But I would never, not for something so serious."

His gaze narrows on me, as if only now realizing how much of everything I've put together. "What is it you have realized?"

I shrug, but his expression only darkens further.

"Your kind were created to protect us. By our own hand," he growls. "Answer me with that in mind."

I gulp. Sure, my parents educated me on our history. But by the time I came into existence, the whole serving-the-gods and beck-and-call thing was pretty much done with. The deities–from all pantheons–became recluse, ensuring their realms were no longer accessible without an invitation.

Still. What was bred into us cannot be taken away, and it's with a bit of annoyance that I answer Hades, feeling as if I owe it to him.

"Your hold on the Underworld is weakened, and top of the line contesting it is Charon. Whether or not he has allies, remains to be seen. But there is definitive wariness among the souls and other creatures here."

His lips twist into something like a grimace. "You think so, hmm?"

I know so. I don't say it out loud, but I might as well, judging by the clenching of his jaw.

"And if you were in charge of my protection, what would you advise?"

My father taught me basic tactics of war, but it was centuries ago. So it takes me a moment to bring them all to mind. By the time I settle on one and meet his gaze again, I get the odd impression Hades already knows what's about to come out of my mouth.

"First would be finding Charon, interrogating him by any means necessary to discover what he knows. Who started this. Evidently it has been in the works for a bit, but it must have been actioned upon by larger forces if you weren't aware of it."

"And what magic can hide things from my sight?"

I chew on my bottom lip, trying hard as I can not to picture Declan somewhere in this castle.

"I'm not sure," I finally admit. "Gods are top of the food chain, no?"

Hades drops his head on the fireplace mantle, his shoulders slouching with the movement. "Yes, one would think so."

"Declan's appearance... My own use of magic..." I hesitate, wondering how to put my question into words, but Hades beats me to it and answers.

"Yes," he says, his gaze lost in the flames. "It will hurt what is already happening. My souls trust that I will keep them safe, that this is their *safely* forever after. The Living are not meant to get in. What the souls see is a breach of privacy, and I am weaker in their eyes for allowing it."

His admission only makes him appear like he has the weight of the world on his shoulders. My own mind is churning with everything that took place, but perhaps because of how my kin came into being–and taught to always put Olympians above ourselves–I cannot help but feel for him.

"Can I help?"

"I will let you know. For now, I need a moment.."

"Alright, but.... one more thing." He says nothing, so mentally I ask, *Should I reveal to Persephone what you told me?*

I'd been wondering, for a long time. But if it's true...

"You may," Hades answers. "Whether from you or me, she will have figured it out."

When only my stunned silence answers, Hades turns. "What is it?"

"I.... I wasn't speaking out loud, just then. It was in my head."

One moment he's a teddy bear, the next

he towers over me, holding onto my shoulders with enough force to hurt me. "You cannot tell anyone. *No one,* do you hear me?"

We're nose to nose at this point, and the entirety of his anger is focused on me. Enough that I feel it like actual heat upon my skin. Yet I cannot back down, perplexed by this new development.

"W-why?"

His gaze darkens. "What do you think souls would do, and the gods, if they knew I can hear their innermost thoughts? Find out their dirtiest secrets and use them against them?"

Yeah, that doesn't sound too good. Already, I'm cringing at everything he must have heard in my head over the years, and especially as of late. Then there's everything else, every*one* else, including–

My eyes widen. "So before, with Declan, you already knew? About him and Persephone?"

A muscle ticks in his jaw. "The moment he walked in, yes."

"But why the charade?" When he only stares at me as if I'm a silly child, I realize. "You didn't want Declan to figure it out!"

"Yes, bravo. Now are we clear, Constanza? This isn't one of those things you can ignore me on. You *cannot* tell anyone." Hades shakes me again, drawing my attention to the matter at hand. "Promise me!"

"Yes, I swear it! But does Persephone know, then?"

"She does. And the less who do, the better." He releases me abruptly, appearing even more exhausted than before. "Leave, now. I need peace."

I scurry out of the room, but the entire time my thoughts are churning. *What the hell just happened?*

Chapter 6

Obstacole
"The greater the <u>obstacle</u>, the more glory in overcoming it."
–Molière–

Constanza

My head is still reeling with what Hades admitted to. If the lord of the Underworld can hear thoughts... My goodness, how can he survive it? All the pain the souls bring with them, not to mention everything surrounding him from the rare creatures he offers protection to. I would go insane.

And I get his point, too. If anyone was to

know, not only would they be afraid of him, but they would also use it to hurt him. He's one of the Originals, after all. Each pantheon has them, the master gods–the children of the Great Ones. Him, Zeus and Poseidon are those of Olympus. I've only met one other set of Originals, and they were from the Egyptian pantheon–I still remember Set's dark eyes on me, and the pure aura of darkness around him.

Suffice to say, the Originals are always the most powerful. And even today, in a world where they are recluse, some would be more than happy to get ammunition against them.

On my way to my room, I push past Persephone's. I wouldn't have stopped–still don't know how to feel about her history with Declan.

The same man who drove me wild and insane with need, time and time again. Who saw through me and held me... distracted me. Our connection was so damn physical, I shiver from the memories. The thought he could have had that with anyone else makes bile rise in my throat.

As I stand there, undecided, a vivid memory of one of our nights hits me with such force, I cannot stop it. For the seconds it rolls into my mind, I'm captive to it, and to the feeling it evokes.

🦢

I'm lying naked over Declan's chest, after yet another night of tumbling in bed.

"It's weird, isn't it?"

He stops rubbing my ass. "What is?"

"These dreams. Feels so real."

He shrugs. "Aren't we entitled to a brief fantasy?"

I tilt my head back to look at him. "That's what my fantasy would say."

He grins. "Who says I'm yours, and not the other way around?"

Before I can answer, he shifts us until he's hovering over me. My hands go to trace his chest, but he grabs both wrists and pins them above my head. Something like a dare glints in his golden eyes.

"Keep them there."

His tone, a mix of dark and seductive, has my core tightening, readying... Declan bypasses my mouth, lingering over my nipples. Within seconds of his torturous attentions, my hands move, one going so far as heading for his shoulders.

And he grabs it, pressing it once more in the cool sheet.

"I said, keep them there, darling. No cheating, or I'll stop."

It takes a tremendous effort, especially when his mouth drives me to new peaks of insanity. That's the thing about Declan—he always makes sure my pleasure comes first. And if I could die, I would happily choose to do so in his arms.

My cheeks feel hot by the time I snap out of it. Only to realize I'm leaning against Persephone's door, fanning myself and acting like a girl with a crush.

Has that all been real, then? His body against mine. All the things we did, said... Well, not so much said as did, but still!

Holy shit. I had dream sex with Declan– and now he's here!

Sooner or later, I'll have to deal with it. With seeing him, talking to him. That time is not now, not when I'm still reeling from the implications, and need a moment to myself.

But then I hear sobs from within Persephone's room, and my heart breaks. She's always been there for me, whether for a fight with my parents, or simply figuring out life. Aside from the skirmish we had this morning, this is the most strain we've ever experienced in our friendship. And all because once upon a time, she had a flirt with Declan. What kind of friend would I be if I let this come between us?

Yeah, the guy gives great orgasms. But he's not mine. Never has been. And if for a tiny second I entertained the brief idea he might be real, well… The coldness in his gaze soon shattered that hope.

Steeling myself, I push the door open softly and walk in. Persephone's sitting on a bench by the window, her forehead resting on the crystalline glass. In the faint illumination from the outside, I can see her tear-streaked face.

"Persephone?"

She turns to me, wiping at her face. "Hey."

I force my feet forward and take a seat opposite her on the bench. And then I wait, knowing she'll talk when she's ready. It's hard, when I was raised to be impersonal and collected at all times, to know what to say and when to say it. In many ways, Persephone is much freer with her emotions than I am. In fact, the only time I've ever been uninhibited was with Declan...

I shove the memories out of my head. *Cannot focus on that. Not now.* Not on how hot he looks, in real life. Or the zing of electricity running through me when our eyes met. Nope, none of that.

"I didn't know." Persephone searches my gaze. "Please believe me, even when you described him to me, I didn't know it was Declan in your dreams."

"I do," I say and reach for her hand. "I was hurt, because in all the centuries we've known each other, you didn't mention him. But I believe you when you say there was nothing between you. Not that it should matter if there was, I mean at least not to me."

Lies, lies, the nagging voice at the back my head says. I ignore it.

More tears stream down Persephone's cheeks, and I reach up with my free hand to wipe them. "Hades does believe you, you know? He just needs a minute."

She looks away, lower lip trembling, and

it breaks my heart to see her like this. Especially given what she told me earlier, of how they're meant to be together. It's on the tip of my tongue to ask her about his telepathy, but I bite it down. Instead, I focus on something else.

"What was Declan doing in my dreams anyway, Persephone? How would that be possible?"

She shakes her head. "No idea. I've never heard of that happening."

"Never?"

Another shake. "Never."

I glance in my lap, playing with the material of my dress. "He said my mom sent him down here to get me. Could that be why?"

"I wish I had answers, Connie, but I really don't."

Silence settles and lengthens between us, becoming its own living thing. I need to understand, more than anything. Perhaps then it'll be easier to explain the pull, the connection, and to shake it off.

"I thought he wasn't real." A shrug. "I'm pretty sure he thought the same, judging by his surprise today."

Persephone chews on her bottom lip. "You're sure?"

I look up sharply. "What do you mean?"

"Only that Declan never does anything unless it suits him. And him in your dreams, now him here..."

"But... My mom sent him."

Persephone reaches for my hand. "All I'm saying is, be careful. I don't want him to use you, not like he tried with me. And he does seem to have a nose for immortals."

I nod. "I still can't explain how our minds even connected like that."

Persephone stands and paces a bit, then stops. Her expression is confused, then she frowns. "Orpheus... You're familiar with Orpheus' story?"

"Wasn't he Apollo's human protégé, who lost his lover, Eurydice? And then he came down to get her in the Underworld, put Cerberus to sleep with his harp playing, and almost had her back. But he broke the one rule Hades gave him, or something. Not a happy ending."

"Yeah, that's him. He was to avoid looking at Eurydice until they were out of here, but he couldn't abstain himself. He lost her to us all over again."

I try and fail to grasp the point of the story. "Okay... I'm not seeing the link."

"What the humans never captured is how Orpheus knew that was possible–to find Eurydice and follow her into a realm meant for the dead only. When he came to us, we realized the connection between him and his beloved transcended death. They were still tied together by the force of their love."

"But it's not like me and Declan are in love." The idea alone is laughable.

Something shifts in Persephone's expression, then it becomes cool again. "Right. But perhaps some other event links you. And it explains this all happening."

"So how do I find out?"

"You'll have to talk to him."

"I have no desire to." If I never see him again, I'll be better off for it. Especially with how he makes me feel, and the fact it's impossible to rationalize it.

Persephone laughs. "Because you don't want to see how unlike your dream Declan he truly is?"

I can't hold back the scowl that confirms her assumption. Based on what she said about him, I'm pretty sure he's an asshole.

"You have to. Because," she sits next to me, "you'll need him to escape."

"What do you mean?"

"I think you know what." When her eyes meet mine, I realize she knows Hades told me.

I look away. "I'm sorry, Hades made me promise. I overheard him by mistake."

"It's okay. He only tries to protect me, as misguided as he might be sometimes. But he's horrible at hiding his true feelings, and I realized a few days back that something was wrong. Tell me everything."

So I do.

When I'm done, Persephone inhales sharply. "This isn't good. If Charon is trying a coup, and now many souls witnessed Declan entering... They'll think Hades is losing his hold."

"But he's the master here. It's not like they can fire him."

Persephone glances away, shoulders slouching slightly. "They can do much worse. Like remove his title and replace him."

"What! With someone who's not a deity?"

She nods, her lower lip trembling.

"You've got to be kidding, Persephone! Hades is an Olympian, an Original! He was gifted the Underworld by Zeus himself."

"Yes, but it is the souls that keep him here, Connie. And you know how some, with their stronger personalities, can actually cause harm with weapons of their choosing? If they were to turn on Hades... He's not invincible. Neither am I."

Her expression shutters, as if she's stopping herself from saying something. I have a feeling I know what it is.

"But... But that's never happened! Can't we round up some immortals, some guards, to protect you?"

Persephone shakes her head. "Do you not remember the Titans, and how easily they were disposed of? This is *one* Olympian."

"But... why? What's the point of dethroning Hades?"

"With the gods living as recluse, many have forgotten how good they can be for them. Humans, especially. They all think it possible to do things on their own, including taking care of their afterlife."

"But Charon isn't human, is he?"

She purses her lips. "No, he is a wraith of the worst kind."

"Ew." They feed off dead people. Enough said. "I still don't get how he could replace Hades, or even convince souls it's in their interest to do so."

"Because they'll say he's not strong enough to protect their ever after."

I shake my head. "But Hades has the satyrs, and that new army. Surely he can find Charon and put an end to this?"

Persephone pinches the bridge of her nose, frustration rolling off her in waves. "I'm not sure it'll be that easy. This feels... more. And the army you refer to, I doubt they'd even be on Hades' side."

"What? Why?"

"Because it was Charon's suggestion he chooses them, based on their skills while they were living."

"And what were those skills?"

"Trackers, of a sort. They hunted down anything that hurt humans, including power-ful shifters. Charon's reasoning was the souls would feel safer."

"Shit." I bite my lip, fully aware now of how bad all of this is. "What can I do?"

Her grip on my hand tightens. "Leave here. If you and Declan are gone, it'll be one less tank of gas to be thrown on the fire. I can help Hades calm the masses, or try to."

"And if it doesn't work?"

"I'll send for help to Olympus."

"Will they come?"

My question isn't meant to be mean. I know her relationship with her mom soured. And in all my time here, I've never seen another Olympian visit.

Persephone hesitates, then nods. "Yes. They'd rather Hades be in power, an Olympian, than anyone else."

"Who do you think is behind all this?"

"There were rumors, a few weeks back. That someone from above was trying to rouse the zmei here."

I gulp. "Zmei?"

Like Declan. He's a zmeu.

"To form an army," Persephone adds with a knowing look.

"And you believe it was Declan?"

"All I'm saying is, his appearance here is a bit too coincidental. Even if he was sent by your mom."

It wouldn't be the first time dear old Mom accidentally made my life harder… But this is not some Cupid-like endeavor. And with her knowing how Hades feels about the Living, something tells me sending Declan after me was a last resort.

"Okay." I grip her hands in mine. "I'll go with Declan. We'll remove ourselves from this mess, and hopefully buy you some time. But I'll also find out if that's the case, alright? If he's involved."

Persephone nods and hugs me. "Thank you. Take this."

She reaches around her neck and unclasps an opal necklace. It's one of her simpler accessories, with a thin chain of silver, and the stone surrounded by an odd design. When she hands it to me, I notice it looks like the opal is hidden–and embraced– by the branches of a tree.

"The opal is magicked," Persephone explains. "Call my name and speak into it when you find out… Or whenever you need me. And

I'll have its matching set here."

I nod and hug her again, trying to clear the lump in my throat. "I'll come and visit as soon as everything is okay."

"Yes." She's also blinking back tears. "Soon. Be safe."

One last hug, and I exit and head to my room. After packing some necessities, I go by the kitchens and grab some rations, then stomp to the holding quarters. Time to face my so-called *prince*.

Declan

I'm tempted to break down the door and take Hades' guards down. But, that won't endear me to the lord of the place. Nor get me any closer to my goal. No, I need to play this smart.

Even as I'm thinking that, I sense a tug from Tytus in my mind again. *What do you want this time, frate?*

Just checking on you. He pauses. *I saw Ileana, not too long ago.*

Da, and?

She mentioned nothing about your little excursion.

Are you really surprised?

No. Another pause. *When we defeated Igor, Fiona hid from them what his true purpose had been. We didn't reveal anything other than the balaur had lost his mind.*

That stops my pacing, and something rubs me wrong in my chest. I smack a fist to it, hoping to get the odd sensation away.

Why would you not tell them?

Fiona had this crazy idea that something else is going on. That things may be bigger than us.

Hmm. No offense, but much as I enjoy our chats, I'm a tad preoccupied at the moment.

Why?

No reason.

Dec…. Tell me.

I glance around the room, and sigh. *I made it to where the immortals wanted me to. But, I might've just landed in a viper's nest with no plan of escape.*

What can I do?

Footsteps outside draw my attention, then the man of the hour steps inside. Behind him, two satyrs close the doors.

Later, frate, I say and force the connection closed.

"Why did you save my life?" Hades questions without preamble.

The smart reply dies on my lips. "I saw a problem and took care of it. Shouldn't I be getting a thank you, versus being imprisoned?"

"Perhaps in another world." Hades narrows his eyes. "How did you enter my realm?"

"I told you, Ileana sent me. Făt brought me to some cave and next thing I know, I was here."

He circles me. "And?"

"And what?"

"It is a long way from the entrance to my doorstep."

"Very true. And you have some unsavory guards, I should say. Like Cerberus. That ungrateful monster attacked me as soon as I helped heal his wounds."

Hades stops pacing and mutters under his breath. "Wounds he got from the wolf shifter... So he did get out."

"You having a hard time keeping your realm under control?"

Hades looks at me, his expression blank. Then he smiles, but it's cold. "You should worry less about my realm, and more about your life."

He turns on his heels and leaves before I can come up with a proper retort. On his way out, though, I hear murmurs. And then another set of footsteps, lighter.

The doors open again, only this time it's Constanza. She steps through and the lock snaps back into place behind her, blocking out the guards. I notice the bundle she drops by her feet, looking suspiciously like packed supplies.

For a moment, she just stares at me. Takes me in. I recognize the look in her eyes, feel the pull I always do with her. How could I have thought what we had was dreams only? Her touch had always been too real. But did Ileana have anything to do with it? Is Tytus right, and there's more to all of this than simply unpleasant coincidences blending together into a clusterfuck?

Constanza snaps to and clears her throat. "We have to leave. Now."

"And what makes you think that?"

She pushes off the door, waving her hand in the air. "Did you not see how everyone was looking at you? Your interference with Hades' business was not well received. They're in the middle of a blasted revolution!"

I move to the bed and sit on the edge. "Really? Everything seems pretty peaceful to me."

Lies, of course. I don't think even she realizes how bad the situation is, but I'm not about to play all my cards.

Constanza huffs and almost inches closer, then stops herself. "Stop looking at me like that."

"Like what?"

"You know what!"

"I will. Soon as we stop ignoring the elephant in the room, darling."

Earlier, I didn't have time to properly take her in, distracted as I was by Hades and Persephone. Now, though, there is nowhere my eyes would rather settle than on her.

Constanza has on way more clothes than I'm used to, but I cannot say I'm complaining. Her soft red dress is tied in at the waist, showcasing its thinness, and the sleeves and bottom flare out, moving with every shift of her hips. With her braided hair, a few locks teasingly framing her face, she is…

An immortal. Remember she's an immortal. And who her mother is. And why you're here.

As if on cue, Constanza stops glaring at me, instead avoiding me. "Right. Well, there's nothing to say. Obviously."

"Obviously?"

I stand up slowly, taking my time until I'm mere steps away. Her scent of violets and fresh mountains wafts to my nostrils, and I can't help inhaling deeply. I want nothing more than to toss her on the bed and conduct this interrogation in a better way.

But, no. I won't give in to that addiction, because if I'm honest it's less about the truth and more about feeling her wet heat around me. And the last time I was so addicted to a female, it didn't end well.

So instead of pulling her to me, I scowl at her. "We've been lovers for weeks."

"We were *dreaming*!"

"Damn real dreams, if you ask me."

"I have no explanation for that."

With each accusing word, my eyes continue to roam her features. The flush of her cheeks–arousal. The blaze in her gaze–annoyance. The blue hue is even more stunning this close by, even more unreal than in our dreams.

"Don't you?" I taunt her.

"Say what you mean already!"

"It's not your mom, causing all this, toying with us?"

That lightning-filled gaze, the rise and fall of her breasts as she's getting more and more aggravated, is damn appealing. *Too* appealing. Suddenly I'm all too aware of the bed behind me.

And then noises outside draw our attention. I move to the window, noticing a group of men and women heading towards the palace. Their glowing forms indicate they're spirits, and they're not alone. The same shapes I'd seen before, dressed all in black, surround them.

"What the hell?"

Constanza pushes around me, cursing softly when her eyes fall on the picture below. "We have to go. Now!"

She runs to the door. When I don't follow, she whirls on me once more. "Were you sent to get me back home, or what?"

"Da," I growl, torn between my mission and finding out what, exactly, the Serafim are doing here. *There is no way I'm mistaken, that's for sure.*

Constanza's glower makes that decision easy. "Then do your fucking job!"

She dashes out and I have no choice but to follow. My freedom is worth more than an ancient order intent on destroying zmei.

Tytus

Night finds me pacing, unable to settle down. Why is it Declan always sees fit to cut our connections, leaving me with an odd feeling of unsettled scores?

And this last conversation... He sounded like he's in trouble. And if he is, and he truly didn't cause any of it, what am I to do?

Ileana won't give me further details, in fact she flat out tried to deny he was in the Underworld. I could press the matter further and ambush her and Făt, but where would that lead me?

No matter how I wish to rationalize this, the tightness in my chest won't go away. This is my brother, blood of my blood. And no matter what our history is, I must be there for him.

Hell knows I wasn't when it counted.

Now's my chance to make up for it.

Chapter 7

Evadare
"Fantasy is hardly an <u>escape</u> from reality. It's a way of understanding it."
-Lloyd Alexander-

Constanza

That insufferable man! Never in my eons of existence have I run across a more impossible being. Ever! And to think I slept with him!? How did I not see any of this?

Because you were too busy licking all over him, that tiny voice at the back of my head reminds me.

Granted, it was all in a dream, or multiple dreams, and can't be construed as real–can it?–but bleeding heck and all the hells below! How could I have been so blind?

Declan's footsteps echo behind me, so at least the big oaf is following me. How did my mom ever think to send him down here? How did she even run across him, for that matter?

I don't bother checking around corners, instead just let my fury rule me as I pass through hallways and go down staircases, all the way to the main floor. I'm stepping off the last marble steps, chewing on my bottom lip, when a crash somewhere up ahead draws my attention.

Then Declan's arm bands around my waist and he tugs me against his chest, pulling us behind a pillar. "What the–"

One big hand covers my mouth, silencing me, even as his hold on me tightens.

"Would you shut up for a second, princess?" He hisses in my ear. "We're about to be found out. If you want a stealthy way out of here, shush."

And then he drags us further into the shadows, turning his body so that I'm more between the wall and him than I'd like.

It does things to me, this nearness. Because I remember how he'd chase me, pounce on me, and take me from behind. How he mastered every inch of my body like he was born for it. How–

"They're gone," he says, and at the same moment he lets me go.

My knees give way and I subtly use the wall for support as I meet his gaze. At his feet is my bundle of supplies, which he remembered to grab–unlike my harebrained self.

It doesn't take me long to realize just how much I let emotions rule me in the last moments. *Mom would hate it.* She drilled it into me from the beginning, from when I was young. No emotions. No impulsive decisions. Immortals are supposed to think, and act rationally. *Robotically,* I'd always whined.

But there was a reason for that, sure. With the power we hold within ourselves, we cannot let emotions rule us. After all, that's what zmei did, and that is how they lost their privilege of defending deities.

Which reminds me, the man in front of

me is one such impulsive zmeu.

I tilt my head to the side, trying to imagine past the human shell. To picture him as the monster I've heard so much about. Nope, can't. All I see is the intensity behind that golden gaze, and the way his hair sticks at odd ends, as if he'd run his fingers through it a few too many times.

I'd seen it look like that, after a good tumble...

"You never did explain," he drawls. "What makes you so sure we need to get out of here now?"

It takes a moment for his words to register, and I frown. A quick look around assesses where we've ended up. Under the massive marble stairs, steps away from the main entrance. Not good–we're way too close if anyone walks in. I'm not sure what Persephone's plan is, but she was clear on one point. We needed to disappear, and fast.

"Follow me," I mutter and head further down.

Declan lets out an annoyed grunt, but he's right behind me again. I stop by a massive portrait of the Elysian Fields and with a wave of my hand, blow some magic to move it. A crack behind it appears–one of the secret passages. I slip within, without waiting for Declan to follow.

I've only gone a few steps, when his iron grip is around my wrist and he effortlessly hoists me up a few paces until we're nose to nose.

"Enough with your orders."

I open my mouth to speak, but he drops the bundle of supplies and lifts his free hand to my lips, pressing his finger against them.

"Shush, princess. Unless you tell me what I want to know, we're not going anywhere."

There is no light in here, but his eyes are gleaming like golden flames in the darkness. Something about the way he holds my gaze, so unafraid and plain out rude, aggravates me. This is not the gentleman from my dreams, far from it.

Mom, what the hell were you thinking, sending this brute after me? I wonder, not for the first time.

Out loud, I say, "Both Persephone and Hades said we have to get out."

"Funny. Because I saw the big bad lord of

the Underworld, and he said the opposite to me."

Shit. Hades had time to see Declan? When?

Shaking my head, I amend my answer. "Okay, fine. Maybe it was just Persephone, then. Point is, our presence here is only firing up things that have been under wraps for millennia. The sooner we're away, the better for them."

"And you know how to escape the Underworld?"

I hesitate, recalling my friend's warning words. "I do. And I can lead the way."

"So long as it doesn't take us past Cerberus," he grumbles and lets go of me.

That draws my full focus—and suspicion. "How do you know Cerberus?"

He arches an eyebrow. "Doesn't everyone?" When I fold my arms over my chest, he scoffs. "Figures. You'll barely give me two words, but you expect me to answer at the drop of a hat. Very well. When your parents tossed me into the Underworld after you, I so happened to run into the big doggie. He was wounded, I helped heal him, and then he attacked me. As you can see, I survived."

A gasp escapes me. "Did you *kill* him?"

That earns me another eye roll. "No. I left him behind to bemoan his fate to anyone who would listen and flew away."

My jaw drops at that. *Flew? Like...* I can't help looking him up and down again, wondering what he'd be like, in his zmeu form. Which does he prefer?

Stop. I pause my train of thought before it wanders. Declan's proclivities are none of my concern, nor are his preferences.

"Did you say you healed him?" I ask, recalling the other part of his story.

This time, it's a snort I get. He's just a full-on caveman, isn't he?

"Don't get your hopes up, I'm no hero. I saw an opportunity for information, and badly miscalculated, is all."

He shifts, his massive bulk brushing against me in the darkness. I plaster myself against the cold wall, only afterwards realizing he's bending down to pick up our supplies again. With his free hand, he reaches into the air itself and does something, some kind of design, that sizzles. Then it parts the fabric of the element, releasing a silver blade in his hand, with a dark leather hilt.

My eyes must have widened because he tosses me a smirk. "You're not the only one with magic, princess."

"Quit calling me that!"

He passes by me, only an inch away. "When you stop acting like one, and more like the Connie I know, I just might."

Then he walks ahead, his steps too damn assured for his own good.

About half an hour later, we emerge from the staircase into a massive tunnel underneath the palace. One can say I've had enough time to explore Hades' home, including all its hidden passages. Good thing, too.

The tunnel expands ahead of us, carved out of the mountain, the gleaming walls lit by sparsely laid torches. It's an odd combination of dark and light, but the wide expanse leaves us without many places to hide, should we be seen.

"This way!" I wave Declan to me, but he's stubbornly looking in the opposite direction from where I'm headed.

"I came the other way."

I huff out a breath. "It wouldn't matter, the tunnels underneath don't reflect what's on the surface."

"How so?"

"They're the exact opposite, inverted."

"That makes no sense."

"Tell me about it," I grumble under my breath. When he still refuses to budge, I get annoyed. "Would you just *listen*?"

Declan scowls my way. "Your mother never said I couldn't tie you up and bring you back. She just said you couldn't be harmed."

I stomp the ground in frustration, and a chuckle echoes from the shadows.

"Wow, Declan, you've met your match."

We both freeze, but it's only Persephone. She steps out from behind a hidden corner, two satyrs by her side. I recognize Hades' most trusted one with her.

"Persephone!"

I run to my friend and hug her as if I hadn't just seen her hours earlier.

"Why aren't you out of here yet?" She whispers in my hair.

"We got lost," I mutter, glaring daggers at

Declan for emphasis. "This one won't listen."

He ignores me, busy scanning the area. Persephone glances between us, then gestures behind herself.

"This way. It's a hidden path that will bring you to the Lethe river, from there you can follow the marigolds out."

"Thanks…" I take a step closer. "Hang on. How did you get under here? And where's Hades?"

Persephone straightens her shoulders, something I know she only does when she tries to appear stronger than she is. "He's… trying to undo this."

"With whom?"

"Some trusted friends, here."

"But it's not working?" I assume by the wariness in her expressions.

She glances over my shoulder, then back at me and nods. It's tiny, but enough to let me know shit has hit the fan, and Hades is barely keeping hold on everything.

"I saw the souls, from Declan's chambers. It looked like a mob."

Persephone only stares, her expression conflicted. I'm already missing our carefree moments from earlier–was it only today?

"What about his army?" I lower my voice, picking up on the fact she doesn't want Declan to hear.

"The new ones–they're no longer interested in protecting their lord."

"What! Why?"

Another glance to Declan. "They've learned of Declan's... nature. And it seems Hades was tricked, once more."

"How so?"

She pulls me into another hug, then whispers in my ear, "They're the dead souls of Cavaleri Serafim, trained knights who hunted zmei for millennia. There's a long, bloody history between them and Declan's kin. Be careful, both of you. And if they catch Declan, for the love of all that is holy, run!"

When she lets me go, I nearly stagger, but catch myself just in time. At the silent pleading in her eyes, I pull in a large gulp of air and change the subject, louder this time.

"You say to follow the marigolds? That's not the path I usually take."

"All the others are watched."

"By whom?"

Persephone glances at Declan. "Those who dislike intruders. Those who believe Hades to be weak."

I catch the undertone of everything she's not saying, and I don't hold back anymore. "I know, Persephone. About his... ability."

A flash of worry crosses her features, then her shoulders slouch. "Does everyone?"

"No! No, not at all," I hasten to reassure her. "If I hadn't spent so much time around him–way more than I wanted to, on the last day–I wouldn't have realized."

"Hate to interrupt the party, ladies," Declan says loudly from behind, "but we don't have time for chit chatting."

"Give us a minute!" I toss the words over my shoulder.

But already Persephone is shaking her head. "No, Declan is right. For once. You have to leave, and hurry. We haven't been able to find Charon, and who knows what he's up to now?"

"Wait. Before we go... Those you mentioned who hate intruders, especially from the Living... Are they the same ones who would see Hades' special gift as weakness?"

She inclines her head, her expression filled with sorrow. "Indeed. Now, follow me. Hades is causing a distraction, but we have little time."

As Declan falls in step with us, he keeps checking the surroundings. "How long will this alternative path take to bring us back in the land of the Living?"

"As fast as your feet will take you, I would imagine."

"And will it pass by Cerberus?"

"It shouldn't... but no one knows where he is. Least of all Charon."

Declan swears under his breath, and I would laugh if it wasn't all so damn worrying.

Once Persephone brings us to the edge, I turn to her. "How can we help once we're out?"

"We'll take care of things here. Just get out safe. Send word once you do." A meaningful look to my necklace.

"Persephone...."

Declan steps up. "Let's go. The sooner we get a move on, the better it'll be for them."

I hug my friend, then reluctantly follow Declan out the dark path, wondering if I'm leaving a safe heaven for a very unsafe one.

Declan

Well, that was interesting. It was even more so for me, given my sharp hearing picked up on everything these two ladies didn't want me to hear.

Which now explains what hunted my brother in the world of the Living... And by the same stroke of luck–read, *bad* luck–it also found me.

The fucking Serafim. I remember centuries upon centuries we fought them until I refused to. Back in those times, I still cared about humans, and something about killing so many of them didn't sit well with me.

What can I say, I wasn't always this smart.

Still. The fact they are here, and evidently placed here on purpose by this Charon, means this entire thing was orchestrated long before.

I am reminded again of Igor's words, when he died of his wounds. His warning that this could not be undone... Was he playing to someone else's tune, same as I was his? And if yes, who? Who would have the power to dethrone an Olympian?

Tytus might be able to do some digging,

since he's on the surface and not restrained by a revolution. But do I really want to appeal to my brother? *No*, I decide, we're nowhere near that type of bonding just yet.

Even if I did contribute to saving his life only a few weeks ago.

Constanza is walking ahead of me–again–and I try to focus my thoughts away from Hades' problem. Whatever happens to him and Persephone is their due. I am here for this little minx, and considering I've gotten her to follow me and we're on our way out of the Underworld, it seems my mission is not such a disaster.

I've got to stop looking at this as such a bad thing. So perhaps there's no explaining Constanza popping up in my dreams or the chemistry we had. But it sure as hell was pleasant. And, if I can get on her good side, perhaps her guard will drop. If she sees me as a friend, a lover, again, it'll be so much easier to have her as leverage against Ileana. Especially if once we return to the world of the Living, she also cares for me. It would be about time I learn to use emotions to my advantage, once and for all.

What's left of my conscience tries to tell me this would be wrong, but I don't pay attention to it.

Instead, I tell myself to focus and school my expression into a neutral one.

"How long have you known Persephone?"

"A while."

"And you always make it a habit to visit?"

Undaunted by my questions, Constanza ducks under some trees, then glues herself to the wall of the garden in an attempt to pass by unnoticed. Hmm. Seems the little minx knows something about sneaking around.

"When I can," she admits.

"And your parents don't mind you spending time in the Underworld, surrounded by souls? Seems dreary."

She tosses me a glare over her shoulder. "Maybe I like dreary."

"Uh huh."

"What's that supposed to mean?"

"Nothing. The girl I knew was all fire and life, is all."

Her side glance says she's not fooled. Nor does she fall into the trap I set and start contesting what we had. Guess this won't be as easy as I thought.

"I'm only trying to make conversation. Otherwise this'll make for a very long few days."

She stops in her tracks and puts her hands on her hips. "Let's get one thing clear. I don't believe you're doing any of this for my benefit. As a matter of fact–"

I catch sight of the souls we're heading towards before she does and improvise fast. I tug her closer, shift my body to shield us, and press my hand over her mouth, effectively shutting her up.

The movement brings us in proximity– again–and my zmeu pokes its head in interest. *Down, boy.*

This close to her, that intoxicating scent fills my nostrils, and kissing her becomes all I can think about. The rise and fall of her chest, the widening of her eyes, and her parted lips under my touch tell me she's not as unaffected as she seems. Despite the souls being gone by now, I don't move, don't put any distance between us. And neither does she...

I remove my hand slowly, and Constanza's eyes don't leave mine. Before I even realize what I'm doing, I'm leaning closer, our lips almost brushing, an ache in my gut–and lower–that I need to fill. At least, until her hands on my chest deliver a shot of lightning and send me flying backwards, straight into some bushes.

When I get back up, she's glaring at me. I point to the glowing forms, now at a safe distance. "Was trying to distract."

She looks from them to me and regret flashes across her face. Then she tosses her head back. "Well, don't go taking liberties."

I stand, dusting myself off. "Message received, princess."

Da, this won't be easy, at all.

Chapter 8

Scântei
"No amount of darkness can hide a spark of light."
-Unknown-

Constanza

I need to keep Declan away from me, period. Every time he gets close, and looks at me soulfully, my knees go weak. And I know it's not because of him, but because of the blasted memories we created in our dreams. My body remembers that, and cannot combine it with this man–the brute.

Worse still, I crave his touch. If I hadn't

blasted him away, I probably would've pulled him towards me within the second. My lips are still burning from a kiss that almost was, my mind reeling at how I almost gave in. I should've known it would be hard to keep my distance, but damn it, I don't want to want him!

Persephone is right. There's something shady about his presence here, and I mistrust it. Yet why did he save us, when Charon tried to attack Hades? Why get involved at all? And more to the point, why is he so quick to act, when my mind around him is a muddled mess? When I yearn for nothing more than to strip him and have my way with him again…?

Questions upon questions churn inside my head, but the answers evade me like fireflies at dawn.

We're officially out of the castle and are now walking through the same gardens I'd been in with Persephone when all this started. Was that only hours ago? Could it be this has all been brewing about, and I've been completely clueless to it?

How many times did I enter the Under-world? How many times did I interact with

Charon, albeit warily? And how many blasted ways have I explored this place... Only to now be stuck, not as savvy as I thought, at all.

I sure would've made a horrible guardian. Perhaps it's just as well the gods don't need us immortals anymore.

And yet.... How true is that, I wonder? I finger the necklace at my neck, wishing to talk to my parents, and get some kind of reassurance that yes, Hades and Persephone will be alright. That there's no way they can dethrone him, let alone harm him.

"Over here," Declan waves me to a corner, and I creep closer, stopping short of being too near.

He's peeking around a bush, then crouches lower, still holding his sword in one hand while I've got the bundle of supplies. When he makes no other move, I hiss, "What are you doing, exactly?"

Rather than answer me, he replies with another question. "What else did Persephone tell you?"

"What?"

"Don't play dumb with me, princess. Earlier, in the tunnels, she said a hell of a lot more than to follow the marigolds. So?"

I say nothing, forcing him to look at me. When his eyes narrow, I stomp my foot and go to move past him. With a muttered curse, he reaches for me and pulls me against him, my back to his chest, his arms wrapped around me tightly.

"Are you done treating me like the enemy?"

"Prove me you're not, then."

He scoffs, his hot breath tickling my ear. "Is that what Persephone told you? How not to trust little old me?" There's a bitterness in his tone that takes me by surprise, almost as much as his sudden release of me. "Fine, don't answer the hard questions. Tell me something easy. How did Hades lose control of his world so fast?"

"What makes you think he did?"

The golden hue of his eyes glints even more dangerously. "Peek around the corner. Go on."

He steps back, leaving me enough room to take his spot and risk a glance around. What I see has me lean on the wall for support, yet unable to peel my eyes away.

If we cross these bushes, we can get to

Lethe, and the way beyond. But... the entire grounds of the castle are covered in souls. They're staring up at the windows above, waiting for Hades to address them. Or something. From their ever-growing furious expressions, he has not yet made an appearance.

Shivers race up my spine, even as my mouth goes dry. I've seen some of these souls around, even chatted with them when I was bored. Yet now they're clearly not friendly, and if they see us here...

I can't fathom what my friend's consort is playing at, but nothing can take away the animosity here. And among the souls, I see dark heads–the knights of the new guard. What had Persephone called them, again?

Cavaleri Serafim.

One thing strikes me, same as it did Declan–there is no way our appearance stirred this amount of animosity. It must have been in the works, time and time again.

"Well?" Declan says, and I realize he's not that far behind me.

On the contrary, his hot breath on my neck implies he is too close. I turn my head slightly. "Do you mind?" When he only arches an eyebrow, I hiss, "Move *back*. I don't appreciate your closeness."

"Sorry, princess, but your feelings are the least of my concern right now." He looks past me, towering over me.

His height used to make me hot, now it drives me insane–and not in a good way. More like I hate how tiny he makes me feel, how vulnerable. Because that, in turn, brings thoughts of how safe his bulky presence feels. Unwelcome thoughts.

"What do you know of Tartarus?"

I frown at him, trying to see where he's going with this. "Not much. It's the hellish part of this place, a secondary realm underneath the one we're in. Meant as punishment for evil souls, basically."

"Uh huh." He's still scanning the surroundings, but something tells me his distracted appearance is only a façade. "So all the bad guys are in one spot?"

"I guess, yeah."

"And that includes the ones from ages ago?"

"Well, yeah. It's not like there's an expiration date for their punishments!"

He grits his teeth when his gaze settles on me again. "And you don't see a problem with that?" He shakes his head. "Stop acting like I'm the enemy here, princess, and see what's right in front of you."

"Which is?"

"Did Charon have a link to Tartarus, yes or no?"

I recall what the ferryman had mentioned in the audience hall, and gulp. "Yeah... He was imprisoned there for a year."

Declan's expression becomes knowing. "Why?"

"Because he'd let a Living into the Underworld... Ah, shit." Now I finally get it. "You're saying Charon had access to all the baddies, since then? That's why we're seeing this increased animosity?"

"Yep."

Does Persephone know? My friend is smart, surely she tied the two together. I finger the necklace she gave me, hesitating to contact her, what with Declan nearby.

"We don't have time for that," he adds with a pointed nod to the accessory. Does the guy not miss anything?

His attention to detail was also something that used to drive me insane. The way he could pinpoint all my pleasurable points and bring me to the edge of ecstasy and back... Few lovers are that skilled at *listening* to a woman's body.

Funny to think something I deemed a quality in my dreams, annoys the shit out of me in real life.

"I need to get us out of here," Declan says, either oblivious or purposely ignoring my glare. His determination is intense. This guy... is not the man of my dreams. He's scary, and more like the Declan I've been told about.

When his golden eyes meet mine, something flashes in their depths. "Do ghosts burn?"

"What?"

"The souls here, princess. Focus. Can they be hurt by fire?"

I recall my previous times here and my interactions with them. "I... I think so, yes. They're not corporeal, but their mind would believe the fire real, and cause psychic pain, if that makes sense. At least enough to be pushed away."

"Good."

He steps further back from me, making room. Too much room.

"What are you doing?"

"Don't freak out."

The moment after, I realize why he tells me that. He tosses his head back, and an expression of agony crosses his features, before it's replaced by blankness. Then flames, large and the color of ice, surround him. More than that, they burn him–wash away the human form to ashes.

A cry gets stuck in my throat, thinking it's a curse that hit him. But, no, it's nothing of the sort. From the flames, an unfamiliar shape emerges. Larger, heavier, with black scales and glinting horns, wings the size of the entire garden.

I hear shouts from a distance–we've been spotted. With his growing bulk, there's no way we wouldn't be. But I'm too entranced by the transformation to even register the danger we're in.

The only thing left of Declan are his golden eyes. The rest... I'm standing in front of the zmeu and feeling damned small and breakable.

Even as my fingers dig into the wall, the beast facing me pants, then lifts his head. The golden stare is even more startling against the dark scales.

What the...? Is he for real!?

"D-Declan?" It comes out on a strangled gulp.

I've never, in my centuries of existence, seen anything so scary and majestic, all at once. And the oddest thing is... the form *suits* him.

Declan nods, then moves. Much faster than I'd thought possible for a beast his size. He pushes past me to the nearing soul crowd and shoots blasts upon blasts of blue fire.

While the souls are screaming, Declan grabs our supplies with one claw and gets me on his back, practically swinging me up by my dress. The moment after, we're flying into the inky sky.

Below us, more cries echo. We've been seen, and yet that's the last of my worries. Because what the hell was my mom thinking, sending this monster after me?

He's *not* the man of my dreams.

Not *at all.*

Declan

Constanza may have been revolted by my true form, but she sure hung tight to me once we were up in the air. Of course, now that we've passed danger, and my zmeu form is too discernable, I should switch back to human. Eventually.

I continue to fly over the Underworld, not knowing where I'm going. What with the tunnels being inverted, and the need to escape, I didn't pay attention which direction I headed in. All I see below is a wide expanse of land, interrupted by woods or rivers. I guess they must not have flying beasts here, since none have followed us. When I glance below again and notice a spot I can use to land, I dive lower.

Within moments of touching the ground, Constanza slides off my back, and I take a few steps away. A moment later, I let the change come over me, burning off my zmeu and leaving the human in its wake. With a snap of my fingers, I clothe myself with a pair of jeans and a human shirt, then open my eyes.

Constanza is staring away from me, a

slight tinge of pink to her cheeks. The same color I've seen after–

Shit. Focus.

I clear my throat and ask, "Where do we go now? Since the marigolds are not an option."

She glances around, anywhere but at me, and gives a slight shrug. "I... I've never been in this area of the Underworld, before. Give me a moment to get my bearings."

She turns away from me and paces around, while I wait. Patiently. Impatiently. Knowing full well she's avoiding me because she cannot deal with what she's seen.

Finally, Constanza stops and faces me. "Let's find our way back to the river. I should be able to direct us from there. There's a crossroads that leads to either the Elysian Fields, where the heroes are, or Tartarus, or the purgatory."

"And, what, you're thinking we'll get some hero help?"

She shakes her head. "Or find out if anyone knows a different way out."

"It's as a good a plan as we have right now." I shrug and jerk my finger to the right.

"Last I saw, Styx was this way."

Without another word, we move again. It only takes me a few more moments to realize there is a point to where she's taking us, and perhaps she's not sharing on purpose.

After another brief silence, I clear my throat. "So, mind telling me where we're going?"

"To the river, like I said."

"I don't believe you."

She whirls around at my accusation, eyes narrowed on me.

"You're heading with purpose, like someone who knows where she's going."

After a slight debate, Constanza sighs and taps her foot. "Alright, fine. You ever heard of Chiron?"

I scratch the back of my neck. "I'm confused. Isn't that the guy who tried to hurt Hades?"

She rolls her eyes, every bit the spoiled princess. "*Chi*ron. With an I."

When I shrug, Constanza says, "Okay, so he used to be this centaur mentor-like guy, for the heroes back in Greece. He helped Heracles, and a couple of others. And when his time came, well, rumor was he became a star, or so the humans said."

"Sentimental fools."

"I couldn't agree more," Constanza grins, and it's so unexpected she agrees with me, that I'm unsure how to react. As if realizing her mishap, she grows serious again. "Anyway, the point is, Hades built him a secluded spot in the Underworld where he could spend his afterlife as he wished—in peace."

"Okay…"

I'm still missing the link to Hades, but I'm sure she's about to educate me.

"Anyway, Chiron knows everything and everyone. If anyone could tell us what's going on, who's behind all this, and maybe even a way out, it would be him."

"I'm not so convinced, princess. Didn't you say he's secluded? How would he know?"

She shrugs. "Chiron knows all."

"Uh huh… And you can vouch for this guy well enough to assure me he won't be trying to kill us?"

"Yes."

Without another word, she starts walking again. I really want to put a leash on her and make sure she stops taking off on a whim, especially when it leaves me scrambling to follow her.

"And how do you know where he lives, exactly?"

Constanza points to a small mountain in the distance, past a forest. "Over there."

"Right." I glance behind the palace we left, a black point in the distance. "You realize we're not going toward any exit, then?"

"Like I said, I'm hoping Chiron might have an answer to that, too."

Silence grows again. The more I let her lead, the more it'll hopefully make her trust me. Enough so that by the time we cross back into the Living realm, I can still use her as my trump card.

Ileana's own daughter... What a stroke of luck. Even if she is as stuck up as her mother is.

As we walk, Constanza watches me out of the corner of her eye, as if expecting me to sprout three heads.

"I don't bite," I mutter. "Much."

Constanza frowns. "I realize that."

"Could've fooled me."

"Excuse me?"

My silence is all she gets as an explanation. She comes to me then, wrapping her tiny hand around my bicep. An unwelcome jolt of electricity runs through me.

"Tell me."

"You're afraid of me."

"I am not!"

"Then would you mind wiping that revolted look off your face?"

Constanza stares at me with new eyes. "I wasn't... That's not it, at all."

I scan our surroundings, refusing to get sucked into those baby blues. A small stream in the distance draws my eye and I head closer to refill our flasks from the supplies bundle. Constanza follows me.

"Declan, stop."

My movements halt when her hands once more cover mine. So much smaller than mine. *She's* so much smaller than me.

I face her and her lips part, her eyes widen. This blasted connection that we created, it's starting to annoy me. Especially because with all the drama going around, I've yet to take anyone else into account but her– and her damned problems, and wishes.

I need to keep things in perspective. She's the enemy, an immortal. Her father killed many of my brethren, eons and eons ago. Worse still, she's a female. And I remember how that ended, last time.

Yet none of that rationalization will shut my zmeu up, or get him to settle. Whenever she's near, he pokes his head, waiting. Biding his time.

The moment lengthens, and we stand impossibly still, and much too close. Everything in her is inviting me. Everything in me wants to take.

Before either impulse takes over, I push off the ground. "Let's keep moving."

To her credit, Constanza doesn't whine at my fast pace, nor the relentless movement. On the contrary, she stays quiet.

Eventually, we reach the edge of a forest. I stop, staring in consternation at the dense trees. Their lush leaves seem inviting, swaying in the breeze. The trunks are a mix of shades of green, each glinting as if from an inner spark. And the sounds... Soft music swells from within, and I catch myself taking a step forward.

"It's the Forest of Forgotten Dreams," Constanza says behind me. Her voice is laced with tiredness. "I've heard souls whisper of it. They come here so they can connect with their loved ones. Send messages. So on..."

I whirl on her. "Is this how you reached out to me?"

Constanza rolls her eyes and plops down on the grass, taking off her dainty shoes and massaging her feet. "No, I didn't. I told you, I don't know how or why we connected in dreams."

"Right." Everything about my tone speaks of disbelief.

"Could you at least believe me on that account, if nothing else?"

It's my turn to seem confused. "Meaning?"

"Meaning, I also meant it when I said I didn't find you or your shifting repulsive. On the contrary, it was... powerful. Awe inspiring." Under her breath, she mutters, "Not that you need further ego stroking."

I hesitate, before sitting next to her on the

grass. My earlier thoughts of using her are fresh in my mind. No time like today to take the opening. "Fine. Suppose you're telling the truth. Why do you think our dreams escalated so?"

She shrugs, a blush coating her cheeks. "Maybe we were both lonely."

I think back to the cave I had been imprisoned in, and my teeth grit. I force myself to unclench my jaw.

"Where were you, anyway? How did my mom even find you?"

I should've expected the question, yet I didn't. To tell the truth... or lie. A shrug escapes me, along with words I can't take back. "She imprisoned me."

"*What*?"

"Your mother imprisoned me. Then traded my freedom in exchange for me bringing you back home."

"My mom wouldn't do that."

"She's an immortal, is she not?"

"But–"

I only stare at her, and watch as my words sink in. "I'm guessing you've had your fair share of manipulations from her?"

Constanza looks at the grass and starts picking at it. "Maybe."

"Then believe me when I say, I need to get you out of here, and soon. Your parents gave me one week."

Constanza sighs. "Sounds like Mom and Dad, alright." She tilts her head to the side. "Why were you imprisoned? How'd you piss her off?"

I shrug. "Not her. My brother."

Constanza waits for me to say more, but I stand instead. "I'll check the surroundings, make sure we're alone. Don't move."

As I leave, I try to tell myself the weight in my chest is because of victory. Because I'm close to being back in control. Because I'm this close to showing everyone what it means to mess with me. And not that it has anything to do with guilt.

Chapter 9

Încredere
-Friendship is built on two things: respect and _trust_."
-Unknown-

Declan

Whatever possessed me to bring up Tytus, I don't even know. It's in the way she looks at me, practically begs me with those eyes and that transparent gaze, to be honest. To say whatever's on my mind. A man could get drunk on a gaze like that.

And I'm not acting much better. Being around her is all but messing with my head, in the worst possible way. Once I get back from my patrol of the area, I try to keep my eyes away. But she's relentless, this immortal.

"Well?"

"Well, what?" I crouch by the fire she started and with a rune in the air, double its size.

No display of prowess is enough to get Constanza to back off.

"You were talking about your brother. And how he caused my parents to imprison you."

I scowl, staring in the distance. "It's a long story."

"We have only time."

I meet her stare, the curiosity in there. Though the shade of her eyes she gets from Făt, there is none of that cold calculation in there, only an openness I'm not used to seeing. Especially in an immortal.

"You sure you want to hear this, princess? It's not a fairy tale with a happily ever after."

She nods, pulling her knees to her chest and getting comfortable. *Well, I'll be fucked.*

"Very well." I settle my gaze on the ground. "Tytus and I hatched around the same time, him a few days earlier. We were real close as we grew, getting into all kinds of trouble in our clan. After a few centuries, rumors started flying around of a prophecy. Of two princes, one Light and one Dark, the latter of which would tear our clan to pieces. As you could guess, that set our elders into a frenzy."

"They thought it was you two?"

"Da." A bitter laugh escapes me. "And their unwavering belief turned the fake prophecy into truth."

"*Fake* prophecy?"

I stare at her, wondering how much to say. Her parents don't know about Igor, no one aside from Tytus, Fiona and I do. If more people were to find out, like Ileana, I doubt I'd ever get my freedom. Not that I trust they would give it to me anyway... But there is a difference in being able to leave this realm, or being hunted out of it.

"Da." I say after a beat. "Darker forces were at work, and one of those, well, he was rather interested in driving a wedge between us."

I turn my gaze to the inky burgundy sky above us. Constanza untangles our bundle to munch on some things, but I feel her ardent gaze on me.

"Bottom line is, over a few centuries, my brother and I became estranged, until we were completely torn apart. When that happened, and the Council accused me of inciting the genocide of our species and humans, he did not defend me, and let them imprison me."

Constanza lets out a low curse. "Just like that?"

I shrug. "I'm simplifying for the sake of storytelling."

"What proof did they have?"

I think back to that time. "Villages around our castle burned. I did not hide the fact it was my doing–killing humans was a favorite pastime of mine back then."

"For pleasure?"

The pain in her tone makes me meet her gaze. "Yeah."

Something flickers in her expression– revulsion? Hate? Something else?

I turn away before I can make sense of it. Whatever it is, it doesn't matter. I'm only telling her this story to get her to trust me more, and lower those defenses. No other reason.

"That, and a certain Order had us in their sights. The Council thought it was because of my actions, thus bringing the prophecy full close."

"What Order?"

I chuckle then, and reach over to her lap, stealing a roll of bread. After a bite, I grin coolly. "The same ones Sephora whispered to you about–Cavaleri Serafim."

Her audible gulp draws my attention again. "Yeah, I heard it all." I point to my ear. "Super sharp hearing is one perk of a zmeu's powers, princess."

"I…" She shakes her head. "Okay, fine. Persephone said that and confirmed they're part of Hades' new guard. But they're not on his side. Charon recommended them and the minute they caught your true nature, they–"

"Switched sides." I snort. "How typical."

Even as I chew the rest of the bread, it tastes like ashes on my tongue. Still, I go through the motions, waiting and thinking. If the Serafim are here, chances are they're on our trail. They would not let go of a chance to hunt down the last of the zmei, even while they're dead.

And if they have my blood… *When I next*

reach Tytus, I'll have to ask him about it.

"Your story..." Constanza interrupts my thoughts, her voice soft, tentative almost.

"Yeah?"

"That wasn't the end, was it?"

A bitter chuckle escapes me then, and I give up on the roll of bread, tossing it back in the fire. "Not even a little bit, princess. I told you there's no happy ending here." I take a deep breath, shift to make myself more comfortable on the cool ground. "My first imprisonment lasted for eons and eons. Over a millennia long, they buried me alive in the earth, unable to fly, unable to do anything but wait. Try to escape. I nearly lost my mind–until one day, the edges of my consciousness picked up a call. A young witch was toying with forces unseen, and I saw my chance, there. Took it."

"How?"

"I seduced her." A glance at Constanza shows her revolted–and slightly jealous?–reaction. A laugh escapes me. "Mind out of the gutter, princess. Why is it you think sex is my go-to weapon, when it comes to females?"

She scowls, not as amused. "Maybe

because you give off that vibe."

"Hmm." I roll to my side, propped on my elbow. "No, I don't think so. If I were to call you out on this, I would say you're thinking like that, because of our history." I let my voice drop to an intimate pitch. "I would also say that's not the case–what we shared was, in fact, unique."

Constanza stares at me, looking like she wants to say something. But she bites her bottom lip, and the words die off before she can voice them.

I grin then, and shrug. "But I'm not calling you out on it. Instead, let me return to the story." I tap my fingers on the ground, then clear my throat. "The witch–I seduced her with promises of power, of more magic. It worked, and I could take over her mind, using her to gain allies. Other shifters, wolves, who were just as greedy. It almost worked, too. They freed me, I tasted air... And then Tytus was there, snatching it away once more. Only this time, your parents were also there. Involved with the wolves on the other side of the battle. And the rest, well, was me back to being imprisoned."

"Wow."

Her simple, one-word reply is enough to break down my walls. I turn to her, desperate to see her expression, understand what she took away from this entire revelation. And what I see…

"I'm so sorry, Declan." Constanza, to my utter surprise, is crying. Silent tears bathe her cheeks in big droplets.

Swear words leave my lips, even as I jerk to my knees, crawling over to her. How is it this immortal can listen to my story and still find the strength to cry for me? When I was obviously the villain?

I reach out and wipe her tears with my thumbs. "Why are you crying?"

"For you! Because what you lived through is unjust."

"They weren't too far off base."

"My parents, maybe. But when you were young? To be condemned, without even much proof? To be told you were Dark, that your destiny was preset? That's barbaric!"

"I was old enough to know better."

"But you *didn't* know any better!"

"That is no excuse, and you know it."

A sniffle, and she leans further into my touch. "You are not what they made you out to be, Declan."

My hands drop from her cheeks. "You don't know that."

"I do, though." She reaches for me again. "Or else you wouldn't be here, saving me, while trying to figure out a way to meet my demands."

It's my turn to narrow my eyes. "Whatever makes you think that's the case?"

She laughs. "Because I know you."

Before I can dispute that, noises around us make us jump to our feet. Constanza stomps out the fire, but it's too late. Shadows move in the distance–darkly clothed ones.

"Run!" I shout.

It doesn't take a genius to figure out that without Hades' protection, we're fucked in this Underworld.

Constanza

Even as we're leaving our supplies behind and trying to run for our life, I can't help but let my thoughts go back to what Declan told me. About his childhood, his past... Does he even realize how much all of that affected him?

To be told from a young age that he was meant to be Dark, to cause destruction... What does that do, to a child? If it had been me, would I be less of the immortal I am now? Probably. I have no doubt about that. It would have affected the way I see things, the way I perceive everything.

It's no wonder Declan turned into the hardened man before me. One who prefers destruction to creation, or salvation. One unable to deal with anything, choosing to take his pleasure from the dream realm.

Now why would I think of that? Ugh.

We're running side by side, contouring the Forest of Forgotten Dreams as we try to get to the mountain peak where Chiron is hiding.

"Does this mentor guy have any weapons?" Declan shouts from behind me.

"Yep!"

I glance behind, and my eyes go wide. In the distance there's a dark cloud hunting us– surely that can't all be Serafims?

"Move it!" Declan yells, grabbing my wrist

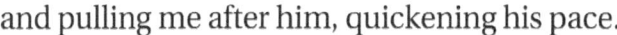

and pulling me after him, quickening his pace.

Arrows shoot around us, and above us. I duck and toss some magic behind. It escapes my hands in jets of white, blinding light. Declan's doing the same, only his escapes via those weird drawings again–runes. But given we're being chased by dead souls, this is only buying us time, at best.

Then, ahead, there is movement. Too small to be one of those knights. We cross to the mountain and curl up behind some bushes. The dark cloud gets closer and closer. I'm panting, trying to regain my breath, and wondering when the comfy bubble I'd been in burst, releasing me into this utter hell of chaos?

Declan wraps an arm around me, pulling me into his side. It's an odd gesture of comfort, but I don't push him away. It would be unfair given what we just shared, and what I tried to communicate to him. So instead, I burrow deeper into his hold, feeling the fast-beating rhythm of his heart against my ear.

"I'm sure this isn't what your parents had in mind when they sent me to get you," he points out.

He turns his body to protect me, coiled and ready to spring for when the Serafim will descend upon us.

"You tried, at least."

He nods, but says nothing. We're both waiting, listening to the hooves of horses, and the loud stomping of feet, as our enemies draw even closer.

"Is there no way to stop them?" Declan's chest muffles my tone.

"No," he says, his voice hard. "Above, with the Living, maybe. My brother fought them not too long ago and defeated them. But here, when they have all their tracking instincts, *and* can hurt us, without being hurt in return?"

A shudder runs through me. "I don't understand. If they're evil, they should have been sent down to Tartarus, not allowed into... here."

"You forget it was Charon who suggested them to Hades as guards, darling. He most likely made sure they *could* enter and continue to live among the rest."

"But Hades would have–" I pause, unwilling to divulge his secret, yet coming perilously too close.

"Would have what?" Declan asks.

The incoming swarm of Serafim buys me time from answering that question. Their shouts grow louder, and Declan's arm around me tightens more. We peer over the bush, watching with dread as they grow closer... and closer...

Then, to our surprise, when the dark cloud is upon us, a blinding wall of light rises and stops them from entering where we are. Shouts of indignation echo across, not that it does them any good.

"Who breaks the confines of my home?"

The deep voice behind us nearly makes me crumple to a heap of relief. I jump out of Declan's hold, and straight towards–

"Granddaddy!"

Declan

I wait for another beat, making sure the shield around Chiron's mountain truly blocks the Serafim, before straightening from my crouch.

Constanza's being lifted in the air by a half-man, half-horse creature–a centaur. A bush of wiry, salt and pepper hair surrounds his face, acting as both beard and hair. His upper torso only holds a leather jacket, and his lower body is on four massive legs, hooved feet and all. Even with my height, he towers over me, and judging by those piercing black eyes, I'm not as welcome as the immortal he's holding.

Noticing my attention on them, Chiron stops hugging Constanza and settles his grim gaze on me. "Who is this, Constanza?"

"Sorry, Granddaddy," she mutters. "We were coming to see you anyway, but then we got chased around the forest, and, well." She shrugs. "Is that barrier a recent addition?"

"Aye, I asked Hades to add it in when souls kept wandering around here. Some of those heroes don't like the peaceful afterlife, they'd rather be fighting."

"Right. Well, good thing you did."

"You still haven't answered my question."

I tug on Constanza's wrist, pulling her to me. "Granddaddy? You couldn't mention that before?"

"He's my godfather," she hisses back. "And he'll kick your ass if you disrespect me, so let me go."

I drop her wrist and settle back to watching from afar. With one last grunt, Chiron gets us climbing halfway up the mountain, until we're in front of a regular-looking cave. Once we step in, it's filled with wall to wall books, a fireplace in the distance, and even smaller rooms down the hall.

"Quite a setup you got here," I can't help observing.

Chiron narrows his eyes on me. "I didn't catch your name."

"Declan."

"And what are you doing with my goddaughter, exactly?"

"We're in trouble, Granddaddy," Constanza says. "And not just us, but Hades, too."

As she catches him up to date on the current events, Chiron moves around his home, preparing a meal and some drinks for us. It strikes me as odd until I realize he's missing that glow around his person.

"Hang on a second, you're not dead?"

Chiron glowers at me. Clearly, I've got a fan. "No."

"But how–"

Constanza turns to me. "Chiron wanted to retire, so Hades prepared this area for him. That's why souls kept coming by. The living aura in him attracted them. And the heroes, well, wanted more of his teachings, and stuff."

That makes sense… some.

But I'm more and more annoyed by how much Constanza kept from me. It might make me a hypocrite, given what I'm hiding, but would it kill her to be a bit more open with her lover?

Chiron gets back to the business at hand. "If I understand this correctly, Charon is working with his cronies, Hades and Persephone are sequestered in the palace, and no one is running the Underworld, nor Cerberus?"

"Basically sums it up," Constanza admits, and takes a sip of the cup he's holding out.

"Well, damn." Chiron runs a hand over his beard, and grumbles a few things under his breath, before settling on the ground. "You can stay here as long as you wish, of course, I'd be more than happy to give you shelter until this all settles down."

Before I can decline, Constanza speaks up. "Actually, Granddaddy, we were hoping for information more than anything else. We can't stay, and we'd rather send word to Olympus to help."

"Is that your best course of action?"

I tilt my head to the side. "What do you mean?"

Chiron glances between us, arching one eyebrow. "Did Constanza not tell you?"

Here we go again. I clench my jaw, trying to hold back from glaring her way in front of this guy. "Tell me what, exactly?"

"Hades and Olympus aren't on best terms. Matter of fact, there's a chance they may not want to intervene at all."

Tytus

I'm dreaming–but I'm nowhere I usually am. The hallway is dark, glowing only from a torch in the distance. Two figures are walking. One grabs the other's wrist, forces them to turn, and my point of view shifts.

Declan?

He is facing off against someone–a blonde woman with eyes the color of an inky sky. And they seem to argue…

I jerk awake. The dream of Declan unsettled me. And what is he doing with an immortal, Of all things?

I force my mind to open, tugging at the

bond between us. *Declan?*

What do you want?

Care to explain why I'm waking up with images of you and some immortal in my head?

A long silence follows. *None of your business.*

It is when you're keeping me awake.

Remember Ileana's quest I got sent on? Well, it so happens the person they sent me down here for is actually Ileana and Făt's daughter.

That small detail is enough to send my pulse racing. *Declan....*

My warning falls on deaf ears. *Breathe easy, frate. She is an immortal, and annoying as well, and I fully intend to return her. For a price.*

Do you realize who you're messing with?

Yes.

And you're prepared to take this all the way?

Absolutely.

Chapter 10

Declan

There's a slight delay to me switching from listening to Tytus, to Chiron's words. "Say that again."

"Olympus won't be interested in Hades, boy."

"First off, don't call me boy. Second, why not? Isn't he one of their own?"

Chiron rolls his eyes. "He is... But he butted heads with Zeus one too many times."

Constanza clears her throat. "What Granddaddy means, well what he's really talking about, is Heracles' resting place."

"Huh?"

I wish I had a more intelligent reply, but I'm getting lost amid all the names.

"Heracles, Hercules... Zeus' son? Hated by Hera, did the Twelve Labors?"

I rub my chin. "Oh yeah, him. That does ring a bell."

Constanza rolls her eyes. "Well, when he died, Heracles was supposed to go to Olympus. Live by his dad's side, etc. And he did... for a while, anyway."

Her weighted silence tells me there's more to the story.

"And?" I finally question, a tad impatient, when her silence lengthens too long.

"Heracles couldn't get along with Hera. Or, the opposite. Whatever the case, he came to visit his uncle–Hades–here and met other heroes in the Elysian Fields." A small shrug. "Well, he never left."

Suspicion creeps through me. "Sounds

like you know this guy pretty well."

"We ran into each other a couple times," she says without getting into it.

I shouldn't care, not really. But I've been burned a tad too much last time I had a female around. *If anything, this is more proof I need to keep my focus on getting her out of here, and using her to regain my freedom.*

If only my zmeu would stop grumbling whenever I think about that.

"Alright." I stand, unable to sit while we're talking about this. "So Heracles stuck around here and, what, Zeus lost his shit?"

"Something like that," Chiron says. "He asked Hades to send his son back to Olympus. Hades refused, and Zeus has been sulking ever since." He pauses, glancing between us. "Do you understand now why it may not be so easy to get Olympus to intervene?"

I pinch the bridge of my nose, sensing a headache on the edge of my consciousness. "Da, I do."

This is getting complicated. Not only have we ended up surrounded on a mountaintop, but now the help we desperately need may be denied. *Well, fuck.*

"Alright," I repeat. "Let's say Olympus is out of the question." When Constanza opens her mouth as if to interrupt, I lift my hand. "I'm not saying it is one hundred percent, but let's just pretend." To Chiron, I add, "Give us information, centaur. Loads of it."

His jaw clenches, the dark eyes glittering in warning. Whatever his problem is with me, he'll just have to deal.

"Very well. What kind of information do you need?"

"First—is there an exit out of the Underworld?"

Chiron sips some tea. "There are many, but Charon knows them all. If Cerberus is not guarding them, he must have these new knights you speak of doing his bidding."

"Even the marigold path?"

He glances to Constanza, as if to verify if that tidbit of information came from her, then nods. "Yes, even that."

"Granddaddy… there must be a way out."

"There is." Another sip. "The marigolds."

Constanza frowns. "But you just said—"

"You cannot do it alone, is all."

"Oh."

"Moving on," I mutter. When Constanza tries to intervene again, I hold up a hand. "No, princess. Not this time. It's bad enough you're dragging us into trying to figure this shit out. No way in hell I'm bringing in more unknown variables."

"I would suggest," Chiron stands from the ground, towering over me as he glowers, "that you watch your tone with my goddaughter."

My fist clenches, even as the primordial magic in me, held back for too long, sizzles down my arm. Chiron's gaze flickers to it, then back to me. Amusement dances in his eyes, as if daring me.

Constanza steps between us, tugging me back. "Declan, enough," she hisses. "What's gotten into you?"

I grace her with a scowl, barely holding back the torrent of words waiting to escape me.

As if sensing my inability to control myself, Constanza turns back to Chiron. "Say we still wanted to, despite the unlikelihood of getting an answer... How do we contact Olympus?"

"I will take care of that," Chiron says. "It's the least I can do, given all Hades has done for me."

I eye him skeptically. "Sure you can achieve that, old man?"

His glare is answer enough.

"Alright, here's the harder question." I settle back into my chair. "Who could have done this? Have all this power, control Charon, all of it. Who's the big enemy we have to watch out for?"

The new puzzle seems to lower the centaur's guard, as he paces around, rubbing his beard. His eyes narrow as he stares into the fireplace. "A few weeks ago, I heard rumors. That some force was trying to open the gates of the Underworld, and free some dead spirits in here."

"What kind of spirits?" Constanza asks.

I froze when he mentioned *unknown force*, dread filling me. Out of everything I told Constanza, this was not part of it. And if she finds out now, from someone else, that I may have had a hand in weakening the Underworld's defenses, in paving the way for Charon and his crazy plan, then I'll lose all leverage. Not to mention she'll hate me, rather than be putty in my hands.

I let that dread rule me, churning in my

gut. Chiron stares at me, but says nothing. Nor do I.

Eventually, he shrugs. "Not sure."

I hold back a sigh of relief.

"And you think this force is at the root of it?" Constanza seems worried.

Impossible. Igor is dead… *Ah, shit.* If he's dead, that implies he's here somewhere, probably in Tartarus. Which means he's right in the middle of it with the dangerous scum of the pantheons.

To my surprise, Chiron disputes that theory.

"No," Chiron says. "I believe it had added onto an already fractured setting."

"Meaning?"

"Let me research a few things, before I go blabbing my old mouth." He smiles at Constanza. "I have rooms at the back, for you to rest. Surely one night, you can afford?"

She shares a glance with me, and as I nod, she returns the smile. "Of course, Grand-daddy."

Needless to say, I barely sleep. When I try, I

see flashes of Alina, and then her face turns into Constanza's. It's enough to jolt me awake, panting and sweating in the tiny bed.

I run my hands down my face, growling and muttering in the dark. What did I ever do to deserve this kind of torture? It's not like I can run into the deceitful whore my ex-wife was and ask her why she had to tear out my fucking heart.

"Sorry, am I interrupting?"

I lower my arm in time to notice Constanza poking her head through the door. My intentions, where she's concerned, are less than honorable. But they do give me a purpose, I cannot deny it.

"By all means," I drawl, and beckon her inside.

She changed out of her red dress into a gray version, and the scent of violets is sharper now, more intense. It wafts to me, and I clench my hand in the bedsheets. What's with this stupid urge to touch her, to taste her all over again?

"Chiron has a shower, further inland. If you want to use it, I mean."

I sit up on the small mattress, arching an eyebrow her way. "Care to join me?"

The telltale flush on her skin is a sign I wasn't too far off in my assumption. Even if lightning flashes in her eyes right after, and indignation coats her tone, she's not here for conversation.

"Excuse me?"

I stand then, pushing off the bed and straightening to my full height. Constanza may want to fight it, but her gaze travels the expanse of my naked chest, and lower, before she turns away.

"Shy all of a sudden, princess?"

I move closer, almost stalking her until her back is to the wall, and I'm blocking her from moving. Her chest is rising faster, and my eyes drop to it, and the lush mounds hidden beneath.

Fuck, just one damned taste. Surely I'm allowed that much?

I press one palm on the wall next to her head and use my other hand to tilt her chin up towards me. "Tell me you don't feel this heat between us. That you don't crave what we had."

Her mouth parts, and for a moment there's a glaze in her eyes that tells me all I need to know. Then she jerks her chin out of my grip, smacking her head against the wall in the process. The hit doesn't seem to douse her anger, as she glares at me.

"I bet you use your charms on everyone, don't you? Including Persephone."

Unbelievable. This shit again!

My nostrils flare, and my hand drops next to her. "Why do you have to bring her up, now of all times?"

"I'm not about to satisfy your needs just because I'm here, and convenient!"

"I assure you, convenient is not what goes through my head when I think of you, princess."

She shoves against my chest with surprising strength, and I move off her, heading out the door and to the shower. If my bed is not what she wants, then the little minx had best be out of there before I return.

My second attempt at sleep doesn't go any better. Despite Constanza's absence from my room once I'm back, her scent lingers in the air, and it makes my zmeu restless. Annoyed. Part of me wants nothing more than to shift and fly out of here, leave all this crap behind.

But then there's the other part, that knows I gave my word, and forces me to stick by it. And, there's always the fact I need the stubborn immortal if I'm to secure a proper second life for myself.

The sounds of a flute echo to me, and I get up from bed to walk back to the living area. Chiron is lying down in front of the fireplace now, and the music is coming from a flute. By his hooves are books upon books, laid open.

"Found something?"

He lays down the instrument on the cool stone and throws me a sharp look. "The better question is, have you?"

I can't fathom what to make of it, so I get closer and take a seat across from him. When I say nothing, Chiron sighs.

"Constanza gave me all the information I needed, except for one tiny piece. Where do you fit in, zmeu?"

My eyes narrow. "So you know what I am."

"I do."

I shrug. "To answer your question, I *don't* fit in. Constanza's mother sent me down here to get her. In exchange, I'll get my freedom. That's about it."

Chiron laughs then, a full belly chortle. "Is that what you think?" He shakes his head, wiping at his eyes. "Thank you. It has been a long time since I have laughed so well."

"Glad to entertain," I deadpan.

Chiron looks at me then. "Your story with Constanza did not begin with your imprisonment, nor will it end with your freedom. That is all I'll say on the matter, but the sooner you get on board, the better off you shall be."

"What are you, psychic?"

His gaze sharpens. "Takes one to know one, no?"

That leaves me speechless. And while I try hard to figure out my next train of thought, the best I can come up with is rolling my eyes. "Sure. I'll pretend I got that. Do you plan to let us know what you've found, at all?"

Constanza walks in at that moment. After a glare my way, she kneels by Chiron's side, trailing her fingers over the books. "Granddaddy?"

He nods and says, "Yes, I did find something. To answer your most pressing question, about who would have orchestrated this mess for Hades? Only one force would fit, only one that would be strong enough to fight against all of this. And that is the Titans. Or, more in particular, a specific one–Cronus."

"What?" Constanza's eyes widen.

This new information should have my full focus, as none of it bodes well for us. Or for *me* in particular, and my future plans. But my attention is somewhere else on noises echoing up to us.

A scrape by the rock, a muffled curse–my ears pick it all up, and the moment after I'm standing, slashing a sword of fire from the flames, and backing towards Constanza.

"What are you doing?" she yells.

I shush her, turning to Chiron. "Is there another way out of here? The Serafim breached your barrier."

"Impossible!"

I grab his leather jacket, pulling myself up until I'm in his face, baring my teeth. "Fucking hell, centaur. I don't know *how*, but those knights following us are *here!* Now unless you want your precious goddaughter caught, answer me!"

Anger leaves his features, replaced instead by worry as his gaze lands on Constanza. He nods, then jerks himself out of my hold. "At the back, past the showers, there's a secret tunnel." He rushes to a corner, grabs a satchel and tosses some leaflets in there, some food, and shoves it towards Constanza. "Take this. All my notes are in there, explaining what I found. Go!"

Constanza's still shell-shocked, taking the satchel with numb fingers. "What about you?"

"It's not me they're after." He gives an encouraging nod. "Go with the zmeu, I will be fine."

I don't wait for more sentimentalities. I grab Constanza's wrist and pull her after me. A few moments later we're through a tunnel hidden behind a portrait and running at fast speed.

Constanza

We're right back where we started–running. And trying to escape from crazy, dead knights. At least this time we have some answers Granddaddy provided, if we ever live long enough to read through them.

Declan sets a murderous pace. His iron grip on my wrist isn't allowing me to slow down. In his other hand shines the sword, glinting as if eager for bloodshed.

I don't know quite where we're standing. Earlier, when we'd gotten so close, vulnerable with each other, he seemed to pull away. To find every reason to pick a fight–so I gave him one, with Persephone. Even if a massive reason for that was my own jealousy, still undealt with.

But none of that takes away from the fact I want him to stop running. Not from the knights, obviously we can't have that. But from me, from what we have–could have? I don't even know. My mind is a mess of confusion, and it's getting harder to breathe.

I feel Declan tense, ready to turn and fight. We've run as far as we can, him and I both know it, because we're getting closer to the Forest of Forbidden Dreams again. Its glowing form teases in the distance, almost within touching distance.

An idea strikes me, crazy as it may be, and I tug on his hand. The same one still intertwined with mine, his strong fingers wrapped around mine, dwarfing them.

"Declan, the forest!"

He glances from me to the woods, then back to those chasing us. It's insanity, he knows it as well as I do. He felt it, the moment we got near... it will mess with our heads. With our emotions.

"Is there any other option?" My gaze shifts over his shoulder, to the darkness and the hunters it hides. "They will not follow. One night, and we can return."

His jaw goes tight, then he lets go of me. My heart sinks, thinking he's rejecting it, but he jerks his head towards the woods. "Go. I'll join you in a second... After I do a bit of cleaning."

The moment after, he tosses the sword to the side, and flames engulf his body. I grab the fallen sword and move backwards, unable to tear my eyes from him. From the change taking over, the zmeu... In mere seconds, Declan is standing in his full beast form, roaring.

He extends his wings, blocking my view of the incoming Serafim, then glances behind him. One golden eye winks at me, and I finally understand what he's doing. A distraction–to ensure I get away, without the knights seeing where I'm going.

I nod to show him I got it, then turn on my heels and run. Soon, I'm crossing into the forest, surrounded by the soft music and whispers of the trees. But my eyes are glued to Declan, even as I make sure I'm hidden.

He's pushing off the ground, flying upwards but only enough to take aim. Then jets upon jets of blue flames escape him, creating a barrier of fire between the Serafim and us. It will keep them away, less their psyche be traumatized once more.

Satisfied, Declan drops back behind the wall of flames, and returns to his human form. Clothes cover him and he makes a run for the trees, and the shelter they now offer us.

When his eyes find mine, he smirks. "Not bad for a zmeu, right, princess?"

I nod, my knees weak with relief. When he turns and goes deeper into the woods, I follow behind him, until we reach a clearing with gigantic trees. Declan clears the ground behind one of them and gestures for me to take a seat.

It's damp. Cold. Between that and the latest events, I can't help my chattering teeth. Declan sees my shivers and conjures something for me to sit on, the entire time silent, and pensive. I fall asleep while he stands guard, the image of his frowning features the last I see.

🐺

Hands on my body. Whispers in my ear. A mouth trailing kisses on my neck, down my collarbone, my midriff… lower….

Moans. Whimpers. A male groan of satisfaction.

My eyes fly open, only to be met with the black sky of the Underworld. Declan's soft breathing by my side calms me, though my skin is flushed with desire.

And then something tells me to glance his way–and I find his eyes glued to me, burning in the darkness. My heart stops, then picks up again at double speed, hammering against my chest.

"Felt it too?"

I swallow past my dry throat. "It must be the forest, acting on our deepest desires."

"Is that your deepest desire, Constanza?" Silence lengthens between us. I'm afraid to answer, one way or another. Declan lifts his head off the ground, moving towards me ever so slightly. "Because if it is, you know I can deliver."

His golden eyes shine with that same

intensity that's already pulled me in, before. *I shouldn't do this. It's madness, giving in... No matter how good it can be.* Memories of just *how* good file through my mind, each more vivid than the last. My body heats, and before long, I know it's a battle I've already lost.

I lick my lips, and in a moment of madness I pull him on me, kissing him like I've only done in dreams. Like this is the end, and he is my redemption. Like we're meant to be. Like he's my one and only... though he cannot be.

He's been in my dreams, the product of my fruitful imagination. He has done things to me that have made my toes curl in pleasure. I don't know how much of that is a dream, and how much is fantasy. All I know is, his mouth...

Reality is so much better, so much sweeter....while it lasts. Then Declan pushes one leg between mine, his hand on my cheek angles my head. He's plundering, taking control, and my body awakens under his touch like it's been too long asleep.

He pushes my leg up higher, and the skirt of my dress rides up my thigh. His fingers smooth over the skin, touching, caressing, already making me beg.

"Declan..." I arch my back, offering my neck, and he's there, kissing and nipping at the tender skin, at the pulse, which is now thundering.

My hands roam his back, then tug his shirt loose, seeking desperately to find skin. Muscle. Steel. I gasp as his hips move against mine, rocking against my center through our clothing, and shooting bolts of madness in my mind.

This man will make me lose my mind.

"Constanza..." The rest of his murmur is lost amid my moans, my pleading. I'm vaguely aware of him muttering in Romanian, and he pulls back at some point, staring down at me like he's lost and I am his way home.

And then his mouth takes mine again, and he's pressing against me more, and this time, I can't hold back. I want everything he gives me. Everything and more.

My hands sink into his back, nails digging in the flesh, demanding more. Declan moves the hand on my thigh higher, at the apex of my flesh, where I'm so needy and ready for him. He strokes me once, twice, and my murmurs become an incoherent mumble.

"Come for me," he whispers like the devil of temptations himself. 'Come for me, so I can remember this moment in the darkest of nights."

I do, then, crying out in the forest unashamedly, clenching my thighs on his hand as I rock against his touch once, twice. Then Declan drops his head on my neck, nibbling on the sensitive skin. I feel his hardness against me, yet he seems in no rush to move. None, at all.

Chapter 11

Mândrie
"It was _pride_ that changed angels into devils; it is
humility that makes men as angels."
-Saint Augustine-

Declan

Constanza's fast heartbeat, and her scent of
violets, surround me. I inhale deeply against
her neck, then allow myself a kiss that sends
her gasping once more. To touch her, in real
life, beats any dream. We had each other in
every position imaginable, but this... To feel
the softness of her skin, like the smoothest

flower petal, and taste her sweetness...

I pull away, allowing myself one last lingering on her lips, tasting her, telling myself this is all done to get her caring for me. The reality, my zmeu knows well, is we both want her. Fully.

He's right there, at the forefront of my mind, demanding, questing–craving *her*. And I cannot allow it. For both of our sake. He's confused, enraged, and it looks like he's not the only one.

When I put some distance between us, Constanza stares at me, confused. "That's it?"

"Would you allow me anything more?"

She bites her lip. Her cheeks are glowing in the orgasm's wash, and there's an odd light to her eyes as they settle on me. But she says nothing, instead standing and dusting herself off. It takes me a moment to realize she's going after the satchel Chiron gave us.

She turns to me, arching an eyebrow. "Since we both won't be getting much sleep, how about we go through his notes?"

Or, I could give in to my zmeu's deepest desire, and ours, and end tonight in ecstasy. Even as the thought hits me, I know it won't happen. These are not the right circumstances. Why do I even care? I don't know. But she makes me *want* to care. Which is a problem all on its own.

I stifle a sigh and nod to Constanza. She hands me a stack of leaflets, while she takes the rest. Seems the centaur was busy during the few hours of down time we'd had, as he traced back all the stories he had of the Olympians… and their enemies.

As I peruse the notes, written in a tiny, readable script, I glance a few times at Constanza. She settled close enough to me that her haunting scent is still there, and I have to clench my fists so I don't reach out to her.

Stopping was a terrible idea. She was under me, ready and willing. I should've gone with it, cemented our connection, and then used it for my purpose. My zmeu growls again at the idea, but I ignore him. Me not carrying it through to term, only means I'm getting attached, which cannot be. If nothing else, I need to drive these emotions away.

I return my focus to the notes, frowning. "Remember you said Charon was imprisoned in Tartarus for a while?"

Constanza looks up from what she's reading. "Yeah?"

"Chiron's notes say here *all* the Titans were in there, too. If the ferryman of the souls got in the same spot as them, what are the chances they influenced him?"

She taps her chin. "Or, maybe *one* particular Titan influencing him."

"Like who?"

"Cronus, like Chiron said." A tinge of fear glints in her eyes. "Or Typhon. He was the father of monsters like Cerberus, the chimera... It would make sense, given everything else that has happened."

I recall the big three-headed dog I'd fought on my way in. "Perhaps."

As we continue perusing the notes, most of them talking about various motives to dethrone Hades, I feel my eyes drifting closed. Soon enough, I'm sleeping, lost in memories and the fog of the past.

I'm walking in a haze of darkness. Figuratively, and literally, given I'm wandering the

unlit corridors of my childhood castle in the middle of the night, a half-drunk bottle of țuică in my hand.

Months ago, my life fell apart.

Months ago, my heart stopped beating.

Months ago, I lost the love of my life.

No. Not true. I lost the cheating bitch I gave everything to. She went as far as marrying me, pretending she accepted all of me, when all along she wished for another.

My brother. I take a few more gulps from the bottle, letting the fiery sensation drill a hole in my already empty stomach.

"Fucking traitor."

I don't know which of Alina's betrayal, or my brother's for sleeping with her, hurts more. Perhaps both.

Not that it matters. She's dead now, and him? Well, he's got another fucking thing coming.

As if the devil himself heard me, a door opens and Tytus steps out, scanning the area. When he notices me, leaning against a wall and drinking heavily, he heads my way.

His footsteps are hesitant. The last few times he tried to talk to me, I almost bit his head off. Now he's about to fight the Serafim again—and I hope he finds the death I wish upon him.

Hate rolls through me, as fiery and ugly as the drink in my hand. How could he betray me, take my wife, when I've always been by his side, always there?

We were brothers, meant to take on the world together. Instead, I will destroy his, and leave it burning to ashes and cinders.

"Declan?"

I swallow another heavy gulp of țuică, silent at his silent query. Used to be we could read each other like an open book. Nowadays, the only thing he can read in me is my pain. Which is just as well.

Tytus' gaze shifts to the drink in my hand. "Can I have some?"

It surprises me, his request. Normally he's all about lecturing me, asking what's gotten into me.

With a bitter laugh, I hand him the bottle. "Sure. You've taken everything else, after all."

When I try to pass him, he grasps hold of my arm. His gaze is relentless, piercing me as if searching for the answer to life itself.

"What's going on with you, frate? I know not how to help you."

I yank myself out of his grasp. "The time for help is long gone." And storm down the hallway, in search for my next oblivion.

The memory, in the dream, turns to more events, before that night. What Igor showed me about Alina, how it gutted me, and the growing pain in me. It culminates to one moment–when I last saw my wife, and the flames that had consumed her, and my heart. I didn't know then that she had betrayed me for the Serafim, and that my brother was innocent.

When my eyes open, Constanza is kneeling next to me, withdrawing her hand as if she'd been about to shake me awake.

Confirming my suspicion, she says, "You were muttering in your sleep. I thought it was a nightmare."

It was. But not the kind she thinks.

I run a hand over my face and shift so I'm half-sitting. Constanza doesn't move, and her immobile form raises the hairs on my neck.

"What did I say, exactly?"

An interminable pause extends before she answers, and even then, her voice is a mere whisper. "Something about Alina." Another pause. "Who was she?"

"No one."

"It didn't sound like that." Her tone now has an accusing tinge to it.

I turn to her, gritting my teeth. "Since when are we on sharing terms, princess?"

Hurt flashes in her features, even as she visibly recoils. "I thought–"

"That, what? I got you off, and now we're pouring our hearts to each other?"

I know my words are hurtful, but it's like I can't stop them. The memories fill my head, clouding my decision, and my emotions. I cannot separate from my hate of Alina, to my... whatever it is... for Constanza.

"Why are you being like this?" She narrows her eyes on me, as if she sees through me. "You know full well it's not just that."

I place both hands on the ground, shifting so I'm leaning over them and almost in her face. "Really? Because unless my recollection is completely off base, our little tryst went exactly as I wished. And if I'd wanted more from you, I would've also taken it. To fill a basic, primal craving. That should be answer enough, no?"

I stand then, dusting myself off and going about shoving our supplies in the satchel from Chiron. My body is tight with tension, but not as oblivious as I'd want it.

Constanza gets up, not deterred by my shitty attitude. "Are you seriously going to be like this, Declan?"

Before I can answer, my ears pick up on something in the shadows. "We have to go. *Now!*"

Constanza

One moment he's yelling at me, the next he's grabbing my hand and dragging me deeper through the forest. I don't even know what we're running from this time, only that we're being chased. Behind us, I catch odd noises, confirming said assumption.

Though I'm panting from all the running, the moment we pause, I whirl on Declan. We've stopped by a small stream, and there's no way I'll let this chance go. Screw kid gloves

with this zmeu! No amount of a shitty childhood excuses the way he's acting.

"What the hell was all that?"

He kneels next to the water, refilling our
flasks. "How do you expect me to know?"

"It's not the being chased I'm talking
about, and you know it."

Declan takes a step towards me, eyes
glinting. "Careful, princess. I'd just as easily
rather tape that mouth of yours and drag you
out of here."

Great, so we're back to threats now.

That alone deflates me. Is there even a
point arguing with him, when he's obviously
shut down? The mere mention of Alina
caused him to close up, and there's nothing I
can do right now, not when we're so pressed
for a decision. Which reminds me about the
purpose of my current stand.

"Fine. Keep your secret past and see if I
care. But we can't leave."

"Beg your pardon?"

"Persephone and Hades. I know what
you'll say next, you were getting ready for it
before we were chased again. But I refuse to
run and leave them here."

"And why not?"

"They're my friends!"

"Friends betray you."

"Not these. They're akin to family."

A darker expression overcomes him. "Family betrays you even harder."

I toss my hands in the air. "I give up! I know you've been through a lot, Declan, but being this cynical? Really?"

A scowl is his only answer.

I shake my head. "I sure wish I'd known and hadn't wasted my time with you."

He snorts. "Good to know."

We face away from each other like two petulant children. My gaze falls in the distance, where I can see the palace. The same place I've spent summers and months upon months enjoying, laughing, and escaping my own reality.

I turn to Declan once more, pushing aside my ego. "Please help me. I know you're not as cold-hearted as you seem."

"Oh, but I am."

"No. If you were, you wouldn't have stopped when I asked you to. If you were, you'd be all about your own interests. Or, you're far from it." I step closer, hesitate, then place my hand on his shoulder. "I'm not mistaken. There's good in you, Declan."

"You're wrong. There was good in me, a long time ago. Not anymore. Find someone else to help you play hero."

He turns his back to me and sets about making camp. *Stubborn zmeu!*

The solution hits me a few hours later. We're lying down behind some bushes closer to the edge of the forest, but still hidden.

I know Declan isn't sleeping, nor am I. My body is still humming from what happened in the woods. From feeling so close to him, until I wasn't. For a moment there–maybe more than one, if I'm honest–I thought there could be more. But if that's to ever be, there's a long, long road ahead. And I have other priorities right now.

With these thoughts comes also a very awake mind. And I know what I need to do.

Declan had cynically spoken of being a hero... Lucky for me, the Elysian Fields are packed with heroes. Sure, they're here for their ever after sleep, but I doubt any of them would balk at saving just one more maiden...

Especially when it's Persephone.

More at peace now, I allow myself to close my eyes, if only for a little bit.

Declan

I wake up with a jerk. Something startled me, got through to me, but I'm unsure what. And then I hear them.... Voices. Female voices, further into the forest.

The last thing I want is to go in the forest again. Especially after what happened with Constanza.

The thought of her makes me search around, but she's nowhere to be seen. *What if she's in the forest, dragged in there by those voices?*

I grind my teeth a little. This immortal is harder to keep track of than I thought.

Part of me wishes to go find her. The other part, filled with annoyance at that, pushes back into the forest. Whether she's there or not, I need to shut up that noise before it drives me insane in the worst way possible.

I don't have to head deep. A few feet in, there's a small meadow. And in it, twelve women dressed in white togas dance around,

humming. Brooches hold their dresses together on one shoulder, and crowns of flowers
decorate their long, wavy locks.

I recognize them at once for what they
are. Sânziene.

In the Carpathian Mountains, they were
the most beautiful maidens of a village. Each
spring and fall equinox they would pick
flowers–sânziene flowers, or lady's bedstraw.

Sure enough, though they dance around
like deers, each one holds in their hands a
crown.

One in particular looks at me, winking
from their circle, swaying her hips. "Join us,
handsome."

"Not tonight."

They keep singing, keep dancing, trying
to pull me in further. Despite my resistance,
two of them come towards me and tug and
push until I'm in their midst.

Then their crowns of flowers go flying,
and I'm too slow to move out of the way. One
lands on my head, perched precariously.
Before I can catch it, it falls to the ground.

A dead silence surrounds me as the Sânziene stop dancing. The trees stop moving.

Even the faint breeze freezes.

The elders of my area used to say if the crowns of the Sânziene land on a house and stay there, it would mean wealth and good fortune. If they land on a house and fall, someone would die within it.

As I stare at the crown, now fading and mixing with the mud and grass, a shudder of something runs up my spine. Then I curse the legends I grew up with, lift my foot, and crush it into the earth.

Gasps echo all around me. When I look up, anger etched on my face, the Sânziene scatter like hares from a hunter. Within moments, I am alone, only the crushed flowers at my feet as company.

And wondering, not for the first time, when in this forsaken Underworld did I lose sight of my true goal? And how do I get back on track... Or do I even want to?

Constanza

"Jason!"

I might've started walking, but by the time I hit the Elysian Fields, I'm panting and running, desperate to find them.

Them being the heroes of human legends, trained by Chiron himself. Persephone and I ran into them a few times. They became regulars to our adventures, or when we needed relaxing of the crazy variety. Turns out eternity doesn't suit guys who are used to fighting, defeating monsters, and saving princesses. These days, they're more likely to throw a good party than save some damsel in distress.

Luckily, I'm hoping to change their minds.

"Theseus!"

A growl of frustration escapes me when I don't run into them off the bat. Where could they be?

A few moments later, I hear giggles and sounds of water splashing, so I head in that direction. I emerge from the meadow across a small lake and, sure enough, I find my missing heroes there–along with another blond god.

"Connie!"

We could be siblings, Heracles and I, with our blond waves and blue eyes. Only, he's three times my size in both height and bulk, and he has no problem lifting me off the ground and spinning me around like I weigh nothing.

"What brings you here?"

Rather than squeal with joy as is my usual way, I slap his back. "Let me *down*! This is serious."

When he listens, I glance between him and the heroes, and the girls they'd been fooling around with. "Leave us."

They scowl but do as I ask, and I wait until the boys put on some clothes, tapping my foot impatiently.

"What's going on, Connie?" Heracles seems the most sober out of them.

Jason's dirty blond mop of hair is all askew, his green eyes glazed as he smiles lazily my way. Theseus is even worse, hiccupping like he's drank an entire barrel of ambrosia or something. His chin-length wavy locks are plastered to his skull from the water, making his sharp aristocratic features pop out even more.

Once upon a time, I thought I'd landed in paradise when I met these guys. And at some time or another, I flirted–and maybe more–

with one or two of them. But like I said, eternity gets tedious. And when the guys are acting more like children or frat boys from the human world than age-old heroes... Well, being around them can get more draining than fun.

I snap out of my thoughts, realizing they're staring at me like I've grown two heads. Right. I'm not usually this quiet.

I clear my throat and start with something simple. "Did you guys not hear anything?"

"Hear what?" Jason asks.

Out of breath, and more than aware of our running time, I quickly bring them up to date. When I'm done, Jason and Theseus appear more sober, and Heracles is frowning, worry etched upon his features.

"Does my father know?"

I shake my head. "Was hoping you might be able to send him a message? I know I'm asking a lot but..."

Heracles nods, waving my apology away. "Yeah, count on it. It's about time I face the old man and maybe help repair his relationship with Hades."

A loud snort from behind attracts our

attention, followed by a hiccup. Theseus raises a goblet in the air and grins sloppily. "Good *luck* with that! Zeus is more stubborn than a bull." His joke cracks him up, and he nearly drowns himself while trying to regain his countenance.

Jason, at least, has the grace to look sheepish and elbows him to shut up.

Heracles ignores their antics, snapping his fingers instead to grab their attention. "Enough with the shit, you two. Jason, Theseus, go back with Connie to meet this Declan character. I'll round up some Olympian forces and more of our guys, and meet you back at the palace."

A relieved breath escapes me. Why didn't I think of this first?

"Like, *now* now?" Theseus looks dejected. "We can't even finish our party?"

Oh yeah. *That's* why.

Heracles rolls his eyes and tosses his empty goblet at him. "Get your head on, T!"

"More and more like a frat party," I mutter.

At the thought of what mixing these guys with Declan will lead to, I groan.

Chapter 12

Minciuni
"I'm not upset that you <u>lied</u> to me, I'm upset that from
now on I can't believe you."
-Friedrich Nietzche-

Declan

With the Sânziene gone, I head back to the camping site, hoping Constanza has returned. The dread in my gut has turned to a rock-solid sensation, but I try to shake it off.

Where the hell could she have gone? And is she coming back, or should I be going after her? Granted, I crossed into the asshole realm again the other night, but it's not like she's not used to it by now. Surely she doesn't expect an apology?

My feet aren't moving, so I guess I'm not going anywhere. In truth, Constanza's abrupt disappearance is a quiet moment I need to take. Especially after our little hot and heavy tryst in the forest. Why did I stop? If all I want from her is her body, then how come when it came to it, I held back?

The answer to that is as elusive as everything else.

I stare in the flames until my sight narrows and my eyes roll at the back of my head. *It's been a while since I've had one of these...*

The vision starts like most of mine—with fire. Everything is burning, a mix of hot flames and cool, blue ones. Out of the blaze emerge knights—Serafim. Their swords glint ferociously, and their eyes are dead. And they're headed towards me as I'm trying to protect Constanza.

I blink back to the present, frowning at my surroundings. "Well, hell." Now what?

ȇ

With little to do, and unable to leave without the sneaky minx, I pace back and forth in front of the forest. Yes, she had insisted multiple times to go back to Hades....I pause in my pacing. Then curse under my breath.

What if she'd returned to the palace without me?

Before I can launch towards it, I hear voices again. Only this time it's one female, and two males. Then Constanza climbs up the hill, followed by my fucking nightmares.

Her defiant gaze meets mine. "Finally awake?"

I force myself to inhale. "What is this?" I gesture to the men with the last word.

Constanza grins and turns to them. "My heroes. I took a little hike to the Elysian Fields while you rested, and managed to get these ones on board."

"On board with what?"

"A rescue mission, of course! I've also dispatched Heracles to see if he can get word to his daddy."

My teeth grind together. "Zeus, you mean."

Constanza smiles bigger. "Precisely."

"Is there a particular reason you seem so at

ease with disturbing the leader of Olympus?"

Constanza steps away from her companions and says, "I'm sure he won't see it as a disturbance."

"I don't follow."

"You don't have to."

I move a step closer to her, gripping her arm. "I need to talk to you. In private."

One of the burliest guys inches towards us. "You alright, Constanza?" When he says her name, it sounds downright intimate, like he knows her well. Naturally, all I want to do is throttle him.

Can I kill a ghost, soul, whatever? I guess I can always find out later.

Without giving Constanza a chance to answer, I pull her after me. For the benefit of our new arrivals, I say over my shoulder, "Private meeting. We'll be back."

Then I pull her into my side, refusing to let go until she falls in line.

Constanza

Of course he has to be a brute. *What I ever saw in him...*

I pull out of his hold and scowl at Declan.

"Is there a reason you're being so handy?"

"Why would you take off like that?"

"I needed to get help. after reading Chiron's notes."

"And I could have come with you."

I tap my foot on the grass, trying to figure out how much to trust him. If Persephone is right, and he's lying.... Either way, I won't know until Heracles come back. Still, I can buy some time. It's hard when he's looking at me like that, though.

"I thought you might've... been hurt." No sooner is the admission out of his mouth, that he breaks our gazes and rubs the back of his neck, looking as uncomfortable as ever.

This is the good Declan, the one who's open and willing to talk again. Should I bring up the past? *Perhaps not just yet*, a tiny nagging voice warns in my head.

"I'm fine. And we got help, so now we're not in this alone."

He throws me a skeptical look. "You sure those two can do anything? They look ready for a party, not a fight."

I roll my eyes. "I interrupted one, as a matter of fact. But that's not important. You remember Chiron's notes?"

"Da."

"Well, he had a point. In every pantheon, the Originals have always been in danger from various forces. And when they turned recluse, if it was because of a bigger evil, not just that humans no longer believed in them, then that explains it."

"You're grasping at straws."

"Could be. But I think Chiron is right, and it's Cronus who's behind this."

"I may have skipped a few history lessons, but the Titans are buried, now."

"No. What if something else happened, another event that sparked them, woke them? Zeus could never kill them, so at best they've been in limbo this entire time!"

An odd look crosses his face, but then it's gone before I can read it. "Fine, princess. We'll wait for your Heracles and see what he says."

Unable to restrain myself, I jump in his arms like I used to, in our dreams. After a moment of hesitation, he wraps them around me, trapping me against the hardness of his body, the safety of his embrace.

When I pull back, his eyes are glued to my mouth.

And just like a dam, I'm aware of the heat of his skin, the electricity tingling wherever he's touching me. My body leans towards his, and our lips brush. Declan lets me take the lead, allowing a short, gentle kiss. The likes we've never truly had.

I break the kiss, and once again he allows me, saying nothing.

Later, once Jason and Theseus pass out, I'm lying down on the grass and facing Declan. His golden gaze lights up in the darkness, and he stares at me in silence. A loud snoring makes both of us chuckle.

"Some guards." He snorts. "Good pick."

"I make good with what I can," I tease back. "Maybe Heracles will have more luck."

Declan stays quiet, but I can't return the favor. Not when my heart demands an answer.

"Who's Alina?"

He closes his eyes and for a moment I think he won't talk. But then he says under his breath, "My ex-wife."

"Wife? As in… a human?"

"Da, a human."

"How long ago was this?"

"A long time."

"Declan…"

He sighs and gets up to a half-sitting position. Arm slung over his knee, he stares in the distance. "A few centuries."

The pain in his voice gets to me. "What happened?"

"She died." A pause. "Rather, I killed her."

The words jolt my thoughts into confusion. *He doesn't mean* kill *for real, surely.*

"What…?"

Declan spares me a glance. "I believed she loved me, but found out she was betraying me with my brother. Or so I thought. The reality was much worse, of course. She was only with me as a spy for the Serafim, feeding them information. When I realized the truth, I killed her. Or, just as good as. I let the information reach our zmeu Council, who took it upon themselves to dole out punishment. I didn't stop them. I loved her with all my being…. And I still stood by and watched her get burned to ashes."

I'm afraid to look at Constanza, but I take

the leap. Her eyes are wide–filled with pity. Not exactly what I was going for.

"I don't need your pity." The words come out harsher than I intended.

"I know," she says. "It was my anger you were looking for, right?"

There's movement in my periphery, then she crawls over the grass and into my lap, straddling me as she cups my cheek. "Too damn bad, Declan. I'm not about to humor you. You had something horrible done to you, and there is nothing worse than betrayal."

She kisses me then, first my forehead, then my cheeks, before finally her lips find mine in the softest of embraces.

But even as I lie back down, Constanza in my arms, the memory won't stay at bay.

I'm returning to the palace, after Alina sent me on an errand to the nearest village. Igor already showed me the truth of her betrayal with Tytus, and I have been good at playing the charade. Every time she gives me her body, I cringe and bear it. The last few days, I have been unable to touch her, which is why I gladly took the excuse to get out.

Before I did, Iris—a zmeu elder—stopped me.

"Your human. We have tolerated you bringing her here and choosing to taint your lineage. But now guards spotted her leaving the castle in the night. Acting odd, even for a human."

I stare at him coolly. "Da, she's fucking some other man."

Iris seems taken aback by my honesty. And then he gets angry. "And you let her? You allow her to disrespect our traditions, to put us in jeopardy through all she knows? What if she tells the wrong people? What if she brings the Serafim raining hell on us? Your brother is out there fighting yet another war, and you allow yourself to be disrespected and weakened by this human in our midst?"

I clench my fists, barely holding back my trembling rage. "Now you know."

Iris calls after me as I walk away, asking what he's to do with the information. I simply toss, "Whatever you damn well wish," over my shoulder.

And then I go to the village. Get Alina's

items. Take my sweet time.

By the time I return to the palace, it is deadly quiet. Except my senses hear something, in the distance. I follow the sounds until my feet bring me to a valley nearby, and a cavern I am all too familiar with. Igor is hiding there—not that the Council seems to realize it.

They are all surrounding a pillar, and the woman tied in its center. Logs of wood are at her feet. I have seen similar executions for human witches, and this seems to meet the requirement.

She's pleading with them, begging them, threatening them. She sees me making my way through the zmei, and shouts. "Declan! Declan, help me!"

Something in my expression must clue her in to the fact I am no longer her loving husband. Tears truly stream down her cheeks then, but in rage, not sorrow.

"You fucker! You've known, all along?"

I say nothing, simply watch. One of my kin, the only one in human form, reads off a paper. "Alina, chosen of Declan, our royal prince, you have hereby been found guilty of betraying your mating bond, your kin. Death is your punishment."

I don't bother correcting them. Alina and I never mated, not in the zmeu sense of the word.

"You are not my kin!" Her screams pierce my eardrums. "You are not my anything, do you hear me!"

The zmei open their mouths, and the air charges with sulfur. Then gusts of fire escape them, charring Alina's body to ashes. Her screams echo in my nightmares that night, and they have ever since. My punishment to carry, forever more.

Hours later, I wake up expecting Constanza to still be draped over me. No such luck. She's far off to the side, chatting with her band of frat boys. And, are my eyes deceiving me, or is there a third one now?

I rub a hand over my face and blink a few times. Da, definitely three of them.

With a groan, I stand, stretch, and move closer. The newest addition is taller and wider than me, and the way he's holding Constanza's hand in his, talking in hushed tones, rankles me the wrong way.

"Who's the newbie?"

She jumps at my voice and turns around. After last night, I'd expected… Not a warm welcome, but something other than the hostility I read in her gaze. *Perhaps she woke up feeling weird.*

I let it go, instead nodding to the new hero. "Heracles, I suppose?" It's only an educated guess.

He nods, letting go of Constanza. I still don't like the way he's positioning himself between us.

"Do we have any news?"

Constanza shares a glance with him, then says, "Yeah, we do."

"And?"

"Heracles raised the alarm in Olympus, and Zeus will look into the Titans. If his investigation works in our favor, he will send troops."

"Great." My eyes narrow on the group. Why does it feel like their animosity is aimed solely towards me? "What about immediate help for Hades?"

"You're looking at it," Heracles says. "I've rounded up a few more heroes, and they have orders to meet us by the palace at sundown."

Theseus snorts and jabs Jason, both of them acting like they're still drunk. I roll my eyes, reach for Constanza's wrist and tug her apart from them.

"What's going on?"

"Nothing," she says, but won't meet my gaze.

"Is this about what I said last night?"

She sighs. "No. Not even a little."

"Hm. Well, care to throw me a bone?"

"Not really, no."

I frown at her, the way she's avoiding my gaze, my touch, and her body leans away from me. Clearly I did something to piss her off, but she's not admitting it.

"Fine, princess." I should've known being honest would bite me in the butt. "Then we're leaving."

"What? No!"

"You have your band of merry warriors, and it sounds like Hades has tons of help soon to come. We have the Serafim on our ass, and I'm not looking forward to meeting them again."

"Well, too bad. I refuse to leave."

"Let me get this straight." It takes every ounce of my self-control to keep cool. "You trekked all over Hades' place, alone, after we'd just been hunted, all in an effort to get to these losers, and now you think they'll help you save your friends?"

"Watch yourself!" Jason grunts, taking a step forward.

"Just because we've been enjoying the last decades rather than have a stick up our butts…" Theseus mutters.

I turn my full glare onto them. "Try *millennia*, not decades, idiots."

Constanza is not impressed. She tosses her head back and returns my glare. "So what if I did?"

"Do you realize your parents sent me to get you out, before everything fell apart? And you're not letting me do that."

"You're keeping me safe." She shrugs. "I don't see what the problem is."

"The *problem*, princess, is not everything revolves around you. Your parents gave me a week. Now, that week is almost over and we're nowhere closer to the blasted marigold path. If you don't let me take the lead on this, then I'm screwed."

"How so?"

"I just am."

She crossed her arms over her chest, and I try to ignore how those globes had felt in my palm just last night. Instead, I jerk my gaze up to hers and hiss, "Come with me. Now. Let Hades handle his stuff. If Zeus is on his way, then what's the rush?"

"The rush is Charon," Constanza says, and turns to Heracles, at the same time taking a step away from me. "Tell him."

"Funny thing," Heracles says as he steps forward. "When I ran into my father, and asked him about the Titans, you know what his first question was? If anyone had caught the zmeu who entered the Underworld."

Ah, shit.

Constanza won't meet my eye, which means, yep, Heracles spilled the beans about Igor and my role in that entire mess.

"Turns out, a few weeks ago someone from the Living world intended to open the gates to the Underworld. That same person was intent on getting through to free some rather unsavory characters. Care to take a gander?"

I don't rise to the bait. "Constanza, I–"

"No?" Heracles interrupts me, glaring. "Very well. It was a group of zmei and, correct my pronunciation, but balauri? Zmei who had fucked with black magic and turned themselves into monsters." When I say nothing in the brief pause he allows, he continues, "That same person made it so Charon, who already had designs on my uncle's throne, saw an opportunity and took it. Started cavorting. But being older, and a little snively weasel, he realized it was time to play two camps. Care to guess who Charon sought?"

"I didn't know!"

Constanza still avoids my gaze, and my outburst doesn't stop Heracles from continuing. "The Titans. Cronus himself. And when dear Charon told him what's going on, Cronus took advantage. Charon is probably holed up right now with him and Cerberus and some other Titans, undoing their binds. And if that happens–" He steps closer to me, jabbing a finger in my chest "–I am holding *you* responsible for this, shithead."

I shove him away, clenching my jaw. "For the last time, I *didn't fucking know*! Da, I helped Igor, until I realized he was playing me." I grab Constanza's shoulders, lowering my voice. "What I told you about Alina, about her and my brother? Igor was the one who fooled me. He made me hate my own brother for centuries! Millennia! How easy do you think it was to get me to believe that breaking into the Underworld was the best thing for me, to regain my freedom?"

A bitter laugh escapes her and she meets my gaze. At that moment, she is truly her father's daughter. "Your freedom? The same one my parents promised you? Let's talk about that, shall we? Or do you want to also deny you had planned to use me as a hostage, to get what you truly want? That you've been playing on my emotions this entire time?"

My hands drop from her shoulders as if scorched, silently admitting my guilt.

Constanza's eyes glint like steel in the dimming light. "Care to tell me again how screwed you are?"

I glance between her and the heroes, now looking less idiotic and more ready to jump on me. And I realize then she's been playing me this whole time, since she returned with them. She wanted to see if I'd be truthful, and I wasn't.

When I look at her, I glimpse hurt for the briefest of moments, before it's hidden from her beautiful features. An impassable mask is left in its place, looking nothing like the Constanza I know.

Wow. I fucked up, and big time.

"I didn't lie. Not about that." My low murmur is nowhere near convincing.

"Right." She scoffs. "I think I'm good, Declan. Go do whatever it is you want to do. I won't be a part of it. Persephone was right, all you wanted from the beginning was to use me. And, foolish me, I fell right for it."

"That's not true!"

She shakes her head. "Doesn't matter now, does it? Your actions do have something to do with what's going on here. And you may be fine walking away from this, but I'm not. I'll help Hades and Persephone. Not because they're my friends, not because I owe them, but because it's the right thing to do. Something you, apparently, have no clue about."

One last scathing look, and she turns on her heels and walks back downhill. I make a move to follow, but Jason stays behind, glaring at me the entire time. By the time he leaves, all trace of Constanza has also vanished.

Tytus

"Again?"

I stop cleaning the sword, and turn to the entrance of the armory. Fiona walks in, dressed in a simple lavender dress that makes her look so damn appealing. But her features are pinched with worry, eyes glazed with tears, even as I nod.

"Again."

I've lost count of the amount of times Declan's little adventure woke me. At this point, I might as well stop trying to rest, as it's useless.

Fiona heads closer, and I place the sword back on the table. I wrap my arms around her, needing her heat, her reassurance.

She shifts slightly and kisses my chest. I'm not wearing anything other than a pair of sweatpants, so it's easy to feel her tears bathing my skin.

"He's your brother," she whispers. "If you have to go save him, you should."

I push her away, just enough so I can read her features. "And leave you here, alone?"

Declan's action nearly tore us apart. And just as we've settled into a semblance of a normalcy, now this...

"I'll be fine, Tytus." She wipes at her face. "But Declan may not be. The peace between you two is so fragile, it would be foolish not to try and save him."

"And if this is another scheme, meant to destroy us?"

A sad, brief smile emerges. "We both know it's not. Judging by the intense emotions I feel through your bond, there's nothing vengeful about any of this. And you did mention an immortal you keep seeing him with."

A sigh escapes me, and I pull her closer once more. "I won't leave, not tonight anyway. Before I go anywhere, I have to figure out what Declan has gotten involved into."

She nods in my chest, kissing me once more. Poured in our embrace is the one thing I've needed all along, since the first nightmare–her blessing.

Chapter 13

Dezamăgire
"Disillusion can become itself an illusion if we rest in it."
-T.S. Eliot-

Constanza

How much of a fool have I been? I've allowed Declan to prance around, fawning over him, nearly giving in to his seduction... Were the dreams his way of ensnaring me? Part of me can't help but go through everything, from the very beginning, to see if there is a reason for everything Declan did.

And the other part... wants to crawl and

weep. Persephone was right when she accused me of wanting something unattainable. Of going after someone I knew was pure fantasy. Yet when I saw Declan in flesh and blood, realized he was here, for real, I couldn't help wondering, as brief as it was.

More than that, I envisioned. Even as we bickered and fought, as we kissed and parted, I've been waiting, wanting him to show me he can be the man I need. The one I desperately hoped he was, deep down.

"Connie?"

I glance at Heracles, not realizing until that moment I've been crying. His features are blurred by my tears, and I stop walking, burying my head in my hands. He pulls me into his chest, rubbing my back in soothing circles, but it does nothing to quiet this burn– this pain–in my chest.

"He's a fool," Heracles says.

"Yeah, a damn idiot," adds Theseus.

I know their words are meant to soothe me, but all they do is restart my sobs even more. Declan isn't the fool–I am, for falling hook, line and sinker for everything he dished out. Persephone warned me, and still I couldn't keep my emotions untangled long enough to see through the web of lies he spun.

I pull away from Heracles, wiping at my tears.

"Are you alright?"

"No." My voice is hoarse when I speak, so I clear my throat. "But I will be. Right now, I want to help Hades and Persephone, so let's get to it."

Heracles shares a look with the other guys. "What if you stay behind? Let us do the fighting instead."

The plan he'd outlined to Declan was still standing. Even as I was busy crying, we've been moving closer to the palace. It seems Heracles and the guys had enough time to explore this unfamiliar area around the Elysian Fields and found a tunnel leading straight to Hades' place. It'll shelter us from any keen monsters or Serafim on our trail, which is a plus.

And it'll keep me hidden if Declan flies by. As if he would... I shake the thought off.

We're on our way to the entrance of the tunnel, and once we get through, we should be by the palace within the next few hours. It's meant to lead straight to the maze of tunnels Declan and I had navigated when we exited.

Easy. Simple.

Not that such simplicity stops my new companions from being worried about me.

I glare at Heracles' suggestion of me staying back, even as my fingers tremble with my rage. It's one thing to be heartbroken, another to be told I'm basically a woman and meant to stay put and let the men protect me. That is *not* how I was raised.

Before I can get a handle on it, a jolt of magic escapes me, tearing into the web of the Underworld, and I pull a glittering sword from it. It's a twin of my father's blade, made from the same steel–the one that kills any shifter, any supernatural. Even a zmeu.

I focus my anger towards something more constructive, ignoring the discomfort in my chest. "Do I need to remind you how many times I kicked your asses these last centuries? I'm not staying out of this fight. Just try and stop me."

Turning on my heels, I stomp towards the tunnel–and as far away from Declan as I can.

Truth is, I was envisioning a fantasy, still.

A perfect man, a hero made of marble and abs of steel. That kind of thing doesn't exist. Declan is flawed, more flawed than most. It's on me that I didn't see it. And it's on him that he wasn't truthful.

Tytus

While reading Declan's journal–the one Fiona discovered and gifted me–I sense a sharp pang in my chest, like it's splitting open. I've only ever felt something similar when I thought Fiona had been hurt, through my actions.

I toss the book away and run out of the library, colliding with her mid-way.

"What's wrong?"

"You're not harmed?" I ask, even as I'm inspecting her body for injuries.

She shakes her head, giving me a peculiar look. If not her, though, then–

"Declan!"

I run back inside, picking up the journal from the floor. His scent is all over it, and if I focus enough, it should let me form a connection strong enough that he cannot kick me out again. I'm tired of the way he

maintains control of our chats, even though I know it's partly done to protect himself.

Declan?

No answer. I push harder, closing my eyes, seeking that link that's connected us since we were mere hatchlings. Surely he's out there, somewhere...

Dec, answer me. Please.

I get nothing back, which is even more worrisome. All our connections have been interrupted, and I thought it was by his hand. But what if it wasn't? What if he's in so much trouble, he refuses to reach out for help, knowing how that ended previously?

If something else happens to him, I cannot live with it. Fiona has forgiven him for his wrongs, and I have made my way along that path, as well. But what use is forgiveness if the person isn't around anymore to receive it?

Declan is my younger brother, and it is my duty to protect him. I may have failed in the past, but this time... This time, I won't.

As I get ready to try again, something tugs on my mind. And then floods and floods of pain, anger and regret unfurl in my psyche, even as Declan opens his mind to me.

Frate… I fucked up. Big time.

Declan

I don't know what possesses me to reach out to Tytus. The desire to not be alone, perhaps, and the fact he is my only family. A faint hope for some kind of atonement? Or a yearning for a solution to this mess, one I crave more than anything I've ever craved?

He answers quickly, as if he'd been waiting. *What happened?*

I run a hand over my face, sighing as I peer at the sky of the Underworld. *Where do I even start?*

A pause answers me, followed by, *How about from the beginning?*

I settle back against the grass, trying to find my words. It's difficult. So much is simmering in my head, obscured by this panic that's seizing my chest, constricting it and cutting off my air supply. Whenever I try to get a deep breath, I fail, as if the thought alone is too much for my lungs.

Weary of the events, I let out a low groan. *Why don't you see for yourself?*

Ignoring his surprise, I allow myself to fall back into the memories of the last days, all the way back to the immortals asking me to come down here. If he's to know everything, he might as well *see* everything. It'll save me time and get to the lecture portion of this conversation much easier.

It's odd, feeling Tytus in my head again. Like a liquid sloshing around my thoughts, touching and releasing them as he sees my memories. We'd been in each other's heads while we fought Igor, but that was in the heat of the battle. This is... scary. And with each passing moment, I'm more and more aware that he could go back to whatever memory he wants, not stay within the scope of this exercise.

Is that how Fiona felt, I wonder? That shitty, powerless, and scared, whenever I got in her mind and controlled all aspects of her actions? The thought takes away some of my pain, but it doesn't help my mood, so I just try to stop caring.

After a few moments where Tytus is digging in my head, his presence lessens, and his consternation echoes through the link. And something else, though it's hard to name at first. Finally, it hits me–it's joy.

Right. So, I take it you're about to laugh at me for the shit I got myself into, huh?

Why would you say that?

Gee, he sounds almost hurt. *Because I feel your joy at my situation, frate.*

You misunderstand. Dec, it's not... I mean, yes, it is joy, but not at what you think.

Sure. If you were here, I'd right on punch you.

He chuckles. *I know. You never were very patient.*

I don't know, Ty. After close to two millennia waiting for my freedom, I'd say I'm fucking too patient.

That silences him for a long moment, and contrition and regret travel down in spades down our bond, enough to make me want to vomit.

Alright, enough with the moping around! Will you help, or what?

Da, of course I will, he says. *But with what, precisely?*

I was hoping you'd have the answer to that.

He sighs. *Do you even realize the extent of your issue?*

Da, I do. I have less than three days to get Constanza back to the surface, and no way to do it. Not to mention she won't come with me unless I'm dragging her at this point. And we both know the immortals won't take excuses.

No, they will not. But perhaps they might understand the circumstances.

Meaning?

Do you really not realize what's been going on, why your zmeu has been so protective of her?

Should I?

Silence is never a good thing with my brother, but sometimes, it's preferable. Like with his next comment.

Maybe you were imprisoned for too long, Dec..

Either help, or shut it, Ty. I'm not in the mood for games.

And neither am I, frate. The answer to your burning question is that you've imprinted on Constanza. Do you recall the stories of the legătură, the împerechere... The bonding and the pairing? Between a zmeu and his mate?

My head pounds in rhythm with my heart. All the blood has rushed to one of the two parts of my body, restricting all manner of normal breathing and rationale.

Images of Alina flash in my mind, the moments I'd had with her. Then they're replaced by Constanza, and the conflicting feelings she brings out of me. Protectiveness. A desire to be good. Deserving. Worthy... And this odd pain since she's been gone, and since she figured out I'm neither of those things.

All I'm able to say is, *Surely you jest.*

A chuckle. *No, frate. That is why you felt my joy. Because you will no longer be alone.*

Stop fucking with me, Tytus. Constanza isn't my mate *or anything else. She's just my... Someone I fucked.*

Hmm. In dreams. So real they felt *physical. Do you know of many who've been through that? Because as far as I know, that kind of connection only happens in fated mates.*

I don't believe you.

Alright, don't. All I'm saying is, the immortals may be more lenient towards you, if they knew what's going on.

Sure they will. Right before Făt drives his sword through my heart. *No! I forbid you to go to them with these tales.*

If it'll save your life, I will do it.

Tytus!

Another moment of silence. *I'd been on my way down to you, you know?*

What? Why? The idea that he'd enter the Underworld for me and risk his happiness, his life, has an odd effect on me. I try not to linger on it.

Because that's what brothers do, Dec. And, yes, I'll help you with this. I will only need one thing from you.

And what's that?

Trust.

Gee, you sure don't ask for much. The sarcasm in my tone makes him laugh.

He's gone from my mind the moment after, leaving me alone with my thoughts. Or, rather, one in particular. I know where Constanza went. The question is, am I ready to follow?

Constanza

"Are you alright?"

I snap to attention, gazing at Jason.

He joined us about an hour ago, right before we entered the gloomy tunnel leading back to Hades' palace. Split by a stream and very little light, we take cover in darkness and march ahead.

After a brief conversation with Heracles and Theseus, Jason starts walking by my side. I stop myself from asking about Declan– refuse to. He isn't worth my thoughts, not now or ever.

And if I keep telling myself that, maybe I'll end up believing it.

The more we walk through the tunnel, the more my body gets tired, and the sword in my arm becomes heavier. But I refuse to slow down or be the first to show signs of fatigue. We're going to get to Hades and Persephone, one way or another.

"Connie?"

I focus on Jason, realizing my attention had drifted yet again.

"Yeah, I'm okay."

His dirty blond hair falls in his eyes, and he looks charming and worried. But he's got nothing of Declan's appeal.

Dammit, stop! Stupid brain and stupid memories. That monster isn't close to being who I deserve, and I need to come to terms with that.

Even if my idiotic heart doesn't agree.

Damn it to all the pantheons and beyond.

"If it makes you feel better, he wanted to follow."

We both know who the *he* is.

"But he didn't, did he?" My low mutter is full of bitterness. "That says enough."

Jason knows my tone enough to back off, retreating to a few paces behind me. I block out their whispers, and everything else but the path ahead. The light at the end of the tunnel.

We must be halfway to the palace by now. At least, I hope so. It's hard to keep track when our surroundings never change, the long corridor never goes up or down, only continues straight on. The stream is getting fuller, though, and I'm hoping that's because we're nearing its source. But even as we get closer, part of me wonders if Declan wasn't right and if this isn't a suicide mission.

After all, Persephone herself told me to get out. This, despite knowing full well I'm an immortal and trained in fighting and magic. If that's not a sign the situation was dire enough...

I have to try. Declan made me waste too much time, and if I don't try, I'll never forgive myself. She's my friend!

Plus, it's not like I came all alone. On cue, I glance over my shoulder at the guys. "Heracles, you did say reinforcements of the hero-type are awaiting us by Hades' palace?"

He nods, his face drawn in a serious mask. "As many as I could gather from the Elysian Fields, if they managed to avoid Charon's traps. Two stayed behind to spread the word."

"And none of them had heard of what's going on?"

He shakes his head. "Same like us, been too busy partying around."

I sigh and turn back ahead. *Let's just hope it's enough forces to contend with Charon, the Serafim and whoever else is helping them.*

As if to spite me, the tunnel climbs upwards. And the river gushes, making it so we're ankle-deep in murky water.

Yuck.

"We must be close!" Theseus yells a tad too jubilantly behind me.

Jason tries to shush him, but it's too late. There's a cloud of smoke, a rumble above us like the ground is broken through, and all the wondering leaves me. Because the answer to whether we'll be victorious is staring me in the face.

And it has three massive heads, ugly eyes, and a tail with a snake.

The heroes close ranks around me, but I know it's useless. Humans cannot best Cerberus, not even those touched by the gods.

Shit.

"He's mine!" Heracles snarls, and for a moment his anger makes no sense.

As we're all struggling to figure out a way past the massive dog and out of the tunnel, the answer hits me. Cerberus had been one of Heracles' Twelve Labors. He'd brought the head of the dog to Hera as requested, only for her to revive the beast all over again.

Given Heracles' history with his stepmom, well, I'm not surprised he's looking like a hulking monster on the verge of a berserker attack right this minute. Sword in hand, he advances, flanked by Jason and Theseus.

I hold back, knowing my blade won't be as useful here–not yet, anyway.

Cerberus seems in tune to our movements, though. Each time we try to catch him by surprise, one of his heads is there. And with his massive bulk, he's stopping us from exiting the tunnel.

"How did he know we were here?" I ask Heracles as we're both pushed back.

"Must've been waiting for us," he groans, sending a glare towards Theseus.

Our friend is taking the brunt of the fighting, as if to make up for his blunder. Then Heracles roars and lunges towards Cerberus– and disappears. I follow in his footsteps, ducking under Cerberus' belly and landing a slash to it, before rolling out of the way.

The snake tail is in my face next and I squeal–embarrassingly loud.

Two of the heads turn towards me, and Cerberus' back paw places itself in such a way I'm stuck, unable to move out.

Shit.

"Connie!" Theseus attacks at the same time as Jason.

Cerberus tosses Theseus up in the air and

he disappears wherever Heracles did.

One last swipe of his paw, and Jason is slammed into the ground, dazed. Cerberus marches over him. I cringe, looking away, frozen. Why has he not killed me yet? Unlike those souls, I *can* actually cease to exist.

But Cerberus only stares. For a long time. Too long. Like he's waiting for someone.

Then, a clap. And another. Someone steps from the shadows, a cloak covering his face, with only his beard protruding.

Double shit.

Declan

I should've stopped being so damn stubborn and moved my ass faster. Then perhaps I wouldn't have lost her trail.

Eventually, I give up on walking and shift to zmeu form. If Tytus is right, my zmeu will know exactly where Constanza is, so I might as well use this connection to her for something.

As for the importance of what my brother divulged… Surely, it cannot be. I've lived for so long, only to find my mate in an *immortal*? The Fates sure have a nasty sense of humor.

Whichever the case, I cannot deny my

attraction for Constanza, nor the fact I care for her safety. And that I've done things completely unlike me, all in an effort to please her. Is this something that can be explored? Not in these circumstances, that's for sure. But...

I push the thoughts aside and let my zmeu take over for the duration of flying, wondering where in hell Constanza and the heroes could be. Then I realize we're heading towards the palace.

Of course she would've followed them there.

Halfway through my journey, something catches my eye on the ground. Glowing forms, only they're not moving, spattered around like after an explosion.

I dive, and shift to human form, clothing myself quickly. It's the heroes, Heracles and Theseus, looking all dazed. But Constanza is nowhere to be seen.

Fear grips my heart as I rush to them.

Then something crawls out of a hole in the ground–Jason.

He coughs and relief spreads over his expression when he sees me. I dismiss the others and run to him, kneeling by his side.

"Where is she?"

Another cough. "Charon–the bastard took her."

I stand, clenching my fists. This particular bastard will soon learn not to touch what is mine.

Chapter 14

Blocat
"We are never <u>trapped</u> unless we choose to be."
-Anaïs Nin-

Constanza

A groan escapes me first, then I blink. It takes me all of two seconds to realize I'm being carried over someone's shoulder. And an additional moment to realize who it is–the stench of death tells me it's Charon.

To top it off, he has his palm on my ass, holding me steady. With every step, every passing second, he sleazes his way towards… somewhere.

A quick glance around doesn't help me figure out where I am. We're surrounded by darkness and nothing else. For all I know, I could still be in the tunnels leading towards Hades' place. Only, we're not going in that direction.

Why aren't we going there? A question for later.

One thing is for sure. I'm alone, and none of my heroes have been able to follow. If they died because of my plan–as in *for real died*, blown out of existence–the guilt alone will kill me.⸱⸱Already it gnaws at me, even though I have no proof of either their survival or doom. And, really, I should worry about my own self, and wherever Charon's taking me. If he took the risk to kidnap me, there's no way this bodes well.

"I know you are awake, immortal," Charon's raspy voice echoes around.

"Then how about you drop me? I'm perfectly able to walk by myself."

"I must say, it's not an unpleasant experience." His hand rubs my ass cheek, and I hold back a gag. "However, you are getting heavy for an old man."

How rude.

Before I can tell him to go to hell, he dumps me on the ground. So I do the next best thing and pull on my primordial magic, as fast as I've ever done it, and toss it at him. Charon goes flying into the wall, and I stand.

"Maybe that'll teach you some manners, pig!" I shout at him.

In hindsight, I really should've run while I could.

Because one moment he's down, a crumpled heap on the floor. Next, he leaps to his feet, his staff pointed at my throat as he backs me into the cool tunnel stone. His blind eyes focus in my direction, even as his nostrils flare. That staff is too damn close to my chest, an odd energy vibrating from it.

"I should have known you'd be trouble." His lips twist in a grimace. "Always an issue, you immortals."

I try to quiet my heartbeat, knowing any sign of fear will only give him more satisfaction. "What do you want, Charon? Surely you realize this is a lost fight."

"It is not."

"Really? Because Heracles already contacted Olympus."

Consternation fills his features, followed by elation. "It will take Zeus too long to move. By the time he does, I'll have accomplished what I set out for."

"Which is?"

I know the answer, but I need to hear it from him. And it's no surprise when he says a single, succinct word.

"Chaos."

Should I be surprised that is his only purpose? The only reason behind his betrayal, and his loyalty switching to another master? Perhaps. Sadly, I am not.

Maybe Declan's got a point with this being jaded thing.

The thought makes me want to kick myself. For a moment there, I'd forgotten all about him. Now that pain is my back in my chest, the lump in my throat, and I have to fight back fresh tears. Why couldn't he just... be what I needed?

Pushing Declan out of my mind, I gulp. I'm eyeing Charon's staff and trying to figure out if I can risk another blast, before he uses whatever ace he thinks he's got on me.

"Try," he says, almost sweetly. "I have

been meaning to test out my toy's new capabilities."

"Which are?"

He rubs it as if it's a pet. "Sucking souls out of the living–human *and* supernatural."

Well, shit. As if this couldn't get any worse.

"And I suppose you didn't just happen to fall upon these abilities, did you?"

He cackles, expelling a furious breath of rotten crap in my face. "Of course not."

I plaster my body as close as I can to the wall, and nod, even though he can't see me. "Fine, I'll come with you."

Between obedience and oblivion, I'll choose the former. Maybe by playing the docile damsel, I'll find out more of his plan and be able to send for help. If there's anyone left to help me, that is.

Declan

"What happened?" I growl.

Jason's back standing now, they all are. Whatever dazed them must have worn off. I remember what Constanza mentioned about the more souls keep of their old personality, the more attacks hit them psychically. Well, this is proof.

Also proof I never should've let her walk away.

I quiet my zmeu's grumbles of displeasure, instead focusing on the heroes. And getting as much information out of them as I can.

"Cerberus," Theseus mutters, rubbing the back of his neck. "We'd been close to the palace, using underground tunnels. I got a bit overexcited, Cerberus was nearby, and...." He shrugs, trailing off.

And I wish nothing more than to rip his throat out. I take a step forward and force a deep breath. *Constanza wouldn't want me assassinating her friends.*

"And *how* did you lose her?" My question comes through gritted teeth.

Heracles doesn't take kindly to my anger and gets up in my face. "Better yet, why is this any of your business? We were walking away from you, zmeu."

"She will *always* be my business."

Jason steps in between us, aiming his words at Heracles. "Easy, man. If we want to find Connie, we need to work together." A glance at me. "No matter how much we hate it."

Heracles glowers at me. "We can do it without *him*."

"I'd like to see you try, considering I'm the one who imprinted on her."

The shock of my words carries through to the trio, and they share surprised glances.

"What does that mean, exactly?" Theseus asks.

Good question.

I'd been wondering that myself, on the entire flyover here. If Tytus is right, and for the first time in my existence I've begun the pairing stage of a zmeu mating, then I'm in deep trouble. Because everything I've feared–losing Constanza, not being good enough–has become amplified.

Rather than admit my insecurities about that particular aspect to the heroes, I glare at each of them, trying to portray a confidence I'm nowhere near feeling.

"It means she's fated to be mine, and I hers."

"Bull*shit*!" Heracles shouts.

I can't help a smirk at his outburst. "If

only you were so lucky."

Even as he cusses up a storm, I pin Jason down with my stare. "Why was Cerberus blocking the entrance to the tunnel?"

"He knew we were down there. After a bit of fighting, we pushed through, but Connie was stuck behind."

My gaze shifts to the sizeable hole the monster left behind, trying to picture it. "No, more like he *wanted* her there."

I step closer and hop through the entrance. Shouts echoing above and thuds of landing tell me the heroes have followed and are right behind me. But it's not them I'm interested in.

Instead, I kneel and press my palm to the ground, attempting to force a vision I truly have no control over. For once, though, it seems the Fates are smiling on me as it hits me with little work on my part.

Constanza is standing, seeking an escape. She has her back to someone as they come from behind, smacking her over the head. She crumples, and the figure bends to pick her up, then turns.

I've seen that ugly face before. *Charon.*

"Fuck."

"What is it?" Jason asks.

"For that matter, what are you doing?"

I stand, dusting myself off and ignoring Theseus. "We don't have time for trifling, so I'll be brief. Some zmei are born with gifts. Mine was an extra dose of the Sight, as well as venom in my attacks that will kill anything supernatural. For once, it seems both are about to come in handy for something other than destruction."

Heracles folds his arms. "I'm listening."

"It was Charon who took Constanza. Now, we've already established he's being controlled by someone else. And chances are, he's bringing her to them."

"To Tartarus." For once, Theseus is on the ball.

I nod, focusing my attention on Heracles. "I realize you hate me, and you have no reason to want to work with me. But I don't fucking know where to go in this place, however I do have one advantage. I can fly, and I can be fast."

His eyes narrow on me. "Why the sudden urge to play hero?"

I roll my eyes. "Don't worry, I'm not about

to kick you out of a job. I want Constanza safe, is all. Her safety is my safety, as far as her parents are concerned."

"What about the imprinting shit?"

"That's between me and her, hero boy."

He glowers, but after a glance to Jason and Theseus, nods. "We can get you to Tartarus."

"Then lead the way."

Constanza

Charon has dragged me to the pits of Hell itself.

After exiting the tunnel via the same way I'd gone in, a black horse was waiting for us. Charon hopped on it and I had no choice but to join him. He started cutting across the Underworld to places I'd never been, the horse running faster than should be possible.

Finally, we come to a dizzying stop in front of another river. This time, the area on the other side is dark, devoid of any flowers. Tall peaks of mountains loom in the distance, and geysers shoot flames up from the ground every few steps.

In one smooth jump, the horse crosses

the river, and Charon dismounts. He spins to me, extending his hand. "Come on, princess."

The moniker reminds me of Declan. *Declan...* My heart squeezes, even as my mind tells me to get a grip. How stupid is it that in this moment of hardship, all I want is him around?

I get off the beast without touching Charon, glaring at him even if he cannot see me. "You got me where you wanted. What, exactly, is my purpose here, Charon?"

"Insurance."

"In which way?"

"Hades and Persephone have taken a liking to you. I intend to use that."

That's what I feared. The last thing I want is to be bait for them. But the ferryman isn't done, not in the least.

"And there is always your zmeu companion. Your presence here will lure him in. It will also ensure he falls in line."

I snort at that. "You may have gotten your wires crossed. Declan doesn't care about me, so your little insurance strategy won't work with him."

"Hmm. We shall see about that."

He points further into Tartarus, but I balk at the idea of stepping any deeper in here. Not that I have a choice. Charon drags me to a small mountain in the distance. Near its bottom is a glowing shape, moving about restlessly.

When she looks up, I notice a pale face, curls that might've been red of her living framing a heart-shaped face, and pretty brown eyes. She smiles at me, but there is nothing warm about it, instead it stops me dead in my tracks.

"Who is that?"

Charon chuckles. "Another insurance."

۲

"Don't look so sour."

I glare at the woman. We've been sitting in silence while Charon paces not too far off, as if expecting someone. Until she chose to talk, in old Romanian, at that.

When I'm silent, she laughs, as if knowing a secret I don't. "Come on, surely you remember the mother tongue?"

It would be bad manners to drive my fist into her face. But I want to with a surprising desperation tinged with fury. Instead, I settle for, "Who the hell are you?"

"Aw, did Declan not tell you?"

I had my suspicions, and that's all the confirmation I need. "You're Alina, aren't you?"

She grins, evidently more than satisfied that Declan hasn't forgotten her, and saw fit to mention her to me. If only she knew.

"After I died, my soul came to Tartarus. But my memories took *forever* to return. Difficult, what with being in here. But, I hung on to those glorious times with my husband for as long as I could, until it paid off."

The way her eyes glaze has bile rising in my throat.

"Why would Charon bring *you* here?"

"For additional leverage."

Before I can ask more, Charon stops his pacing and walks back to us. "It is time. Alina, go hide." He points the staff towards me again. "If you say anything to warn him, I'll let loose the Serafim on your precious Hades and Persephone. Remember, you're the only thing protecting them right now."

I merely glare at him and don't move from my spot. A good thing, too, since a moment later a massive shadow covers us, and flaps of wings beat a fast wind. Declan, in his zmeu form, prepares to land, forcing Charon away from me as he does so. When the flames disappear and he's human and clothed once more, his back is to me.

I stare at his broad shoulders, unable to believe my eyes. He's actually here. Declan, villain extraordinaire, come to play my hero. But he doesn't understand the trap he has walked into.

"What are you doing?" I hiss.

He glances over his shoulder. "I should've thought that's obvious. Saving you."

Charon chooses that moment to intervene. "Welcome to Tartarus, zmeu. I should think it is time we have a proper conversation."

As if on cue, the dust behind Charon also settles, and another shape comes out. For a moment, I assume it's another zmeu, but he looks nothing like Declan. His scales are murky, his eyes as blind as the ferryman, and he looks… sick. There is no other way to describe him.

"Fuck," Declan grumbles.

"What is that?"

"Not what. Who." He reaches into the air and draws out a sword. "That's Igor, a balaur."

The moment he says the word, I remember what Heracles told me, about the plot that had been undergoing... The one Declan helped with, when he was siding with the bad guys.

My tone comes out a tad accusing. "Isn't he your friend?"

He shoots me another look, this one I can't interpret. If I didn't know him better, I'd say he's hurt, but I'm probably imagining things. Again.

My eyes move past him to the massive beast, then to Charon. He's just out of reach of the chaos he created, and his impassable stance warns me he has more planned.

"You cannot win against that thing."

Declan's expression hardens. "Watch me."

He faces the monster again but without shifting to zmeu form. That's when I start panicking. Jason and the others were strong, bred to do this kind of stuff. What in the name of all pantheons is Declan playing at?

Change to zmeu. Change to zmeu. I keep

chanting in my head, hoping by some miracle he'll hear me.

With everything I've learned, I shouldn't care. If anything, I should use this distraction as a chance to get the hell out of here. But I can't make myself look away from the balaur, getting closer and closer. Declan draws him further from me, sword in hand. He's muttering under his breath, and the massive beast tilts its head.

Then *words* pour out of its mouth. "I warned it would not be the end, did I not? Now, you will regret having turned against me."

"Yeah, yeah," Declan says, loud enough I can hear him. Is that *boredom* in his tone?

He draws something in the air–a rune– and a shield comes over him, like a million little stars. This only seems to amuse the balaur.

As I stand watching, unable to move, I also notice another thing. If I'm to believe Igor's words, Declan hadn't been lying. When he told me he ultimately turned against him... Could it be that he wasn't lying about using me, either? Or, at the very slightest, that he changed his mind halfway through, same as I did?

My thoughts shatter with their next flurry of motions. Moving way too fast for a beast so large, Igor gains on Declan and paws him through his magic shield, sending him flying backwards.

Shit.

Declan

Change to zmeu. Change to zmeu.

I can hear Constanza's plea in my head, and aside from the surprise of it, I can't follow through. I've already used the zmeu form to find her, and if I change again, we won't be able to get out of here as fast as we need to.

Fighting against Igor is idiocy in human form, but then again, I'm not thinking clearly. The moment I saw her, relief like never before coursed through me. The fact she's alive, and unharmed, goes a long way towards me not killing Charon on the spot. Not that I have the tools for that, anyway.

Igor smacks the surrounding air again and I jump, landing a useless blow on one of his paws. My sword clatters somewhere in the distance, repelled by his scales. The moment after I land, I reach for air again and pull out a steel sword. It's heavy in my grip, so I twirl it a few times, getting the hang of it. Good thing muscle memory is a thing.

If only Igor *could* be killed, I might actually have an advantage. But the entire time I'm fighting his glowing self, I'm wondering how the hell we'll survive this. The heroes are waiting for us on the outskirts of Tartarus, and I wish now I'd have let them join me.

Too late to change my mind.

Igor comes at me again–only, this time, Charon lifts his staff. An odd light surrounds it and shoots straight for Igor, dissolving the balaur in front of my eyes. And not a moment too soon, as my body protests me getting up.

Constanza runs closer to me, panic in her features. "Declan, I have to–"

I tug on her wrist, pulling her behind me, and clutch my sword tighter. "What the fuck is your game, ferryman?"

That's when Charon completely fucks me over. He glances in a corner, and a shadow moves out. At first, all I can make out is a blurry shape, hidden by the ever-permanent red fog in Tartarus. Then I catch sight of red curls and, a few moments later, a figure I'd recognize anywhere.

My grip on my sword slackens as I stare at the human who tore my heart out. The one who single-handedly ruined a millennia-long bond with my brother. The same one whose cries have filled my nightmares non-stop since her death.

Alina.

Chapter 15

Șansă
"Maybe sometimes love needs a second <u>chance</u> because it wasn't ready the first time around."
-Anonymous-

Declan

A myriad of emotions runs through me. Rage at seeing Alina's face again, hurt for all the shit she pulled, and yeah, a tad of something like nostalgia. What the hell is she doing in Tartarus?

"Heya, Declan," she says, switching to old Romanian.

To see her is one thing, but hearing her voice is even more unreal, and I can't tear my eyes away from her.

For so long, I cared for her. Loved her. Gave her everything and was even willing to set my clan aside. To live as a human.

My very character changed, and I allowed it so. Alina's love, the pure joy at being in her presence, was all I needed. I became someone else, someone softer… All because of *her*.

And when I lost her, because of *how* that happened, the rage led me to commit acts of unspeakable vengeance. I killed innocents, da, to soothe my own wounded soul. I sent many probably here, when they did not deserve it.

And now she stands, glowing form, a tentative smile on her lips, looking as beautiful as I remember. It's so easy to recall all those memories, the soft touches, the bliss.

It's even easier to recall the lies.

The sneaking out in the middle of the night, the utter shattering I felt when Igor showed me images of her cheating on me with Tytus. Fake as they were, those images broke my connection with my brother, ensuring I forever blamed him for the betrayal.

Perhaps even blamed him more than I ever did Alina.

After I found out the truth, I still stayed by her side. Undecided in what I should do next, I couldn't walk away. Instead I spent day and night observing her, driving myself crazy... Until it was done. Until the Council burned her body.

"Declan?" The haze of memories breaks when Alina speaks again.

Constanza's behind me. At first glance, I didn't see any obvious signs of Charon hurting her, but I plan on checking as soon as I can get a breather. It's understandable she'd still be angry with me–given our last conversation and everything I held back–but I'm not about to let shit get out of control. Not again.

It also doesn't escape my notice that I'm more aware of her than the woman who once had my heart. And trampled all over it.

I arch an eyebrow Alina's way, striving to remain cool-headed. If there's one thing I hate, it's being manipulated through and through. What is Charon's purpose in bringing back Igor, and now her?

"What the hell do you want, Alina? How did you even get involved in this shit?"

"You know how." She inches ever closer, trying to be seductive with a sway of her hips.

I grip my sword tighter and lift it in her direction. "That's far enough, *draga mea*."

"You won't even allow me closer?"

"I think you lost your privileges long ago, no?"

Her smooth expression drops, and she shares a glance with Charon. Not that he can see her, judging by the tilt of his head. *Must be figuring out how his little scheme is going.*

Realization dawns on me at what I must do. If I want this not to be a wasted rescue attempt, I should figure out why it happened. And before I can get Constanza to a safe place—preferably out of here—and show her how I feel, this mess has to be dealt with.

I force my voice to remain even, not knowing whether Charon understands what we're saying in Romanian, or if he's going by our tones only.

"Did you really think this would work?"

There, this comes out smoother. Almost... pleading. I hate it, but it seems to do the trick, as Charon relaxes.

Alina frowns, clearly not understanding the game I'm playing. I only need a few more minutes, not much longer.

"I only meant to say I'm sorry." She lowers her voice. "To apologize for the part I played in hurting you."

"Hurting me?" I scoff. "You were a blip on my radar, Alina. A minor one, at that."

"You and I both know that's not true."

I move closer, keeping my tone as saccharine sweet as possible even as I allow myself to within an inch of her. Constanza's sharp intake behind me warns me she's reading this the wrong way, but I'll have to deal with that later.

"Fine. You want the truth? I loved you with everything I had. And for too long I thought you betrayed me with my brother, ignorant of the fact you fucked me over in a worse way, still. I gave you *everything,* and you trampled all over it." I smile. "But it's alright, Alina. Because I've since learned there are better things out there, and more worthy than yourself."

As she glares at me, she opens her mouth,

presumably to alert Charon. I jerk forward, clamping my hand over her, shushing her before she can express anything.

Charon, oblivious, says, "Well, zmeu, it seems I have you at an impasse."

"Uh huh."

"Here you have your former flame, and now, your current one. But only one can survive, and you will have to choose which you bring back to the world of the Living."

A monster draws up from behind him, looking a lot like Cerberus' older–and uglier–brother. It's clear he's threatening both women with that monstrosity. And with its appearance, I finally see the point of this entire charade. Charon doesn't really mean to kill me, he only wants to tire me out. Enough for whatever else he has in mind. Too bad for him, this is his latest, and biggest, miscalculation. Because there's only one female I care for.

I pause for a beat, waiting to see if there's more to it, and when Charon says nothing, I burst out laughing. "Are you fucking serious, old man? You actually think there's a *choice* here?"

I glance at Constanza, noticing the regret

in her gaze, and shake my head. "I choose the immortal, any day. You can have Alina."

Without further ado, I grab and toss her towards Charon. Then I spin to Constanza, grabbing her wrist. The monster roars, moving closer, and in the distance I hear more noises–like backup, for Charon. But I also hear something else much, much closer.

Screw waiting. With a tug, I drag Constanza after me.

"Let's go!"

Behind us, Heracles and the two others pop out of the woodwork, launching themselves on Charon and the monster with glee.

About fucking time. Good thing they also don't take orders from higher authorities.

I don't care where Alina's gone off to, or where she'll be for the rest of eternity. It's only Constanza I need, and I need her now.

Constanza

"Wait, wait!" I pant, digging my heels into the ground. "Heracles and the others–"

Declan whirls to me, a wild look in his eyes. "My priority right now is to get you safe. Let's go."

Without another word he pulls me after him, and we run and run and run until my legs wobble and tremble. I don't fight him, only follow him, knowing deep down that he's taking me somewhere safe.

It's the oddest sensation, really. A few hours ago, I shunned him, scared by the truth Heracles confronted me with. All the bad Declan had done, how could I ever be with someone like that? Especially when our peaceful existence here had been disturbed, massively so, as a direct result of his actions.

And if he had stuck by those actions, perhaps I would still need to be away. To avoid his touch. And I wouldn't be as happy as I am now that he came to my rescue.

But… Declan did.

Not only did he show up, he also chose to save me. And he fought off his old mentor–or whatever Igor was to him–*and* chased off his ex-wife. He made the hard choices, no matter what it cost him.

And that… That builds a measure of trust. Enough for me to follow him, even as I try to disentangle my mind from my heart.

Finally, Declan slows down and eyes

something in the darkness, pulling us towards it. It's a massive tree, its trunk hollow at the back. Enough to shield us... hide us.

He pulls me inside, making sure I'm as deep as I can get, then turns to the entrance. The air sizzles with his runes as he draws them and a barrier–much like the one he'd used in battle–wisps out of them and ties across the tree trunk opening like a spider's web.

I watch him work until he stills, panting in the darkness. His head rests away from me on the rough bark, as if he's run out of energy.

I never expected him to come to my rescue. Even less that he'd shun his ex-lover for me, especially after our last conversation.

"I know what you think," he says, "about everything I held back. Everything Heracles told you. But not all of it is true, or not in the sense you assume. Da, Heracles was right, I worked with Igor. Blinded by vengeance, I didn't care who suffered."

"Do you still feel like that?"

He gestures to me, his head still resting on the tree. "Do you mean have I changed, am I a reformed man, selfless and heroic?" A snort. "No, I am not. At times, I crave nothing but to burn everything to ashes, and leave everyone behind."

"Me, as well?"

His eyes shut, and he inclines his head in an unfamiliar gesture—one of contrition. "No. Never you. That's one thing I've been fighting against, and failed, time and time again." His golden eyes open and latch onto mine again. "You've shown me what it's like to live, Constanza."

I don't know how to respond. My mind stutters to a stop, scared to say the wrong thing, scared to say the *right* thing. Because those emotions, the tug of war in his heart, it's also in mind. And yet despite everything he could have done, or *not* done, Declan still showed up.

"Thank you," I whisper, attempting a step closer. "For coming back. For saving me."

"Of course."

I dip my head, confused. Plagued by a different kind of insecurity. When he was speaking with Alina, he was so soft, so... I couldn't hear his words, but by his tone, I thought he was caring, that he'd fallen into the trap.

"With Alina–"

He straightens from the tree, runs a hand over his face. "It was a ploy, Constanza. To get their guard down."

"And choosing me–"

"There was no choice."

"Why?"

He faces me fully, but in the darkness I can't figure out his expression. I only hear it in his anguished voice. "Don't you know by now, Constanza?"

I do. And he may not be my perfect guy, but he's willing to try. Even with his flaws and messed up past, everything he's done has only proven he is even more worthy of my attention. Of my caring. Of... my love. And perhaps my salvation.

So I step closer to him and hear his breathing stop. After a slight hesitation, I reach up to smooth his brow, and the deep frown that won't go away.

"I know, Declan."

He stares at me, his eyes searching mine, filled with hope and restraint and regret and so many other things I don't have time to name. He lifts a trembling hand to my cheek, cupping it, and I turn to kiss his palm, never once breaking eye contact.

With a groan, he bends his mouth to mine. I'm expecting one of our furious, breathless kisses. Yet as desperate as we both are, the embrace is tender, almost tentative.

Declan's hands tremble as he caresses my body, as if there's too much inside him he cannot hold back. I can tell, because I feel it too. Like a dam about to break and consume us both. We've held on the edge of this precipice for so long, teasing each other, holding back for fear of realizing the reality of what we had doesn't compare to the fantasy. But I have an inkling that if we were to give in, it would be even more explosive, even more earth shattering, and not only on a physical level.

Just as I want to push it, to get us where we need to be, Declan freezes.

I pull back from the kiss. "What's wrong?"

"Shh." He glances around, then his body relaxes and he pops out through the barrier. "Over here."

A moment later, Heracles, Jason and Theseus join us in our little hideout.

I search their faces for an explanation. "What happened?"

"Killed the monster," Heracles grins. "Or what was left of it."

"And Charon?"

"He escaped."

"Fuck," Declan says, and I couldn't agree more.

He doesn't ask about Alina, and that warms my heart. But for my own sake, I need to. "And the soul who was there, the woman?"

Jason shrugs. "Escorted her back to the depths of Tartarus. You know, nicely."

"Right." I have a feeling threats were used, not that I'm complaining.

They stare between us, and a blush creeps on my cheeks. Declan says nothing, deep in thought, but it's apparent the heroes are itching for more fighting. A fact confirmed by Jason's next words.

"So, what now?"

I try to think through everything we've learned. "Charon was tight-lipped about what his purpose is. I think we can assume, based on what Chiron dug up, that we definitely will face Cronus at some point or another. Which means we need a weapon, something to fight any Titan."

"Isn't your sword enough?" Heracles points out.

I nod. "Yeah, but there's something else, too. My parents were guardians to Hades, way back when."

Declan chokes on a sip of water and throws me a look. Oops. I did forget to mention that... *Oh well.*

"And?" Theseus frowns.

"They may have hidden more swords like ours here, the kind that can fight anything. If we can find those, and get them blessed by Hades, it'll give us an edge when we fight souls like the Serafim."

The heroes nod.

I hesitate, before admitting, "There may be something stronger, too."

"Like what?"

"A spear with special qualities. But, that could also be a rumor, one of those old legends."

Declan arches an eyebrow. "Who would know?"

"Persephone, maybe..." The necklace around my neck feels heavier. "I tried reaching out to her, when Charon took me captive. With no luck."

"Hmm." He goes back to pacing.

"If such a sword exists…" Heracles rubs his chin. "Any idea where it would be hidden?"

I shake my head. "Your guess is as good as mine."

Jason shrugs. "Well, I'm up for another quest."

"No." Declan says. "You'd be going in blind, and wasting time. This is for me and Connie. We'll do it, and try to reach out to Persephone. You three need to ensure Zeus' forces can enter here. No more surprises like Cerberus and all these monsters. Go back to the entrance and get rid of Charon's people guarding it."

Heracles looks at me. "Are you good with that?"

I know what he means. Am I okay with being alone with Declan, for the duration of this so-called quest?

"Yeah, I am."

For the second time, Declan's body relaxes, and I feel in my bones it's the right decision. I've seen enough to know there is good in him, no matter how much he denies it.

While the three heroes set guard around in a perimeter around the tree trunk, Declan and I get some rest, to prepare for leaving as soon as possible.

In the darkness, with his heartbeat in my ears, I almost fall asleep. Until Declan speaks.

"When that's done, and we have the weapons... I'll join you to save Hades."

I snuggle closer against him. "Thank you."

Declan

I cannot fathom what this sorcery is, but for once I am at peace.

I never expected to see Alina ever again, to ever get all the resentment off my chest. Now that it's gone, I feel... less burdened. Like a weight has been lifted off my shoulders, and I'm able to view things in a less grim light.

It's probably all in my head, though.

And if it's not, well, I can only attribute it to the immortal in my arms. The one my zmeu wants nothing more than to claim.

Since Tytus got that stupid idea into my zmeu, he won't stay at bay. The need, the craving, the want to be with her. Something about having Constanza back soothes my soul. Makes the darkness inside me leave. Has me hoping for better times.

Which is stupid. Given her parents intend to imprison me again once I get back. I'm not an idiot, there is simply no way they'll let me go free.

And perhaps Constanza might fight for me. Perhaps she might win. More than likely, she will turn against me. And no amount of pleading will get me back in her heart.

"What are you thinking about?" she murmurs against my chest.

I tighten my arm around her. "Just that I'm glad you're safe, darling."

"Is that all?"

I kiss her forehead, willing my mind to shut up. "Da, there is nothing else."

Even as she settles deeper in my embrace, and her breathing slows down, the thoughts are back to churning in my head. I'm not used to such chaotic emotions, such deep ones. Even with Alina, they hadn't been this strong. Which only means if at the end of this I cannot have her...

Impossible.

My zmeu rebels against the notion, but it's not too out of bounds.

So what do I do? Cut off all emotions and pretend this never happened? Keep going as if everything will be alright? Try to change, so I can hopefully prove everyone that I'm better now?

Foolishness.

Yet with Constanza in my arms, hope blooms in my chest. Perhaps it is stupid. Perhaps I have gone soft.

Tytus

In a rare moment of rest, I've been able to shut off completely and sleep. I'm woken up by Fiona shaking my shoulder.

"Ty, wake up!"

The urgency in her tone has me jolt awake.

"What is it?"

"Ileana's here."

I'm out of bed and heading down the stairs before she can say more. Fiona joins me by the entrance a few moments later.

"Immortal," I greet Ileana. "What brings you here?"

Her eyes flash lightning, warning me I won't like her next words. "You didn't tell us everything."

"About what?"

"Igor's plans."

I take a step closer, and in the same movement intertwine my fingers with Fiona's in a silent reassurance. We had chosen not to divulge anything, specifically to save Declan from their wrath.

"They no longer mattered, given he was dead."

"They did," Ileana hisses. "And because of your silence, my daughter is about to pay the price. As will Declan."

Chapter 16

Comoară
"Knowledge is the _treasure_ of a wise man."
-William Penn-

Declan

I must've fallen asleep, because the way I wake up is nowhere as sweet.

Declan!

I jerk awake and try not to disturb Constanza. Tytus sounds mighty pissed, though.

What is it?

Where are you right now?

I glance around and give a mental shrug. *Safe. For now.*

And Ileana's daughter?

With me. I frown. *Why the sudden interest?*

Ileana was here, rather panicked.

How unsurprising.

Constanza stirs, as if sensing we're talking about her mother. She lifts her head off my chest and sits up, rubbing at her eyes. Her sleepy appearance is endearing, and my heart softens towards her even more. No matter much I want to avoid it. *Shit.*

When she senses me watching her, she frowns. "What is it?"

I hold up a finger and gesture to my head. "Tytus."

"Your brother?" Realization dawns on her and her mouth forms an O shape. "He's talking to you?"

"Da, and he mentioned your mother came by to see him. Give me a moment."

I close my eyes, trying to block her image from her mind. *Tell Ileana her daughter is safe with me, but we won't be making that one week deadline.*

Why not?

Because shit has hit the fan here, and we can't leave.

Can't, or won't?

Both.

He's silent for a bit. *What's gotten into you?*

I don't know. And I don't. As far as I can tell, I'm going to get Constanza out of here safe and sound, and that's my only priority at the moment.

You sure about that?

I scowl and try to relax my expression, mindful of Constanza watching me. *Did you wake me up just to annoy me, or was there a point to all this?*

There was. A pause. *Ileana knows about Igor, and what you almost did for him.*

Shit.

The leak didn't come from us, he hurries to add, and oddly, I believe him. Fiona had no reason to protect me in the first place, so it's a wonder it lasted so long.

I figured as much. Did she say where it came from?

Da. And you won't like this, brother… It's Olympus. If you guys are waiting for help from them, it's not coming.

Why the fuck not?

Zeus. It seems the big guy isn't too keen on cleaning up his brother's mess, or yours.

A low growl starts in my throat. Constanza touches me softly, and I open my eyes. Her worried expression hits me with a pang, and I sigh. *Hold on, frate.*

"Your mother is fine," I tell her as I sit up. "But Olympus isn't sending us help. We're on our own."

She gapes. "No!"

"Yeah."

She gets up and goes to find the heroes, and I take advantage of the moment of silence to get back to Tytus. *Did Ileana say anything else, something useful this time?*

No. But if you explain to me the issue you're having, I can try to dig on my end here, before joining you.

There's no reason both our lives need to be in danger.

I'm not discussing this with you, Dec. I told you before I would help you, and you have to trust me. Now, details. I sense we have little time.

My brother is as stubborn as I am, and I realize when a fight is lost. So I give in and fill him on everything.

Right before I sign off, something occurs to me. *Tytus?*

Da? He already sounds distracted.

If I know him well–and I do–he's planning a million tasks to find me a solution. And for once, I appreciate how hard this must be for him. And how I shouldn't be taking it for granted. But when I try to express as much, the words remain stuck in my mind.

So I clear my throat, and instead ask, *Have you ever heard anything about weapons? Specifically, blades or spears that might kill a Titan?*

No, but I will leave no stone unturned.

Thank you.

As soon as I'm done with him, Tytus signs off, and I get up. Splash some water from a flask on my face, then Constanza joins me. The heroes follow her, looking less than happy.

"Heard the news?"

Heracles' jaw looks like it's ready to snap. "Yeah, we did. Typical of the mighty Zeus."

"Do I sense some daddy issues?"

He scowls my way, and I shrug. "What's our second option, then?"

Despite all our heads together, we don't come up with anything. Until Constanza touches her neck, and her eyes widen. A second later, she's gripping the pendant and saying Persephone's name.

"Constanza?"

The voice comes from her palm. My girl glances in it, and sure enough, there's Persephone's face reflected.

"Yes! How are things? Where's Hades?"

"We're locked in our quarters in the palace. The Serafim have taken over and..." Her voice drops even lower. "They're searching for both of you, Connie. Be careful."

"I am. But that's not why I'm calling." She quickly brings her up to speed, ending with, "Do you or Hades know of anything that could give us an advantage?"

"It wouldn't be any use. You should get out while you can, my dear friend."

"NO! Absolutely not. Think, please."

Other noises echo out of sight, and Persephone disappears for a few moments as we wait in tense silence. When she returns, her expression is confused, and a tad wary.

"Is Declan there?"

Constanza glances at me. "Yes."

"Can you get away for a bit?"

"No. I trust him."

Her faith in me does something, and instead of inching closer, I find myself moving away. To be given that trust, I also have to make sure I don't break it again. It's a daunting thought, one I am not used to.

For her, we can, my zmeu says.

I ignore my own doubts, instead perking my ears and listening to their conversation.

After a beat of hesitation, Persephone sighs. "Let's hope it's a trust well-placed. Hades says there is something. Only him, Zeus and Poseidon know of it, because they gave their blessing for it to be created."

We all turn to Heracles, but he only shrugs. "No clue."

"It's a spear," Persephone says, confirming Constanza's story. "And it's buried under Chiron's mountain."

"Then why did the old fool not tell us!" I growl.

"He's not aware. When Hades created the

spot for him, he didn't tell him."

"And what's so special about this spear?" Jason questions. "No offense."

"The way it came into existence," Persephone admits. "Hades says when they imprisoned the Titans, they collected their blood and got one immortal and one zmeu to forge a spear, using primordial magic, out of the blood itself. It was burned in zmeu's breath and it can kill any Titan. For good."

"And what if we don't face Cronus?" I'm thinking of Charon and his many fucking creatures.

"It will give you an edge, regardless. Much more than any simple immortal blade."

"So you're saying we should use our efforts to find this spear," Constanza says. "Drop everything else."

"That's what I would do, yes, my friend."

I glance at Constanza, then everyone else. "Sounds good enough to me."

As she says goodbye to Persephone, I wave the heroes to me. "You three should stick around here. Me and Constanza can move faster on my back. And if you can give the illusion that we're hidden somewhere

here, you may buy us time. Even if Perseph-one thinks no one else knows about this, I don't buy it."

Heracles nods, surprisingly docile. "Good for me."

"And me," Jason adds.

Theseus shrugs. "Same."

I turn to Constanza, who's done with Persephone by now. "Fancy a trip back to your godfather?"

Constanza

As soon as we're away from the heroes, Declan shifts again and I climb back on him, holding onto his spikes for support. We fly into the night sky, and I'm grateful that we're together, if nothing else.

When Persephone had wanted to talk to me alone, I could've given in. But I didn't want to. And I noticed something else in Declan's gaze, for the first time. Trust. An odd vulnerability. I would lie if I said my heart was closed to that.

When we land next to Chiron's mountain, I don't avert my gaze from Declan as he shifts back to human. My eyes take him in greedily, remembering his hands on me in the forest. When our gazes lock across the few paces, the air becomes almost tangible with tension.

My breathing comes out faster, and my body tightens in expectation of... something. Declan's eyes smolder, and it looks like he's fighting an internal war of whether to act on what he undoubtedly feels, or let it go.

He draws a rune and then he's dressed once more, the moment broken.

"So, do we yell out for Chiron?" he asks.

"No need. He sensed you coming a mile away."

I turn around, finding Grandaddy perched on the slab of mountain above us.

"Perfect," Declan drawls. "This'll save us time."

I ignore him and move up, hugging Chiron. "How bad was it, with the Serafim here?"

Guilt at leaving him behind has weighed on my shoulders after our last visit, but it had been unavoidable. Hopefully, things won't end the same this time around.

He shrugs. "They destroyed a few things, but once they realized you were not here, they were quick to leave. I can't say the same for Charon."

"He came by?"

Granddaddy's expression darkens. "You've only missed him. He seemed to go on and on about some kind of weapon the Olympians created. He left when he realized I had no information on it."

Declan and I share a glance. *How the hell did Charon find out?*

"Right, about that, Grandaddy..." I catch him up to date, brief as I can be.

When I'm done, he's rubbing his beard and looking thoughtful–and a tad annoyed. I don't blame him. The least Hades could've done was tell him he's sitting on some super-important weapon that could end all Titans.

"I'm tired of gods who act like we're their playthings," he mutters and his gaze narrows on us. "You're sure of this?"

"Yes."

"There is no hidden passage in my mountain, other than those I myself created. But if I was Hades, and I wanted to hide something, it wouldn't be around the top that I would do it. It would be towards the bottom, where I would be sure no one would think to look."

"So how do we find it?" I'm ready to cry, frustrated at all the dead ends.

"Head on down to where the mountain starts. See if there are any fissures or ways in, or sense of magic."

"What if we have to blast something, to get in?" Declan has a point. Last thing we want is to destroy Granddaddy's home.

"This area is stable. I'm sure it will be fine."

"Great to know."

I ignore Declan's grumbles, instead trying to think back to Hades, and the way his mind works. It would've been great if he'd given us a map, but since he didn't…

My fingers trail the pendant at my throat, and my eyes widen. "Grandaddy! Are there any minerals and semi-precious stones here?"

Chiron rubs his beard, thinking. I want to stomp my foot and tell him to hurry, but then his glazed expression clears and he nods.

"There is a pathway to the back of the mountain, and I've seen bits and pieces of such stones there."

I try not to get too excited. "What kind?"

"Mainly amethysts and onyx, some opal. Why?"

I turn to Declan, grabbing his arm and trying to ignore the jolt of electricity running through my body. "This is it!"

"What's *it*, princess?"

"The stones! Hades is always gifting Persephone stuff with minerals and semi-precious stones, because his satyrs mine the area. It must be a clue!"

Declan looks doubtful, but before he can voice his opinion, he jerks his head to the side. Tilts it, as if in tune to something he alone can hear. Dread builds in the pit of my stomach, becoming a full-blown volcano when his expression darkens.

"Fuck!" Declan swears. "Not again."

"What now?" Chiron groans.

Declan steps closer to us, grabbing my wrist as if ensuring I won't be taking off. He meets Grandaddy's glare and says, "We've got company. Again."

Chiron hops upwards, to a peak that gives him a full view of the valley. By the time he returns to us, his features have filled with anger. "Give me a sword and leave them to me. Find that spear, and I will buy you some time."

I don't want to leave him. But I need not look at Declan to realize we're pressed for time. And Chiron can take care of himself... I hope.

Declan tugs on my hand. "If we find it fast, we can get it, then return and help."

I nod, and we run away, leaving Granddaddy with Declan's sword.

~

"What about here?"

Declan retraces his steps and comes back to where I'm pointing. A tiny crack in the mountain's façade, enough for an insect to pass through. We've passed three more like these, and I'm starting to lose hope.

I peer over my shoulder, wondering if he's still alive, if he got swarmed by the Serafim...

"We may have something," Declan says, distracting me.

I rush and kneel next to him, not seeing what he does. Sure, there are a few minerals glinting about, but...

"The inside," he says, "it sounds hollow."

"You would know, with your super hearing."

He flashes me a quick grin and sets about tracing three runes across the line of the fissure, then backs away, me with him. They sizzle and the wall of stone crumbles, as if someone had taken a hammer to it.

"Much more silent," I whisper.

He shrugs. "I try."

Declan goes in first, and I follow. The moment we're inside, my hopes are dashed. Yes, the place is hollow, but it's also a dead end. Like the inside of a tree trunk, there's enough space for us to move about, but an immovable wall stops any further progress into the mountain.

"I don't understand. There were stones outside this entrance..." I move closer to the wall, looking for a hidden mechanism, anything to show it was placed here on purpose to hide a mythical weapon. Nope. No such luck. In frustration, I slam my palms against it, uselessly so. After multiple attempts, I move away and rub the soreness settling in my wrists.

Declan takes my place, and presses his hands to the same wall I tried to punch. Then his forehead. If I didn't know better, I'd think he's exhausted and trying to catch his breath. But, no, he's not.

Something rolls through him, and his outstretched palm clenches into a fist. A low groan escapes him. When he turns to me, the whites of his eyes return to normal and he rubs his head as if he had a headache.

"Hades was here, alright," he says. "But it looks like only a mix of immortal and zmeu blood can open the way."

"Okay, so what are we waiting for?"

When he simply stares, I roll my eyes and pluck a dagger from thin air. I cut my palm and hold it out to him to reciprocate.

"Together?"

"Together."

We both press our hands against the wall, and it rumbles, groaning–then it *moves*, deeper into the mountain. And there, laid on a simple beige cloak, is the spear.

For all intents and purposes, it looks like a regular version. Only the tip seems to shine oddly, but that could be the light.

Declan's relieved sigh echoes around me. "Finally." He rushes in before I can stop him and grabs both spear and cloak, before exiting once more. His grin is brighter than all the stars combined. "Let's go save ourselves a centaur, da?"

Without thinking about it, I run into his arms and kiss him. It's full-bodied, putting my everything in it, and his arm tightens around my waist as he pulls me closer, groaning. We kiss for what must be only seconds, and the hardness of his body presses against the pliancy of mine. I want to give in to this desire, this fire burning between us, overriding my senses.

But Declan pulls away, setting me back down.

"Later," he tells me, ignoring my disappointed expression. "If anything happens to Chiron, you won't forgive me."

I nod, and move away, but he grabs hold of my hand. "Doesn't mean this is over... princess."

Only the way he says it now, it's more an endearment than anything else. I give him a shaky smile, before leading the way out. Once he's in zmeu form again, and I'm nestled on his back with the spear, we take off. His bulk should hide me from view of those below us, or at the very least conceal our newfound treasure. Still, for added protection, I make sure it's wrapped in the cloak, and secured to me.

Wouldn't do to drop it in the hands of the enemy.

With a powerful push off his legs, Declan jumps in the air. As we fly over, he has no trouble spotting Chiron. He's fighting against a group of Serafim, and some other creature that looks like a big worm with ugly antennae. I shudder as it slithers around, ready to attack from behind.

Declan's already on the move, though. Jets of blue fire escape him, burning through the creature. It turns, stuck in the flames, trying to toss something towards us–it takes me a moment to realize it's a web of some sort.

I react on pure instinct and shoot a blast of primordial magic, at the same time Declan does his bit. Our combined effort detonates, and the beast explodes, bits of it flying everywhere. Unlike the souls, it was very much alive.

Yuck.

Chiron is slammed back into the mountain by our blast, but so are the Serafim—on opposite ends. Declan takes advantage and shoots more fire. Then he roars to Chiron, who seems to get the gist. With a salute towards us, he takes off, hooves beating the ground, and disappears into the darkness below.

That's one person saved. Which only leaves us two more... Hades and Persephone.

Chapter 17

Neprevăzut
"To expect the <u>unexpected</u> shows a thoroughly modern intellect."
-Oscar Wilde-

Declan

I fly over the Underworld, hoping Chiron gets away safe, the old bastard. Those Serafim won't be too happy and they'll hunt us down next. Which means they'll be looking at the skies... Not the ground.

A different set of woods extends under us. I check the distance between it and the area towards Tartarus. It can't be more than a few hours' walk. *This'll do.*

Air whooshes past me as I dive through, landing a few moments later. I can't change back to human, if I do I won't have the zmeu around for the rest of these fights, and that's risky. So I wait until Constanza is off me to meet her gaze.

After a beat, she frowns. "Won't you take human form?"

For a moment, I debate if it's even possible. With each conversation, each passing day, I've felt closer to her, as if something has sparked my zmeu into full protectiveness. Everywhere I go, she is around me. Thus, it would make sense that our connection would extend to the mental.

I decide to try speaking to her mind anyway. *I cannot.*

Her eyes widen. "How are you…"

I lower myself further until my massive head is eye level with her. *Remember what I told you about my brother and I?*

"Oh." She glances around. "So why did we stop?"

The Serafim will look for us in the skies. If

they don't see us, they'll go back to Charon and it will cause a dispersion of the forces again.

"Which makes it easier to pick everyone apart."

I nod.

She hesitates for a beat before moving closer to me, reaching out to pet my muzzle gently, her expression softening. It feels so good, I sense my zmeu purring like a cat.

"And why aren't you changing to human form?"

I've reached the maximum my body allows in such a brief time span. Any further transformations will only weaken me, ensuring I won't have the zmeu for when I truly need him–the last fight. And we need all the help we can get.

Constanza stares at me for a moment longer, as if trying to determine if that's all there is to my decision. In the end, she nods and settles down on the ground next to me, her back leaning against my head.

It's weird, being like this by her side. Quiet, waiting. I'm aware of the heat of her body, and my own tremulous thoughts. Am I using this, in a way, to escape facing her?

Perhaps. I don't want to see the hope in her eyes, the high regard she holds me to, for having rescued her. Not when I know I'm not deserving of it, of her.

ɛ

An hour, two, must have passed, as we lie down quietly. The spear is by Cassandra's side, bundled up, and we both glance at it every few moments.

"Why do you think the gods created this?"

Insurance is my best guess. If they ever lost control of the Titans, they didn't want to be eradicated.

"Dad once told me the war was bad… Between the Olympians, but also between our kin."

Hmm.

It's odd to think of Făt as her father. Perhaps because my few interactions with him were strained, downright violent. Perhaps also because it makes me aware of the differences in our upbringing, in where we come from. We couldn't be more different if we tried.

"What are you thinking about?"

Nothing.

My answer is too quick, and with her usual perceptiveness, Constanza sees right through it. She turns around, kneeling next to me and gazing into one of my eyes. Her expression, as far as I can tell through the vivid colors, is annoyed. Our bond confirms that.

"Declan..." She flicks her fingers against the top of my massive head, and I pull it to the side, shaking it and snorting. Puffs of blue fire dance out of my nostrils.

Did you just flick me?

"I did." She folds her arms over her chest. "Why have you been acting so weird? After rescuing me, and everything."

Don't know what you mean.

She calls on magic, her hand glowing as she arches an eyebrow. "We can do this the easy way, or the hard way."

It's cute that she thinks her little trick will work.

It's downright annoying when my zmeu actually lets it, forcing me to relent.

I give up. Fine. You'll wish you hadn't asked me, but let's pretend for a moment you'll even consider it. Without pausing to find my words, I stumble ahead. *Tytus says the reason we connected via dreams, and everything since then between us, is because my zmeu picked you.*

The magic dies out of her hand. "Picked me? How so?"

There's this thing… I sigh, and more wisps of blue fire escape me. I wish I could be in human form as I'm telling her this, not appearing as a massive monster ten times her size. Then again, maybe it's a good thing, since the ugliness is more alike to me than I'd like to admit.

You know how your parents have the consort thing going on? As do the gods? Well, zmei also have something similar, like mating. It's called the legătură, the bonding, which leads to the împerechere, or pairing. Either way, to make a lengthy story short, it's always the raw, primal part of us that picks the female, and builds on that connection, which is almost always purely physical from the get go. Until… Until it's more.

Constanza couldn't look more stunned if I'd smacked her with a tree trunk. "You… So your zmeu…"

I nod. *He chose you. I didn't know, it's not like I could have hidden this from you if I had, but... It's happened. And there's no actual way of stopping it, I guess.*

She moves towards me, touching me again. "Why would you say that? About stopping it?"

Because we both know I've never been what you wanted. You deserve so much more, darling.

It's easier, somehow, saying all this while in zmeu form, knowing she cannot see the truth of the emotions on my face. It allows me a semblance of protection. Hilarious to think I actually need it... But truth be told, Constanza has managed to dig her way into my heart despite my protests, and this is not the easiest thing to admit.

"Declan, look at me."

I give her my undivided attention, waiting for a soft discourse on why our trysts were great while they lasted in dreams. And how that's where they should stay.

Instead, Constanza says, "Would it be so crazy, if I told you I don't want any of this to stop? That no matter what you've done, I still feel safe with you? That I still... want you?"

It would be easier if she were saying these things to manipulate me. But she's not. I see it in her innocent gaze, I feel it in our mental connection. This immortal goddess truly means *everything* she's saying to me.

And, idiot that I am, I know not how to respond.

As my silence lengthens, Constanza's voice changes. "Declan... Thank you."

What for?

"Everything you did, that you were never asked to."

I'm no hero.

"I know. And... that's what I like about you. Despite what you believe, there's more to you than meets the eyes."

I snort, and tiny blue flames escape my muzzle. *Sure, princess.*

She stands with her hands on her hips. "I'm serious." She bites her lip. "Will you please change to human form?"

There's a pleading in her gaze, in her voice, that answers the most primal part of me. I couldn't resist if I tried. Screw the limitations of my changes, and the war going on outside our little bubble. I allow my zmeu to burn and step naked out of the flames.

Constanza moves forward before I can conjure clothes, and wraps her arms around my waist, tilting her head back to watch me.

"We have little time. And who knows where this fight will lead…"

"What's your point?"

"Kiss me. Take me. Make me yours again, Declan."

I search her gaze, her expression, for a hint of this being a scheme, another way to control. There is none. Constanza's lips are parted, her eyes darkened by desire, her body soft and pliant against mine.

So I surrender to the desire burning between us, allowing the fire to ignite the ice in my heart, and melt it away to nothingness. Permitting these unfamiliar emotions to burn away the past, making way for a future as uncertain as can be.

When our lips touch, it's burning and raw, and I move my hand to her neck to pull Constanza closer. Our joinings and tumblings before, in dreams, were always earth-shattering. And this will be doubly so.

Blind, I steer us backwards, until Constanza's back is against a tree. She hitches one leg around my waist and I bend slightly, picking her up and wrapping both her legs around me. A groan escapes me when her dress falls open, and I come in contact with her heated center.

"Constanza..." My words become growls against her skin, fervent whispers and pleas. My body is afire, demanding hers, needing hers like I've never craved anything in my life.

With one hand, I conjure some furs for the grass, and gently lay Constanza on them. I keep myself propped on my elbow, parallel to her body, but taking my sweet time caressing her–if only to hear her beg.

She arches her back with every sweep of my hands, with every touch of my fingers on her sensitive flesh. A gasp escapes her when my thumb traces the material around her chest, tweaking a taut nipple.

"Declan!" Her frustrated mewl amuses me, but not for long.

Soon, she pushes me on my back, and moves atop me, removing her dress in the process. And then she's naked, my golden goddess, straddling me and looking at me with her azure gaze, a satisfied smile pulling the corners of her lips.

"Let's get one thing clear." She bends lower to kiss me, her breasts brushing my chest. "In bed," she murmurs against my lips, "you can have your control. Take everything you want. But I demand *everything*, Dec. And nothing less than."

When she pulls back, her eyes are glittering, and I return her grin. "As you wish, princess."

I shift just so, making sure her legs fall apart before I'm thrusting inside her. Constanza gasps, and it ends on a long moan as she throws her head back. One experimental shift of her hips, followed by another, and before long she's riding me to her ecstasy.

When her heat tightens against me, and her cries become harsher, I grip her waist and flip us over so I'm on top. Grab her hands, pinning them above her so I can better touch her with my free hand. I graze my fingertips across every dip of her curves, until she's squirming underneath me, pleading for more.

"Declan…"

Her growling plea comes out as a demand.

I answer it with a deep thrust.

And that growl turns into a long moan.

I laugh, lowering my mouth to hers again, stifling that moan and all the others after. My pace increases and before long her heat is all I feel, her scent is all around me, and my zmeu is there, ready... demanding...

My hand holding hers lets go, digging instead into the ground. Constanza reaches for my back, digging her nails into my skin, making me wince in both pain and pleasure.

A roll of something comes over me—fire. Blue flames dance all around us, and I pause in my movements, mesmerized. The blaze merges with my body, coating me, and Constanza, and our surroundings.

"Constanza..." Her name on my lips, I shatter, unable to hold back any further.

Constanza nuzzles my chest and props her head on it, making a contented sound at the back of her throat.

"You alright?"

She nods at my question, lifting enough to meet my gaze. "You know I am." Then she chuckles as if at an inside joke.

"What's so funny?"

"My parents are going to freak."

That's one way of putting it.

"I should warn you, they really don't like me."

"I don't care." She hugs me tighter. "They have eternity to get over it. And if they don't, that'll be their problem."

"You're quite opinionated, princess."

She laughs. "You have no idea."

Lulled by her soft touches, and the quietness everywhere around us–not to mention the physical exertion–I soon sink into a dreamless sleep.

Constanza

A few hours later, we emerge from our post-sex bliss and get dressed, before heading back towards Tartarus and the heroes. We stick to the forest, Declan ahead and me carrying the spear, avoiding anywhere the Serafim can track us.

As I follow Declan down the path, I try to tear my eyes from his strong back. He doesn't check behind to see if I'm there, but I'm pretty sure he's as aware of my presence as I am of his.

Which is... scary, to say the least.

Persephone, in her relationship wisdom, had told me, *once you know, you'll know it's worth it.* Am I at that point? One romp in the hay, and I'm ready to change Declan?

Only... that's not true. I've known him for weeks, and the connection has always been strong between us. What doesn't change is the fact he's still as insufferable.

But to change him?

There is nothing in him I would want to affect. Not even the parts that are dark.

On impulse, I quicken my step and slide my hand in his. For a second, I fear he'll pull away, but instead he glances down at me and smiles. There's a new softness in his eyes, right next to that possessive streak, that I can't resist.

When his larger hand intertwines our fingers and squeezes, I try to push down the butterflies. We're doing this backwards. But I don't care. Not now that we've cemented this bond between us.

A warmth hits my chest and I stop walking, pulling the opal necklace up. "Persephone?"

"Connie!" There's a panicked aura about

her, visible even in the small opal reflection. "All kinds of creatures joined the souls around the palace, including Cerberus and some hydra!"

"More monsters?" Declan scowls. "That's one hell of a bad luck streak."

"Where's Hades?" I ask Persephone.

"He went down to control them, so they don't turn on us."

"Shit!" I look at Declan, panic filling my gaze. "This isn't good."

"Do you have the spear, Connie?" Persephone's lower lip trembles, her eyes filling with tears. "Please tell me you do."

"We have it."

I can't make out the expression on her features—is it relief, or something else?

"Come fast," she pleads before I can ask. "Please... Hurry."

The image vanishes, leaving me stunned. Declan doesn't give me time to breathe. He grabs my hand and pulls me after him.

"We're almost there."

I'm trying to quiet the dread in my gut. "Did you catch that, at the end?"

"Catch what, darling?"

"That look on her face."

He shakes his head. "No, but you know her better than I do."

Something about this feels wrong, but I can't figure out what.

And then we reach the heroes, and they're swarming us and ooh-ing and aah-ing at the spear like boys in a candy store. Only Heracles stands back, his eyes going back and forth between me and Declan.

"We good?" he asks.

I nod, smiling. "Yeah."

Declan says nothing, instead points to our new weapon. "Now that we have this, a bit of an update. Persephone reached out to Constanza, told her more monsters are attacking the palace. They may hold Hades back with them."

"So we have to move, and fast," Jason says.

"Yep." A grin stretches Theseus' face.

"What did you two do?" I narrow my eyes on them.

They grin at each other and whistle in tandem. Hooves beat the ground and before we know it, we're surrounded by....

"No fucking way," Declan breathes.

Unicorns.

As in, white horses, fluffy manes blowing in the breeze, and ivory horns atop their heads. Their soulful eyes catch sight of us, and one even gets closer to Declan and nudges him.

Much like me, he seems in a trance. I snap out of it first. "How the hell...?"

Jason shrugs. "Remember my Golden Fleece quest? Let's just say I made some friends."

"But in the... Underworld?"

"Where do you think they come from, Connie?"

I blink. I'd never really thought about it. In all my eons of existence, I've only ever seen one.

"The purest of souls..." Jason spurs me on, amusement dancing in his gaze. "They're born out of here, which is why they only show themselves in certain instances in the world of the Living."

"Oh."

Declan chuckles by my side and raises his hand, hesitantly. When the unicorn doesn't move away, he pets it, until excitement rules the enormous beast and it almost impales Declan with its horn by mistake.

"Jeez. Take an eye out with that, why don't you?"

With a shake of his head, he hops on the first unicorn, and I glance around. All the guys have one, except me.

Jason shrugs. "We figured you'd ride with Declan."

Rolling my eyes, I let my zmeu pull me atop the unicorn's back, and get settled in front of him.

Declan

I sneak a glance at her when she's not paying attention. The flush on her cheeks reminds me of her moans last night.

Soft. You're getting soft.

Yes, I am. And I can't help it. I thought I'd be the one leading her to temptation. Instead, I find myself ensnared by her innocence.

Without thinking, I reach for her chin and tilt her face up to mine. Constanza freezes at first, but before long leans her back against me the way I knew she would.

I bend my mouth to hers, getting lost in the feel. *Addiction.* That's what this must be.

A whoosh in the air has me lifting my head, eyes narrowing on our surroundings.

Heracles and the others have also stopped. I pick up on the worst sound possible–an ambush. Right when we're this near to the palace.

Fuck.

I jump off the unicorn, ignoring Constanza's startled cry, and smack the beast's flank to get it moving. The moment after, I conjure a sword from mid air and block another arrow.

"Take cover!" I yell for Constanza.

I don't even care about the desperation coursing through me, all I know is I refuse to let Charon hurt her, or anyone else around her. The heroes move with me, but I raise my hand.

"No. He's mine."

And we both know only one of us will survive.

Heracles, Theseus and Jason flank me, and we advance the forest in an arrow-like formation. My ears pick up another whoosh of arrows and I duck. Follow it by tossing runes towards the trees, causing fire to catch. As the flames burn, the assailants hiding behind screech and move through to the front.

The heroes attack them, but I'm only focused on one–Charon. And finding the fucker before he finds Constanza.

Without realizing it, I'm moving alone through the forest, getting further and further from everyone else. And then something moves out of the shadows behind me, and I turn to face him.

Charon stares at me, his blind gaze unblinking, his cloak covering half his face. When he removes it, it shows a bald head with a few wisps of oily hair. He's holding onto his staff, pointing it towards me.

I can only hope Constanza keeps that spear safe. The more we can keep him from realizing we have it, the better it'll be for us long term.

"Thanks for saving me the hunt," I smirk, circling him.

He inclines his head to the side, presumably listening for my footsteps.

"I aim to please."

I lunge at him, fully intending to strike, but his staff stops me. Sparks fly when it connects with my sword, and I grit my teeth. *What did he do? His staff didn't spark like that when I stopped him from hitting Hades.*

"If only you had stayed out of what does not concern you." He laughs. "Too late, little zmeu."

He pulls back, and this time the staff comes to hit me again with uncanny accuracy. I jump out of the way, and the true fight begins. Each time I get close, Charon pushes me off. He's *blind* the fucker, and still I can't get ahead of him.

Declan!

Tytus' voice in my head distracts me, but luckily only for a split second. I still avoid Charon's hit, and land a slash on his shoulder.

I'm a tad busy, frate.

This is important. You know the weapons you mentioned? I didn't find records of anything in particular existing, but there was something else.

What?

It says out of all the Olympians, a select few could bless certain blades to ensure they could cut through anything—living, dead, and in between.

Yeah, and?

And, whoever is touched by such a blade,

forms a link to the Underworld immediately. One that cannot be broken.

I eye Charon's staff with newfound suspicion. *Can anything be blessed, frate? Even if it's not made of steel?*

Da. Steel is best, but wood or bone can also become weapons.

Fuck me.

Why? What is it?

I'm not about to tell my brother what's going on. *Nothing. Later. And thank you!*

I force my mind closed and focus on the staff. Only one moment Charon is there, the next a fog rises from the ground. By the time I draw a rune to blow it away, I'm aware of a presence behind me. A stuttering breathing.

When I whirl, it's too late. Charon shoves his staff into my chest, sending me flying backwards.

"No!"

The last I hear is Constanza's voice as everything goes dark.

Chapter 18

Erou
-A <u>hero</u> is someone who knows how to hang on one minute longer."
-Novalis-

Declan

Sharp pain reverberates in my chest. When I blink, Constanza's soft locks brush against my cheek. She's pressing on my wound, staunching the blood flow, even as her healing energy rolls into me.

"I'm alright," I mutter.

Part of me knows I won't be. I can't be.

Tytus' warning was clear, and I didn't listen to it. And now I don't know how much time I'll have, but it has to be enough. I cannot let Constanza get through this alone, especially if what I fear has happened, has truly come to pass.

Hell to the no.

"Damn better be," Heracles says from somewhere to my left.

I move my head from Constanza's lap, but everything swims around me, so I lie back down. Something wet and soft nudges my hand and I crack an eye open. One of the unicorns is kneeling next to me, and its wet muzzle is what I'd felt.

"I'll be fine," I repeat. To Heracles, I add, "Did we get them?"

"Yeah, we did."

At the finality in his tone, I open my eyes again. "What is it?"

"Will you be able to fight?"

"Da," I mutter. "No question about it."

Wetness hits my cheek and I look up, noticing her crying. "Constanza..."

She grabs my shirt in her tiny fists. Her lower lip trembles, the tears coming on stronger now. "Don't you dare die on me!"

A strangled laugh escapes me. "No such luck, princess. I'm afraid you're stuck with me."

Eyes filled with tears, she bows her head and rests her forehead against mine. A soft energy flows through me, making my zmeu grumble softly.

"I'll hold you to that," she murmurs in my ear, right before brushing her lips over mine.

"Alright you two, enough with the kissing!" Heracles says, though amusement, rather than annoyance, coats his tone.

Constanza pulls away, and he helps me to my feet, dusting me off. I wince when his pats are a tad too heavy around my recently healed wound. When I lift the shirt to glance under, sure enough, my skin is smooth.

But the minute I touch the blood on my shirt, a vision smacks me with such force I lean into him, squeezing his shoulder as I try to get my bearing.

It's dark everywhere around me. Cold, too. I feel none of the heat I usually do, surrounded by four walls. There's a tunnel at the end, but when I get out, it's not into the sun—rather, into the arid ground of Tartarus. I'm turning round and round, but I'm all alone. And when I glance down my body, it's no longer living… but encompassed in the shimmering glow of souls.

"Declan!"

Constanza's voice, her touch on my arm, brings me back, and I'm panting. Only then do I realize my entire weight is leaning on Heracles, and I've remained upright only through his strength.

I clear my throat and push off him, avoiding everyone's worried gazes. "I'm alright."

"Are you sure, man?"

"Yeah, you don't look so good."

Jason and Theseus earn themselves a glare from me. Only Heracles remains silent, even as I sense Constanza's worry increase.

"Bit of dizziness. No worse than your hangovers, I'm sure."

It's a testimony to their worry that neither of them correct me on the fact dead people can't feel hangovers.

"We don't have time to waste," I say in a firmer tone. "Come on."

Jason and Theseus are first to move, followed by Constanza–but not before she delivers me one last questioning glance.

Heracles sticks behind, grabbing my arm before I go further.

"How badly were you injured?"

I grit my teeth. Only worry for Constanza makes me talk. "Bad enough. If anything else happens to put me out of commission, swear you will escort her out of here."

Our gazes meet, and for once, there is no animosity in his regard. He only nods and squeezes my shoulder, before letting go and following the group.

I drag my feet behind them, feeling my energy lessening by the second. Who would've thought I'd find myself not only visiting the Underworld, but also *staying* here? Fuck.

Dec…

Da, frate?

What happened?

Charon and his bastard army did.

And where are you headed now?

To Hades' palace.

Be very careful. If you see any Titans around, get the fuck out of there.

Not without Constanza.

He's silent for a bit. *I'll be down soon enough.*

Ileana has to show you the entrance. How else are you going to find it?

I have my ways. She's not the only one who entered, once. See you soon.

I want to tell him no, to stop him from coming to my rescue. But it's proof of my selfishness that I'll take all the help I can get, if it means getting Constanza out of here alive.

Some things never change, after all.

We inch closer to the palace, our treasure wrapped in Constanza's bundle. She's still glancing at me when I'm not paying attention, probably afraid I'll topple over.

I won't. Not yet. But I'm even more aware of the urgency now surrounding us. I need to bring her to safety before it's too late. Before I can't stand anymore.

Constanza stops ahead, and I bump into her. "I think Charon set guards even further from the palace."

I glance past her shoulder and notice who she means. "Alright. We can take advantage of this."

"How?"

Heracles backs up. "Leave it up to me."

No sooner does he disappear, that Constanza whirls on me. "What's going on?"

Jason and Theseus smartly give us space. Not that I desire it. Space means being alone with Constanza, and lying to her. Which is the last thing I want to do. But admitting the truth would hurt her even more, right now. And for once in my damned life, I'm going to think of someone else.

"Nothing, darling."

"Don't *darling* me! You're acting weird."

"Da, being impaled by the staff of an old dinosaur will do that."

She searches my gaze, and I do my damndest to make sure she doesn't see my sheer panic. At losing her, at losing this second chance, at not being around when she needs me most. To get her out of here. To try out this thing between us when we don't have to fight for our lives, or save her friends.

And worse, still, panic at getting what I deserve. Would my soul really end in Tartarus? If I was to die, would that be my fate, given everything I've done? Is it pointless, then, to seek a fresh path for myself, when it has already been written?

No. I made the mistake of thinking that before, as a child. When I overheard a bunch of elders talking about a fake prophecy and taking it as fact. I let that dictate too long of my life, and I'll be damned if I allow the same to repeat.

Not now.

Not when I have something to fight for.

Not when I have something to look forward to.

Before we can continue with the argument, there's a loud sound, and Theseus runs to check on it. A moment later, he signals us to follow.

"Coast is clear," he says. "Heracles distracted the monsters. But there are knights everywhere, hidden in various areas."

Constanza and I share a glance. "Perhaps it's best you go with him. Get rid of them, clear the area, and we'll find Hades and Persephone."

The heroes take off at my suggestion, leaving us alone. Thankfully, Constanza doesn't continue with the barrage of questions. Instead, she moves through the darkened grounds, focused on getting to her friend.

I only wish my attention was on that alone.

Constanza

I know Declan is hiding something from me, but he's also a bullheaded zmeu who won't talk until he's ready. So I bury my worry for whatever it is under a wave of dread. What will I find in Hades' palace?

As we cross through the gardens of Lethe, I hear something. At first I think it's my imagination, but it grows louder. I head towards it, but Declan is faster. *He must have heard more than I did.*

Sure enough, as soon as we pass some bushes, I stop dead in my tracks. Declan rushes to the bundled form on the grass, muttering something. It's only as I get closer that I make out his words.

"Did you drink from the water? Hades, *did you drink*?"

I kneel next to the two men, trying to see past the mess of beaten up and burned clothes and scars that Hades is. One blackened eye opens and stares at us, only to be closed again.

"Leave.... here…" he says.

"We came to help!"

I run my palms over him, healing the wounds, until Hades is once more the god I know. But there is a dead glint in his eyes, something I haven't seen before. And it scares me shitless.

"What happened?"

Haltingly, he runs through the brief events that took place since we left them. How the souls kept the palace surrounded. How Charon returned, followed by his monsters. How the knights Hades had taken on as his guards turned against him and helped drag him down. How the dead had seen him weakened, assaulting his mind with their thoughts, until he was at Charon's mercy.

"I have lost."

"No, not yet." I clench my fists. "There is always hope!"

He snorts, meeting my gaze. "If you think Olympus is coming to the rescue, you are wrong."

"We know," I admit. "Zeus refused."

Hades slumps back over, running a hand

over his face, before letting it drop to the ground, boneless. "I am weary of all this. Of everything I hear. Everything I cannot block out."

I lean over him, clasping his hand in mine. "Hades, listen to me. All is *not* lost. You trusted my parents once with your safety… Trust *me*, this time. Trust in both of us. We can help fix this."

He says nothing, only gives a faint squeeze in return. I settle on another subject, one I hope will drive the fire of life back into his veins. "Where's Persephone?"

It does the opposite. He looks up towards the window of the palace, a tortured look on his face.

"They took her… Charon's knights."

Declan swears, and I notice him quickly checking our surroundings. "Why would they bring you here, near Lethe?"

"They tried to make me drink. When that didn't work, they tried mental torture." Another anguished look. "This is a lost battle. You both have to leave."

"No. We have this."

I unravel the spear, and Hades stares.

Then his gaze meets mine, and a hint of the old god is back in his expression. "How?"

I shrug. "We make an excellent team."

His glance goes from me, to Declan, and back to me. "Always breaking the rules, Constanza."

I only grin, even as Declan helps him up.

"You should still go," Hades says. "Leave the spear with me and get yourselves out. There is nowhere safe, not here."

"Persephone, though. We have to help you save her."

That tortured look. "*He* must have her."

"Who?"

But I already know. Before Hades can finish, I'm running away, spear in hand, and ignoring the shouts behind me. There's only one who would dare cross into this palace, only one who would go so far...

The inside of the palace feels wrong. Like there's an energy here that shouldn't be, and it creeps me the hell out. I know I shouldn't be here without back-up, holding the one weapon that could help us all. If I'm taken, we're all screwed. But Persephone is all alone. And I'll be darned if I let her spend one more minute with that bastard. I trust Declan and Hades will be hot on my heels, and hopefully this is something we can handle.

Moments later, after taking the steps two by two, I get all the way to their floor. That same sensation of foreboding runs up my spine, but I shake it off and move towards the main bedchamber, pushing the door open. Darkness coats everything, and again, that energy that shouldn't be here.

"Connie!"

It's a whisper in the darkness. I move closer, and Persephone steps out.

"What are you doing back here?" Panic coats her voice.

"Came to rescue you."

"Connie, I–"

She falls to her knees, clutching her head and shouting in pain. Another shape steps forward, and I stagger backwards. Only, it's not Charon, as I had thought. It's someone way damn worse.

Hair as dark as Hades', eyes as blue as Zeus', but taller than them both. Stronger.

He's twice the bulk of Heracles, and he's a freaking big human. But this guy... is no human. He's not even a god. He's a creature much, much older, and the energy I'd been feeling all along comes from him.

"Thank you for finding my weapon, immortal." The man grins, showing a line of white teeth, filed like canines. "I suppose I should introduce myself. My name is Cronus."

Declan

"Who has Persephone?"

"Cronus," Hades says, and it's like the name itself weighs him down.

I take a step towards the palace, but Hades grabs my wrist. "He is not one to be trifled with. We have to tread carefully."

"What do you mean?"

"We cannot kill him."

I yank myself out of his grip. "You must be joking. Why not?"

"Too many reasons. I will give you one– the rest of the Titans will be sure to step in his footsteps, and there is no way I can contain that uproar."

At the end of the day, the Underworld is Hades' domain. I'll defer to him, but that doesn't mean I'm about to cower from a fight. "And the spear?"

Hades glances towards his home. "If we find a shot, perhaps. But I fear we may not. Cronus has had millennia, longer than even your imprisonment, to get himself ready for this moment. He is prepared, and we cannot underestimate him."

"You don't think we can win."

His expression darkens. "This is not a fairytale or story of olden times. It is real life. And in real life, the good guys don't always win. Sometimes, the best thing they can do is stop the evil ones from generating more chaos."

What the hell has *him*, lord of the Underworld, so afraid? Before I can ask that out loud, Hades continues talking.

"While we cannot win, we can drive Cronus further into hiding, even back into Tartarus until I convince my brothers to come help me bind him, and the rest of the Titans. But make no mistake, there is no way to win this war. The best we can do is win this particular battle."

"Then what the fuck was the point of sending us on some wild goose chase for a weapon that's supposed to fix this?"

"To give us leverage."

I'm already moving towards the palace. "I need to help Constanza."

He's right on my heels as we go through, and climb the stairs. We burst through their bedchamber, and find Persephone clutching her head. Constanza is gripping the spear, and Cronus faces them both.

When he sees us, he smirks, showing a row of filed teeth.

"Not had enough, Hades?"

I understand now why Hades was so broken when we'd found him. It hadn't been just Charon or his cronies that tortured him. Cronus himself must have taken part, and judging by the gleam in his eyes, the bastard enjoyed it. I'm afraid, for a moment, that Hades will back away.

But Hades is deaf to Cronus's words, his focus on someone much more important. He falls to his knees near Persephone, clutching her hands in his. His forehead drops to hers and his groans of pain fill the room, even as

Persephone's grow fainter.

He must be pulling away her pain. But how?

My feet shuffle until I'm behind Constanza, letting her know I'm there. *I have no fucking clue how we can win against a Titan, darling, but I'm right behind you.*

She surprises me by responding. *I have a plan.*

Of course you do.

"Let Hades and Persephone go," she says out loud. "Surely you've had your fun with them?"

Cronus grins at the pair, still on the ground. "No, I do not think so."

"Perhaps I wasn't clear," Constanza says. "It wasn't a request."

Cronus smirks. "You think you can fight me off? Four of you, against a Titan?"

"No," I interrupt as I move to the front. "Only *one*."

Move back! I toss to Constanza, knowing she'll hear me, as will Hades.

A second later flames erupt over my body, and my zmeu form grows and grows, breaking apart the entire room until it's in shambles. The last thing I should do is morph again, and putting myself through the transformation. But I have more to lose if I don't.

By the time I'm done, blue flames are burning everything, but Constanza, Hades and Persephone are near the door.

Run! I tell them, before lunging towards Cronus, my bulk breaking apart the palace's remaining walls. Cronus in my clutches, I burst through the windows and drag him with me, down into the depths of hell below.

Tytus

The cavern is darker than I thought, split by a river as reflective as the moon. Ileana was only too keen to help once I explained how much trouble her daughter is in. Surprisingly, I feel no remorse using that bargaining chip.

If she hadn't shown me how to get through to the Underworld, I would have taken Lucas up on his offer. The head of the wolf pack back in Rockland Creek has had his own adventures down here.

Yet now that I'm in, alone, all thoughts of others escape me. Declan occupies them instead, as does the fading link between us. I hope to use it and locate him, as fast as possible. And if I can gather some help along the way, it probably wouldn't be rejected. Something tells me the upcoming fight is big, bigger than we'd ever have thought.

I step to the banks of the river Styx and toss my head back, taking a moment to marvel at the blood-red ceiling above. Then I let the change come over me, the flames burn my human form, until only my zmeu with burgundy scales is left.

As I emerge from the blaze like a phoenix reborn, my focus is sharp. Clear. There is only one I have come here for, and I do not intend to leave without him. And if that means helping him in whatever messy insanity he's become involved in, so be it.

I'll be damned if I let my brother fight this battle alone.

Chapter 19

Frică
"The only thing we have to <u>fear</u> is fear itself."
-Franklin D. Roosevelt-

Constanza

"DECLAN!" I run towards where he disappeared, but can see nothing below.

How did this happen? One moment he was there, and I thought we were on the same wavelength. That we *all* felt Cronus' power and knew it's time to get the hell out of here. And then he goes and does something so...so... reckless!

I go as far to the edge of the caved-in wall as I can, but the dust and darkness below leaves me no way of knowing what's happening.

Someone's pulling me back–it takes me a moment to register it's Persephone.

"We have to *go*!"

I follow her and Hades out the door, glancing behind me every moment, hoping Declan will be there, by some miracle. But he's not. He's somewhere down below, fighting Cronus–and the spear is in my hand.

When I recognize the way we're heading as the secret tunnel Declan and I had escaped through, I stop. No. No way I'm escaping this palace again. Last time, I had to leave my best friend behind. Now, it's to be my lover? *No.* Hell no. My heart, my mind, my entire being rebels against the idea with a force that surprises me.

"What is it?" Hades turns to me and, judging by his expression, he already knows.

I think back to Declan injured before, to him fighting like that, to turning to zmeu when he shouldn't have. Before I can say anything, Hades holds out his open palm.

"Give me the spear."

"Why?"

"Because I'll go help him."

"No!" Persephone cries.

He turns to her, cupping her cheek. "Nothing will keep me from returning to you. Believe me." He bends and kisses her, and I look away to give them their moment.

Despite Persephone's pleading, Hades moves to me and holds out his hand again. "Spear, now."

My hand trembles when I hand it out. "Please... Be safe."

He takes off down the hall, and we're left alone.

Tears streaming down her face, Persephone runs into my arms. "Now what do we do?"

I pat her back, trying to console her, but feeling my heart disintegrating with dread. What *can* I do, to save Declan before he dooms himself?

Declan

I can only blame my impulsivity on wanting to protect Constanza, and perhaps a bit of a crazy edge. As we fall, entangled together, Cronus pushes off me. While I hit the ground–hard–he lands on bended knee, then stands.

Eyes glinting, he pulls out a double-edged sword and grins towards me, his canines on display.

I can't keep my zmeu form. The flames shimmer and leave me human, and with a tired rune I clothe myself. But my muscles are weak, both from the change that never should have happened, as the wounds from before.

As a beast, at least, I could have used the venom to gain an advantage. But I have nothing now, not even the damn spear. So I drag myself to a standing position and conjure a sword instead.

The energy surrounding Cronus is nothing to be played with, and I know I can't win. Hades was right to fear this guy, and I'm more the fool for thinking I knew better than a god.

Still, I'll still try. Until my dying breath, I'll try.

When I get up, gripping the sword tighter, Cronus laughs. "This is not your fight, zmeu."

If only you knew. I force myself to meet his gaze. "I beg to differ."

He tilts his head to the side. "Why be involved in this, at all? The Olympians cast aside your kin. Much like they did mine." A knowing smirk. "In fact, a few of your brethren were kind enough to help with this coup, you know."

"I do know," I scowl. "And they are *not* my brethren. Get your facts straight."

He moves around, eyeing me up and down. I imagine I look like shit, sweating all over the place. A pitiful excuse for an opponent. And he's not wrong to underestimate me, considering I've never felt more out-manned than in this moment.

"I'll let you and your immortal leave," Cronus says. "No harm done. Simply stop interfering with my plans."

I grit my teeth. "Not happening."

There's no way Constanza will leave without knowing Persephone and Hades are safe. And, realistically, neither will I. Because this guy–Titan–has a way of rubbing me the wrong way. I remember what Hades said earlier, near Lethe. That sometimes good guys don't win, they only stop the bad ones from creating more chaos and destruction.

Well, that's my purpose here. I grip the sword tighter. *Even if I'm not really a good guy.*

Before he can say anything, I lunge on Cronus, striking. Our swords clash with a resounding clang, and I feel it all the way into my muscles. Cronus' eyes shine brighter–he's enjoying this, the fucker.

He kicks me in the stomach and I go stumbling back. Hades chooses that moment to storm out of his palace, placing himself between us. The spear we'd retrieved shines in his hand.

"Get back," he tosses over a shoulder. "I said before, this is my battle to fight."

Cronus laughs. "Son, do you really want to start this war?"

Hades' knuckles are white on the weapon when he faces him again. "More than anything I've ever wanted."

Cronus smiles, and then he moves. With me, he'd been slow. I realize now it had been a test, or some kind of taunt. Because if vampires are meant to be fast, this Titan is nothing compared to them. He zooms right and left, in the blink of an eye. Hades matches him strike by strike, though he's still getting acquainted with the spear.

Still, whereas I thought he'd get smashed

to pieces, he holds his own. I want to help, but when I try to, a wave of dizziness unlike any other hits me, and I fall right back on my ass.

Hades throws me a warning glare from afar, and I can read it clearly. *Stay the fuck down.*

I would've listened. Probably. If I didn't start seeing patterns in Cronus' attacks, or the fact that some Serafim wayward souls were taking positions at various corners of the gardens. Exactly as one would in an ambush... One Hades was being led into.

Watch yourself, I think out loud. *He's trying to trap you.*

For a brief second, I fear it doesn't work. I'd suspected the lord of the Underworld had the ability to read minds from a few things Constanza mentioned. But I'd only clued in for good when we'd found him in Lethe, all beat up. The last thing I want is to open my mind to Hades now, but there is no other option if I don't want him dead.

I can only hope he'll hear my thoughts amid all this ruckus. *Watch yourself!*

He narrowly avoids one of Cronus' strikes, but the bastard pulls out another sword and this time slashes Hades in the shoulder. He staggers back, panting hard. I push myself to my feet.

Keep moving backwards, towards me, I tell him.

He does so, with Cronus following, on the prowl. But right as he's ready to attack again, and the Serafim seem prepared to jump in, a barrier lifts from the ground upwards, surrounding the immediate palace grounds, and keeping Cronus out.

The Titan's eyes glitter menacingly and he moves closer, striking the barrier with his fist. Luckily, it holds, and he's left on the outside. For now, anyway.

Hades walks over to me, holding on to his bleeding shoulder. He towers over me and extends a hand, helping me to my feet. I try to hide the weakness of my legs, but his frown deepens.

Under the guise of pulling me up, he yanks me a bit closer. His harsh whisper reminds me whose presence I'm in.

"What did you do, to tie yourself to the Underworld?"

I meet his gaze. "Protected Constanza."

Hades says nothing for a beat, two.

Behind us, I hear my name and Constanza's rushed footsteps.

"Is there anything you can do to help?" I hate the pleading in my voice. But if anyone can, it's him. Only, Hades never has time to answer me.

I whirl around as Constanza collides with my upper body, sending me moving backwards. Hades holds up a steadying hand to my back, but removes it before either her or Persephone notice.

I dip my face in Constanza's neck, inhaling her sweet scent.

"Let us move inside," Hades says with a meaningful look to the fuming Cronus. "While we can."

Hades brings us to the dining room, where food of all kinds awaits us. Ruled by hunger, Constanza and I devour everything in sight. When all that is said and done, the food rests heavy in my stomach, unease coursing through me.

We only bought some time. Hades and I realize as much, having felt Cronus' glare on our backs once we'd walked away, protected by the barrier. It won't hold for long, though, and we are lucky to have even this small moment of peace.

"What's the plan?" Persephone surprises us with the impromptu question.

Hades freezes. "We go at it with all our forces. And hope to hell it's enough."

Silence at his statement descends on the table, but Constanza breaks it. "Is there anything that would send Cronus back to Tartarus?"

"Not willingly," Hades says. "But I'll keep thinking on it."

He leans over Persephone, holding her hand, as if he can't bear to be without her. I understand the feeling all too well. And he knows my time is limited, I see it in the odd glances he shoots my way. Probably expecting me to admit everything to Constanza, but I'm not about to.

"Do you think the heroes survived?" Constanza asks.

"Yeah," I nod. "They must be off to the side, waiting for a signal from us." I shake my head. "Did Cronus say anything, Persephone?"

"Other than try to change my mind to join him? No."

"What's his motivation?"

She shrugs. "To escape his prison. He says the balauri in there had long since been devising plans to get out, get back into Olympus. He found out about the zmei and everything else from them. Monitored things, developed spies." She shudders. "They have spied on us, in our own home."

"They will pay," Hades promises, his tone dark. "I will find each and every one of his spies, and *they will pay.*"

I don't doubt that for a second. Since we healed him, there's something less soft about the lord of the Underworld, and more... dangerous. Like he's about to blow a fuse, and we'd all best not be around when he does.

"Declan?"

I glance up at Persephone, noticing her hesitation. What the hell did I miss now?

"I'm sorry," she says. "For misjudging you."

"You didn't. A long time ago, I was exactly the guy you thought I was." I shrug. "Still am."

Constanza rolls her eyes, but Persephone only smiles, glancing between us. "I am glad our paths crossed again, even if it's in these circumstances. At least... it allowed for closure."

I nod. What else can I say? If I tell her she'd been a mere blip on my radar, she'll only get pissed again. Already, out of the corner of my eye, I see Hades stand straighter, and I shift my thoughts elsewhere.

Constanza, thankfully, notices I'm having a hard time focusing and makes our excuses, leading me upstairs. Within moments, we're finally alone in her old chambers.

I drop to the bed and she follows in my arms, curling up close. "I was so scared…"

I hug her waist. "And I, darling. Never been more aware of my inadequacy than in that moment."

She kisses my chest, then finds my lips, and the soft press of her body warms me.

"We finally have a moment of peace."

I nod, my gaze glued to the ceiling. "Finally."

"Do you want to talk to me about what's really bothering you?"

Yes. But it will ruin this moment. "No," I say out loud. "It's not important, I swear it."

She sighs. "Fine. How about you tell me about your home instead?"

As I describe it, I feel a pang of panic. Will I ever see it again? Tell Tytus I'm sorry? He's on his way down here, but no amount of what he does can help dig me out of the hole I'm in. which means I have no choice but to lie. Only, instead of like before, I'm not lying for myself, but for them. So they don't feel guilty, when it all comes to pass, and they have to leave me behind.

"And your brother?"

A sharp intake of breath. "What about him?"

"You said you have a rough relationship."

"That's putting it mildly."

"But he's talked to you, no? Since you've been down here."

"Da, he has. Wants to make up for the past. Start again."

Her mouth is pliant when I kiss her again, but she moves back, smiling at me. "And?"

I groan in frustration. "And what, darling?"

"Do you think it could happen? You two, making up?"

I drop on my back, sighing. "I don't know."

"Talk to me." She rests her head on my chest again, relentless.

"I.. Perhaps. We've been away from each other too long, have changed too much. Now he has his soulmate, and I have you, and… I don't know. We may have time for each other. Or we may not."

"That's a load of bull and you know it."

I run a hand over my face. "You really don't let go of things."

"Never."

"I know he was acting out of misplaced information. And I didn't make it easier, with all my stunts. We are both at fault for how our relationship has turned out so yes, I take responsibility for my part in it. Do I forgive him? I do. I cannot forget the eons I spent imprisoned without him coming to my aid… but I forgive him for the part he has played in it."

Constanza grins. "I thought you might. And here you say you're not a good person."

"That's because I'm not."

"I beg to differ."

I move over her, my body pressing hers on the mattress. "I'm not, darling. Case in point, I'm about to take what I want."

She laughs, nuzzling my neck. "You know I freely offer it."

"Good. I'm done talking about my brother."

"Why?"

"Because we're pressed for time."

She chuckles. "Then what do you want?"

"This."

My mouth moves against hers in a new kiss, and our tongues battle for dominance. Her small hands go to the back of my neck, pulling me closer, even as she arches against me, rubbing her body against mine.

This time, I take no prisoners. I work my way down her curves, kiss all the little dips and nooks I know have driven her insane in our dreams. And only when she's writhing on the bed, panting with need, do I give in to what we both need and thrust inside her.

We're fire together, the flames licking up our bodies, binding us closer than it should be possible. Nothing else exists but Constanza's body under mine, her nails raking my back, her whispers in my ear... And I surrender gladly to the burn. When I fall asleep, still connected to her, it feels more like home than anything ever has.

Constanza

Long after Declan falls asleep, I stay awake, holding him.

Something's wrong. I don't know what, but there's a resignation to Declan's gaze that I don't understand. As if he knows time is limited.

Is it the upcoming fight? It cannot be, he survived worse. The only other explanation must be he's afraid of when we go up, back to the Living, and what will happen to us.

My hold on his waist tightens.

I'm under no illusions. Based on what he's done, and the fact my parents imprisoned him, it's pretty clear they won't accept our relationship. Not so easily. But like I told him, we have all of eternity to change their minds. And, yes, saving the Underworld may play a role in that.

Despite what may happen, I won't let him leave. No matter what Mom and Dad say.

He's not perfect.

He's flawed. And damaged. And insufferable.

But he's mine, and I am his. And we'll get through this, together.

A repetitive knock wakes us up. We hurry to get dressed, and I open the door to my room. Persephone hugs me, and I cling to her a moment longer. To think I'd been so close to losing her.

Hades ushers us in, and he goes to check on Declan. Their voices are too low for me to hear, but Persephone tugs on my hand.

"Hades thinks we have a shot at driving Cronus out. At the very least, back near Tartarus. But only if we get the monsters to switch sides."

"How can we do that?"

Declan stands, nodding to Hades. "That might work." When he sees the question in my gaze, he says, "My zmeu form, darling. Monsters will answer to the alpha, and I'm the biggest one…"

My eyes widen. "Are you serious?"

"Yes," Hades says. "With the heroes helping us out, and us trying this, yes. It might just work."

"And then, what? You push Cronus' forces back, simple as that?"

Hades inclines his head. "That's the hope."

"And Charon?"

"That bastard started all of this," Declan growls. "There's no way I'm letting him get off."

Hades' expression darkens. "I will take care of him, make no mistake."

"Fine. But we want to help."

Declan doesn't miss a beat. He comes to me, tilts my chin up and holds my gaze. "I thought as much." His lips press against mine, and I don't realize he's turned us around, and he's got his back to the door, until he pulls away.

Hades is by his side, and they share a look. Then Declan smiles my way.

"This is where we part ways, princess."

"What! NO!" I move forward, but some kind of barrier stops me and Persephone from the exit.

"This is for your own good," Hades says. "The minute we exit, the barrier will disappear. If you need to run away, if we lose the fight, make for the tunnels. Try to seek asylum in Olympus."

Declan's eyes are filled with something I cannot identify, but I feel tears in my own. "Please don't do this."

"I have to." His voice is low, hoarse. "I'll do my best to come back to you."

The moment after, they exit, and the lock clicks behind them.

"They cannot be serious!" Persephone says, gaping at the door like it personally betrayed her.

I stomp to it–past the barrier which, as Hades promised, disappeared–and bang my fists against the oak panels.

"Bastards!"

As predicted, my shout goes unanswered.

Chapter 20

Dă drumul
"When I <u>let go</u> of what I am, I become what I might be."
~Lao Tzu~

Declan

For the first time in my life, I'm not thinking about how to get out of here safe. I know I can't. And while that should make me more resigned, it only fuels my anger, my rage, my determination to see Constanza safe and sound.

At least with Hades by my side, we may make some headway into this shit.

I didn't want to imprison both our girls, but

when he pitched me the idea, knowing how stubborn they both are... Well. Heartless as it may seem, all we wish is to protect them.

That's what I think, anyway, until we emerge out of the palace. And into the biggest mess I've ever seen.

Massive monsters surround us in a semi-circle. I count two more hydras, three chimeras, and two other dogs that look like Cerberus but in distinct colors. And then there's Cerberus himself, and by his side is Charon.

"Slimy weasel." I clench my fists, craving nothing more than to punch him until he's bleeding.

Hades notices where my gaze landed and scowls. "Where is Cronus, though?"

Another sweeping gaze around doesn't show the bastard. Shit.

"If I was a big badass Titan," I mutter, "I wouldn't be in plain sight. I'd wait until I tire everyone before attacking."

"Good point."

Before we can think it over any more, the Serafim move in one united line at the front, and attack. I pull a sword out of the air, and head towards them. Hades follows me, spear against his back, sword in his arm. Before long, we're surrounded.

It's a good thing Hades blessed my sword. Thanks to his little voodoo trick, every slice of my blade against the souls of the Cavaleri dissolves them into nothingness. Do I feel slightly bad they'll never get a peaceful rest? Not in the least.

These bastards killed my kin, drove us to extinction, and it's only fair. Balance, right in the world once again.

Oddly, it also feels good to be making up for the fact I wasn't there when Tytus was fighting them. Multiple times through the ages, I had my chance to help, to bring them to justice, and I didn't. Until I made everything worse, that is.

It's all in the past.

I duck one knight's sword, only to impale him on mine, before slashing through his body and moving on to the next. In my periphery, I notice Hades advancing just as quickly.

Where the hell are the heroes?

Shouts in the distance draw my attention, and not a moment sooner.

Unicorns burst through the ranks of the

Serafim on both sides–must be a dozen or so!–using their horns to get rid of the spirits. They disappear as easily as with my sword, relegated to nothingness.

Interesting.

On top of the unicorns are Hercules, Jason, Theseus–and a few others I don't recognize. Soon as they're in the midst of the fight they jump off the horses with a roaring, unified shout, and start cutting through the souls.

"Hades!" I yell. "Their swords! Do your magic trick."

He rolls his eyes and mutters something about it not being magic. A blast of white energy releases from his body in little orbs, and travels through to the swords. When it touches the metal, it becomes absorbed. The blessed blades now burn brighter, and the next time Heracles hits a Serafim, they dissolve.

His surprised gaze meets mine and I grin. "Good of you to show up."

"Good of you to help out."

It's as close to a compliment as we'll ever get. So we keep going at it, slashing and fighting our way through, surrounding Hades as much as we can so he doesn't get taken unawares.

And throughout it, I'm aware of Charon sitting way too fucking quietly, of the monsters lying in wait, as if waiting for something... Or someone.

For an order to let loose.

And I hope it's not what I think.

Constanza

"This is ridiculous!" I try the door again, rattling it off its hinges. "How could they do this to us!"

Though anger rolls over me in waves, it's overshadowed by the pure fear running through me. That Declan will be harmed, and everything else will fall apart.

"It's no use," Persephone says. "Whatever Hades commands in the castle, is done."

I turn to her. "Did you know he was planning this?"

She shakes her head. "No, but they want us safe, Constanza. Gods know they've worked hard enough to keep us out of Cronus' hands, so can you really blame them?"

"Yes!" I run a hand through my hair, accidentally pulling a few strands out. "No! I don't know. I just..."

She comes close to me, grabbing my hands in hers. "You want *them* safe, too, I know."

When she sees I'm not to be reasoned with, she returns to the window, biting her nails to the bone. Despite her reassuring words, I can tell she's as worried as I am. Only, she hides it better.

I shuffle closer, planting my butt next to her. "How are you?" This is the first real, quiet moment we've had since I left the castle days ago. Might as well make the most of it.

Persephone glances at me, then back outside. It's pitch dark, we're unable to see much other than some glows in the distance. "Fine, I suppose."

I nudge her knee with mine. "Seriously. Cronus had you imprisoned here, and they tortured Hades. You're not *fine*."

"Maybe not, but I will be." She gives me a shaky smile that's somehow all Persephone. "I'm a queen, aren't I?"

I nod, unsure what to say.

"What about you?" she asks. "You seem happy. With Declan."

A snort escapes me. "I was until he locked me in here. Just wait until I get out."

She laughs, and leans over to grab my hand again, squeezing it. "I'm happy for you. He seems... changed."

"I hope not. Thing is, I don't desire him changed. Not for me. I want him the same way he's always been, even if that's flawed."

Persephone grins wider at that. "Who would've thought you'd finally learn what it is to love?"

A chuckle escapes me, but the moment after she's bending over as if in pain, gasping. I crouch by her side, worried Cronus might have done something from afar. When I see the tears running down her face, that worry shifts to dread.

"What's going on?"

Her answer is not what I expected. "They're winning," she whispers, turning her head to me. Relief shines in her gaze. "Hades and I, our own bond... They're winning."

My heart threatens to rush out of my chest. My knees grow weak. I sink to the ground, gasping and crying all at once. Persephone joins me, hugging me.

As we calm down and wait for them to return inside, she smiles at me, hope shining in her eyes. "So, was Declan everything you thought he'd be?"

"That, and more."

"And you're sure your parents will approve?"

I chuckle. "Nope. But like you said... the good things are worth it."

We share a smile.

Declan

I hear them first, before everyone else, and my eyes shift towards the skies. "Ah, fuck, fuck, *fuck*!"

Everything had been going well. For the first time since I'd seen Cronus, I was starting to think we might win. And then... of course more shit has to happen.

Hades hears my shout and turns to me. "What is it?"

I cut off one Serafim and move closer to him. "We're about to have company. And I think it's Cronus with the fucking balauri."

His eyes narrow on the skies, and his features go into what I can only describe as outright rage.

"Enough is enough."

Yet he does nothing, instead letting the

ominous cloud we both see in the distance approach us, getting closer and closer, until it's right above us.

Well, at least he didn't bring the entire party. To my knowledge, throughout the entire zmeu history, we'd had over a dozen balauri created. They're zmei that couldn't control themselves and went over to the evil side, stuck forever in their monster form.

Well, Cronus only gathered a few, so I count myself lucky. Perhaps killing Igor scared the rest, who knows?

Hades moves closer to me. "You're still able to change to zmeu?"

"Da." I nod, hoping that I'll be able to hold the change, if it comes to it.

"Good. Let's do that first."

"First?" I frown at him, but he's already moving forward.

Not only that, but he tosses his sword to the side, stands tall and proud, and gets within arms reach of the monsters, and Charon.

"What the fuck is he doing?" I mutter under my breath.

"I was wondering the same thing," Heracles says by my side.

Everyone has stopped fighting, the Serafim included, as the souls navigate towards us, trying to hear Hades out. And when he speaks, I'm finally starting to understand why he's ruler of the Underworld.

"I know you think I have failed," Hades says. "That you have joined Charon's side because you believe I have betrayed you, and what this Underworld stands for." He takes a deep breath, as if ready to admit to some sin.

"Shit," Heracles says.

I'm about to echo him, but Hades surprises both of us.

"I have *not* betrayed you," Hades says, firmly and unequivocally. "What they have fed you are lies, by the worst of the worst. The bane of the world, the evil scum buried in Tartarus to spare us *all* a world of pain. And now, here they stand."

He walks around, pointing towards Cronus and the balauri.

"You were told the immortals I allowed in here were the enemy? That I have grown soft?" A dark chuckle. "How easily you have all forgotten that these same immortals protected us gods, not so long ago. As did the zmei."

The Serafim don't seem moved by the speech–if anything, their rank tightens around us. But the passive souls that were previously watching on, are now more interested. And, dare I say, appearing repentant?

It's not them I'm worried about. Rather, the monsters. Each of them is within striking distance of Hades, and we have to be ready to protect him when that moment comes. There is no way to say whether his speech is affecting them, at least not yet. And that worries me more than anything.

"If you want the truth, you should have asked me. I have always been truthful, and I will not begin with lies now. The immortal and zmeu were here at *my* request and given *my* protection in my realm. Despite it, that protection was tossed in the air as *some* saw fit. Is that how loyalty to your lord goes nowadays?"

Hades shrugs. "Perhaps I have grown too soft, over the years. Offering a shoulder to cry on, rather than lectures. Offering solutions, rather than punishments. Perhaps it is time this Underworld goes back to the olden times, the darker times. No? Is that what you prefer, poor souls? Is that what you wish, my loyal creatures?"

"Uh..." Theseus has joined us. "Is he trying to make us lose here, or what?"

"Shh," Jason shushes him. "I think it's working."

I don't want to believe him but sure enough, heads are shaking here and there. No one agrees with his propositions. So Hades closes the loop.

"Well if it is not tyranny you wish, tell me, what do you believe will happen under Charon, under Cronus? Or have you forgotten the stories of old about the Titans, my fellow friends?"

More shared looks. Whispers of agreement with him. Shuffles of feet, in Hades' direction, but none threatening.

And then, culmination of all things, Cerberus steps away from Charon. A hushed silence falls on everyone, and even Cronus' interest seems to have peaked.

The three-headed dog steps to Hades, and my hand moves to the hilt of my sword. *Say the word, Hades.*

Stand down.

And this is why I hate wars and answering to authorities as a general rule. They never see what's right in front of them until it bites them. I fully expect the enormous lump of a beast to bite Hades' head off, or even pull the spear out of his hands.

To my utter surprise, Cerberus does neither. Instead, he drops to one paw, and another, and... bows his head. In submission.

"What the fuck just happened?" Heracles lets loose.

"I think... the tide has turned."

A clap starts off to the side. We all turn and watch Cronus slide off the balaur, grinning.

"Nice speech, son. Very eloquent, if misleading."

Hades only stares at him, even as Cerberus moves to his side.

"I mean, after all, you have already lost your kingdom. Is that not right, Charon?"

The sleazeball bends at the waist. "Very true, sire."

Cronus shrugs. "So what is it you're promising my monsters, anyway?"

"I am only promising them what has always been theirs."

I change to zmeu form then, towering over the monsters and backing Hades up. The beasts either back away from the fight, or join our group. *Fucking yes, we're finally on to something.*

Cronus laughs again. "Is that all the backup you need?"

In that moment, a loud roar echoes in the distance, and I tilt my head sideways. Something red and shiny bursts out of the clouds, and for a moment I fear I'm hallucinating. Until a voice reverberates in my mind.

Hello, frate.

Tytus?

Fury fills Cronus' expression, even as a new wave of hope runs through me. Perhaps I'm not so dead just yet… Especially considering Tytus is not alone. Instead, glowing forms surround him—our fallen zmei kin.

How…?

He lands next to me, forcing some of the heroes to the side. The rest of the zmei surround us in a circle, blocking all escapes. These are our dead comrades, and I even recognize some old Council members among them. Some, I notice, are just as surprised to see me here.

Sorry I'm late, I had to make a pit stop in the Elysian Fields.

You're forgiven.

I feet the jolt in the link, the sense of hope, and I nod towards him. Yeah, I probably mean for more than just the lateness, but no more words need to be said. Not now.

Tytus focuses on Cronus, as do I.

"I've had enough of this," the Titan yells. "Get them!"

The monsters move first, followed by the rest of the Serafim. And before we know it, it's a mess of everything. Fights, roars, pains.

Cronus is taunting Hades, and I see him ready to blow. We aren't ready for that. I move closer, enough to catch the last of it.

"When I have your kingdom, I will also take your queen, son. Teach her what a true king is like."

The spear drops out of Hades' hand, and I lunge to grab it before Cronus can. Before either of us can move, a shield of something escapes Hades. It's a solid energy, hitting everything and everyone in the vicinity, leaving them on the ground with their ears ringing, their minds torn apart. Hades drops to his knees, panting, the weapon pointing towards Cronus.

I shake it off first, and Tytus. We both turn to Cronus at the same time.

Let's go.

While he's completely out of it, we grab the Titan—me with my talons around his arms, Tytus around his legs—and hoist him in the air. We fly as fast as we can until the arid desert of Tartarus is beneath us. We drop him in, but not before I shoot a dose of venom through my claws, and into his body. It'll be enough to knock him out for a few more hours, one can hope. At least until the Olympians can work their magic.

By the time we return, Hades is back on his feet, fighting the remaining Serafim. Between the heroes and his spear, he makes quick use of them, leaving only Charon in the middle.

I approach him, each step of mine shaking the ground, my tail swishing. When I'm close enough, I toss my mental power his way. *Your mistake was you thought you could win. Against Hades. Against myself. Disloyalty is punishable by death where I am from.*

I glance at Hades, and he throws the spear my way. It lands on the ground and I pick it up with my talons.

It seems Hades agrees.

Like he did with me recently, I impale the sharp tip into his body, watching as his soul curls into itself and dissolves. He disappears, and I feel no remorse. Only peace.

When all is said and done, I return to my zmeu form, and fall to the ground on shaky knees. Tytus is there in a second, his gray eyes filled with worry even as he clothes us both with a simple rune.

"What happened?"

I shake my head, gripping his shoulder so I can stand. "Nothing. Changed one too many times."

"Is that all?"

I nod, trying and failing to hold his gaze. Part of me wants to tell him, if only to hear there is a miracle cure. But I know such is not possible.

Tytus glances around, his eyes falling on Hades. "Where is your immortal girl? We should get out while we can."

I frown at the urgency in his voice.

Something Hades is quick to agree with, it seems.

"Your brother is right," he says. "This was only a skirmish. Now that one Titan has escaped Tartarus, more will follow. I have to go to Olympus to warn my brothers and issue an all-out warning to every pantheon out there."

"Why every?"

Hades scowls. "Because Tartarus doesn't just hold our Titans. It holds every Evil from the beginning of time. And the sooner everyone is aware of it, the sooner we can all work towards a joint solution."

I snort. "You think that's possible?"

"Only time will tell. It is good us gods measure it differently." He jerks his head. "Go, before you have to stick around for good."

I turn to Tytus and steer us a safe distance from the mess. "Thank you for coming, brother."

"Anytime."

"I mean it." I meet his gaze. "This means a lot, given our history."

He nods, understanding more than I am saying. *And now for the hard part.*

"I need you to do me one more favor."

"Anything," Tytus says.

"Fly away from here, outside of the Underworld. Get Ileana and Făt, tell them to wait for us there, too."

He frowns. "Why?"

"So they can get Constanza." *And stop her from coming after me,* I think, but don't say out loud.

"I can do that, though I am not looking forward to it." Tytus grips my shoulder tightly. "And there's nothing else you wish to tell me, frate?"

"Nothing."

He nods. "I will do this, for you. And I'll be waiting on the other side."

With another squeeze, he backs away, and flies off. Leaving me to face one more person... And tell one last lie.

Constanza

I don't understand why it's such a rush to leave the Underworld. Declan practically drags me out, saying Tytus burned a path to the exit or something, something only he can see. So I follow him, perched on a unicorn, while Declan rides another.

"We didn't even get to say goodbye to the heroes!" I shout over the wind.

"Another time, darling," Declan says. "Believe me, they know you are grateful for their help."

I would hope so... I draw solace knowing Persephone will say all the thanks I cannot, and ensure they are returned to the Elysian Fields and their eternity of partying before long.

Once we get to the edge of the path Tytus burned for us, we dismount and go on foot, Declan lags behind me. He stops right before we exit the shadows and tugs on my hand, pulling me into a breathless kiss.

His mouth moves against mine, cajoling, taking everything... And then releasing me just as fast. He leans his forehead against mine for a brief moment.

I stare at him, but the darkness in the tunnel hides his expressive eyes. Instead, all I see is the hint of a smile.

"Go," he finally says. "I'll be right behind you."

I hesitate, but from a distance hear Mom and Dad calling for me. How did they even know we were coming out?

"Constanza!"

The quiver in Mom's voice is what decides me, spurring me out of Declan's arms, and across the barrier. "Mama!"

Sure enough, Mom and Dad are a few meters away, waiting for me. They open their arms to me and I rush into them, crying and laughing all at once.

After they squeeze me to their heart's content, I turn around, ready to introduce Declan.

"I need to.... Wait. Where's Declan?"

He's no longer behind. Nor in the shadows at the entrance of the cave. He's... gone.

Chapter 21

Absență
"*Absence* is to love what wind is to fire; it extinguishes the small, it inflames the great."
-Roger de Rabutin, Comte de Bussy-

Constanza

"Where is he?"

"Where is who?" Mom asks.

I turn to her, frowning. "Declan! He was right behind me."

She shrugs. "Not important, dear." An arm around my shoulder. "Let us take you home. The zmeu did what he promised, which is to bring you to us, safe and sound."

I pull away from her. "And in exchange you were to give him his freedom. Or did you forget that?"

She shares a glance with Dad, who's been way too quiet. I don't like this. Any of it. My parents love me, but I've seen their dealings with other immortals and shifters. They're not *always* just.

"We did, da," he finally says. "But seeing as Declan is not here for us to hold our word, that is a moot point now."

"Convenient, no?"

We all turn to the side as a dark-haired man emerges from the shadows. His gray eyes glint with something fierce, as if he's holding back from spewing everything he wants to. But what could that be?

Either way, there's only one guy who would be out here, facing off against my parents.

"Tytus, is it?"

He tilts his head towards me. "Have we met?"

"No. But I know Declan."

"Ah." He smiles, recognition appearing in his eyes. "Constanza, I take it?"

I nod, well aware how weird this entire situation is. Wondering what it is Declan has told him about me. And, more to the point, what Tytus knows that I don't about his brother's sudden disappearance.

As if reading the questions on my face, Tytus says, "Declan asked me to wait for him here, after the fight with Cronus."

"Cronus!?" Mom's voice rises to a pitch I'm unused to.

I cringe. "Yeah, you guys missed a lot."

Without giving them a chance to ask questions, I explain to them as briefly as I can what happened, and Declan's part in it. Namely, how he helped save me. When I'm done, I gaze at them.

I don't know what I expected. That they endorse my love? Send me back down to the Underworld? Offer to go for me, and bring Declan back? Whatever it was, it's not what I receive.

Which is Dad shrugging. "That's all well and done. What's the point?"

"What do you mean the *point*, Daddy?"

"Declan did his job. He got you back, safe. As far as I'm concerned, that takes care of it."

"It does NOT!"

"Honey, I realize you want to save everyone and their grandma," Mom says, talking to me as if I'm still a child. "But this is a bad man. There is a reason we imprisoned him."

"Yeah, he told me everything."

"Did he?" Dad asks. "Even the fact he killed his last lover?"

I roll my eyes. "Yes. everything. And I love him anyway."

That gets Daddy riled up. "You *what*!"

"I. Love. Him."

He arches an eyebrow towards Mom, at a loss on what to say.

Tytus, silent until then, chooses that moment to address my parents. "Well, I suppose that settles it. Or, rather, is a suitable point to intervene. Before you consider anything else, you should be aware the legătură bond has taken hold with them. My brother may be too stubborn to admit it, but I see it. As do you, Ileana."

"My daughter is not mated to a zmeu!" Dad scowls.

Tytus shrugs. "Deal with it."

"She is not!"

Mom looks just as pissed. They don't

even allow me to argue my case. Instead, they create a portal and drag me through it, closing it before Tytus can follow.

Declan

I skulked away as soon as Constanza was out. What would be the point in lingering behind, only for her to realize what happened?

Yet there seems to be another I've angered, who is not too keen to give up.

DECLAN! Tytus roars in my head.

For a second, I consider not responding. Would it achieve anything, other than more guilt on both sides? Probably not. Still, I give in, if only because the tunnel is long, and my heart is too heavy to be dealt with alone.

Da, frate.

What the hell just happened?

Rather than answer, I try to distract him, knowing full well it's futile. *Thank you for being there when Constanza got out. I hope the reunion with her parents wasn't too harsh.*

It went as expected, he says, *though you would have enjoyed Făt's expression when she admitted she loves you.*

I stop dead in my tracks, my heartbeat thudding painfully in my chest. *She said that?*

Joy, elation, pain, pure agony. Can a single heart hold all that in the span of seconds? Apparently, it can. I turn to the closest cavern wall and punch it, refusing to hear Tytus out until my knuckles are bleeding and I have fallen back on the floor, panting.

I've done this to myself, created this situation I cannot escape from. Again. Only this time, it crushes me even more, because there is something good waiting for me, out there. Someone that is now forever unattainable.

I cannot leave the Underworld, I finally admit.

Is this Hades' doing?

No. it is mine.

How so?

I was injured fighting Charon in the Underworld.

And? You are a living soul.

Da... Do you not remember? I can almost hear the wheels turning in his head, and the pieces falling together. *He impaled me with his staff, probably blessed by Cronus, and Charon drew blood. It's a thing of the Underworld, frate, you read more upon it than I. Point is, I am linked to it, now, and I cannot break that.*

Surely Hades can undo that link, after everything you helped him with?

One would think so. But no.

In truth, I hadn't even asked Hades. There was no time, and I was not keen to have the last of my hopes dashed so swiftly.

I don't believe that. Are you trying to stay there?

Why would I choose that over freedom?

There's less anger, and more exasperation in my brother's tone now. *Because you feel guilty over everything else you did. Maybe even see yourself deserving of this.*

That is not the case.

Though... certainty eludes me. Perhaps, in a way, it is what I am doing. Rather than seek escape, I perceive this as my punishment, and knowing I do not deserve to get away, after all I did.

I caused enough harm, Tytus. Surely even you can attest to that.

I can. And that doesn't stop me from wanting to save you.

Save your breath. Return to your witch, and be happy.

And who will you return to?

No one. As I deserve.

I cut the last of the communication off, refusing to continue further. No point in punishing myself even more, is there?

My footsteps are heavy as I make my way back to the palace. I don't have to walk for long, before running into Hades himself.

"Lost your shine, zmeu?"

I glance at my body, noticing I'm resembling more and more the other souls. Wonderful.

"What's it to you?"

He sighs and moves closer. "I owe you a debt for helping out."

I don't want to hear his thanks, so I try to move past him. "Good to know."

"You will not ask me to undo this?"

I stare at him for a beat, then shrug. "Constanza deserves better than I. She has an entire lifetime ahead of her."

And she does. My walk here, all by my lonesome, has convinced me of that. An *eternity* she should spend with someone worthy.

Not someone like me. A villain in disguise, a fallen hero, a lost soul.

Hades narrows his eyes on me. "She loves

you. Do you not realize that?"

"She will love another."

I walk away, ignoring the pain in my gut as I say that.

૮

Lethe is alluring. I almost give in, wanting to forget her. How can I? She is in every breath, every waking and sleeping moment.

Like fire needs oxygen, I need her to breathe. To grow. To live. Without her, my heart has closed in on itself, and nothing has any meaning.

Not the beautiful paths.

Not the various souls.

Not the peace that was so hard earned.

Not even Heracles' attempts at drawing me into their parties.

All I feel is desolation, and pain... And da, a bit of anger mixed in there. For not waking up earlier. For not seeing what I wanted earlier. For letting so much time go by...

I've been here three nights, but have not slept in any. Hades says souls don't need sleep, and perhaps they don't. Either way, I had hoped to see Constanza in those dreams, yet also feared I would. What I would say, what I would explain, how I would say goodbye.

I ran away because I was a coward, knowing she'd be happy with her parents. I wish to hell I had given her a better last kiss, something she could truly remember me by. I already fall asleep with her taste on my lips, her moans in my ears, her whispers in the wind.

It's not sane. None of it is. But if insanity will keep her memory alive with me, does anything else truly matter?

Out of my periphery, I notice the waters of the river change, and a face shows within. Or perhaps it's in my head, another vision that hits me.

Either way, instead of the limpid silvery waters, I see my brother.

"Frate.... You survived."

I scowl at him. "You could call it that, I suppose."

He shakes his head. "Always so stubborn...." He peers closer at me. "You don't look well, or rested."

Is he seriously trying to rub it in right now?

As if to spite me some more, he adds, "Has love truly saved you?"

"I guess we'll never know!" I snarl, splashing at the water, then backing away.

I don't want to forget. Or cease to exist. I just want...

Sighing, I lie onto the grass and stare at the inky sky.

Constanza

After the portal, I've returned to my parents' house. Nestled between mountains as old as time, under a blood-red sunset, lost amid fog... Our home was never a mansion. Shaped on the outside like a regular building with white walls and windows, it has a slanted tip, as if the architect had decided to throw some chaos into an otherwise symmetrical creation. Under the nascent night sky, it sparkles like a thousand diamonds. And with the sun bathing it, it appears bathed in hopes, dreams and warmth.

And I have no intention of entering it.

I yank myself out of Mom's hold and stand, practically stomping my foot.

"I'm not going in there."

Dad folds his arms and arches an eyebrow.

"Really? And what do you plan to do instead?"

"Go back to Declan!"

"Over my dead body," he hisses.

Tears sting my eyes. "You don't know me, then, if you think I'm letting him rot in the Underworld."

"Oh, but I do." He comes closer, cupping my cheek. "And it's because of that misplaced faith that you try to save him. But the zmeu made his grave. This is not our concern."

He turns away as if the issue is dealt with, and the first tear escapes me. "Will you really not even hear me out?"

"There is nothing to be heard!" he roars, turning back to face me, lightning blazing in his gaze. "I will not have my only daughter's mate be a zmeu."

I turn to my mother. "Mom? Please?"

Her expression is as blank as the sky. "Beloved, it shall pass. It is only an infatuation."

I clench my fists. "No, it's not. And you two don't get it!" Sobs choke me, but I clear my throat and force myself to continue, drawing strength from Declan, from everything he could do. I need to stand by him, now. I won't let him down.

"For the longest time," I tell my parents, "I was such a mess growing up with both of you, seeing your love. I feared I could never have anything like it. What were the chances that I would find my perfect pair, as you did?"

"Honey…" Mom tries to step my way, then stops.

"But I did." I sniffle, wiping my nose. "Declan is *it*. And I understand that you hate him, and you think he's a terrible choice and that he manipulated me, but he didn't. He's what I want."

Dad snorts. "What, a murderer and pillager? That is what you desire in a mate?"

It's my turn to get angry. "No. I want a man who'll stand by my side, even when it's hard. Even when all he wants is to be selfish, but he's self*less* instead. I never looked for someone with a dark side, but it is what I found. And I am thankful for Declan, thankful for the chance I'm given." I blow out a breath, steeling my spine. "And I will not give it up. If you two won't help me return to him, then…."

"Then what?" Dad asks.

I lift my chin. "Then you'll break my heart. But I still won't let him go."

I take a step backwards, ready to create a portal of my own. Before my parents can say anything, though, a dark shape looms above, then lands.

Tytus.

I must be gaping, as he shifts from zmeu form to human and grins at me. "Family reunion not going the way you hoped?"

I scowl in my parents' direction. "Not in the least."

"I will not allow it," Dad says for the upteenth time.

I look at Mom. "And you?"

She shakes her head, tears in her eyes. "I am sorry."

"As am I." Deep down, my heart breaks. But knowing I have eternity ahead to fix this, to get them to see how good Declan can be... I hope it'll turn out alright. Maybe. And if it doesn't, well, at least I found what I wanted all along. Even if I didn't realize the price to pay would be so steep.

I nod, and wave sadly to them. "Take care of yourselves... Until our paths cross again."

To me, Tytus says, "Ready to get Declan?"

"Yes." My eyes are still on my parents. "One day, you'll see I was right. That he's the one for me."

Then I turn my back on them and hop into the portal, ready for Declan. For having my heart mended. For a new future... even if it's not fully the one I'd wished for.

Chapter 22

Consecințe
"Sooner or later everyone sits down to a banquet of
consequences."
~Robert Louis Stevenson~

Declan

I'm back by Lethe again, unsure why I even bother. To torture myself? To expect a link to the Living that will never come?

It's not like they'll answer. Neither will my zmeu, so buried inside myself now, as if he's not even there. Nothing is left of the old me. With each passing hour, day, whatever, I see the glow of my skin pale, and feel myself waning away.

My gaze lingers on Lethe.

Why should I stop myself from drinking its waters? Erase all knowledge of my past existence, be reborn anew. Who's to say I cannot have a better life in a few years? Even if it might be a mortal one?

Lies. I do not believe the cloth of a man can be changed, not when it is so ingrained in me. No matter how I wish to drink from the alluring river, it will be the coward's way out. And I cannot stand losing all memories of Constanza, of what we had together. Not when they're all I have left, all I can cling to.

"You look like hell when you're moping."

I glance up, notice it's Persephone, and return my attention to Lethe. "Sure."

How can she appear so damn radiant, when I'm feeling so shitty?

Because *she* still has her mate. Right.

She sits on the grass, uninvited. "I never took you for someone to give up."

"I'm not."

"Aren't you?"

I glare at her, but it doesn't seem to faze

her. "There is no way out."

"Did you even search for one?"

"I don't have to." I pick at the grass stubs, tearing them and wishing I could do the same to this pain inside my chest.

"Because you punish yourself."

"I deserve punishment, don't I? You said it yourself."

She leans back on her elbows, giving me a coy look. "Maybe I've been convinced of the contrary."

I snort. Ignore her. She still doesn't leave.

After a moment, she straightens up. "Have you ever thought, despite all the evil you did, that perhaps you have already atoned?"

I give her a blank stare. "There is no such thing as atonement for someone like me."

She stares at me, her eyes dancing with mirth. Then she glances over my head, and another voice says, "I beg to differ."

I stand, whirling, only to face my brother. In flesh and blood. My jaw must hit somewhere on the ground, as he chuckles and pulls me into his arms, hugging me fiercely.

Before I can return it, he lets me go. "Well. I dare say you seem better in person than via the damn river."

He grabs at his neck, then tosses something to Persephone. "Thanks for that."

"My pleasure," she says, and it sounds like she's smiling.

I'm not turning to check what the object was, though, too astounded to find my brother here. In the Underworld.

"What are you doing?"

"Come to rescue you, of course."

"I cannot be rescued. Didn't I tell you that?"

He rolls his eyes. "Multiple times, as a matter of fact."

"But... I don't...."

He places his hands on my shoulders, looks me in the eye. "We're brothers, Dec. Through thick and thin. And we've had our drama, but through better or worse, I never forgot you. I know you never forgot me, that you spent millennia cursing me."

A deep breath, a squeeze. "There's a lot of shit between us. None that can be handled in one conversation, or twenty. But are you willing to try, at least? To not attempt to kill me?"

I shake my head. See his expression drop.

Try to fix what I accidentally caused.

"I don't… Da, of course I'm willing to try. But I *cannot*, don't you understand? I'm never getting out of here!"

He laughs, and lets go of my shoulders, patting me on the back. "That is where you're mistaken, frate. I have someone working on your release as we speak."

"Someone working on my…." I whirl on Persephone, my gaze latched onto what's in her hand.

She grins, opening it and showing the opal necklace Constanza'd had all along. Which had left the Underworld *with* Constanza.

My gaze lands on Tytus, and his smug grin.

And then I'm running, heartbeat pounding out of my chest, hoping… not daring to… yet still…

Constanza

"You have to let him leave, Hades."

I'm in the gigantic audience room, with Hades facing me. He's being insufferable, making this way more painful than it should be. And I want to smack him, but I doubt that'll earn me any brownie points.

"Please."

He takes a seat in his throne made of bones. "Tell me why, and perhaps I'll consider it."

"You're really going to make me have an audience, like I'm some poor soul?"

"I cannot be seen to play favorites. Surely you understand."

It's only as he rests his chin on his palm that I see the amusement dancing in his eyes and decide to humor him.

"Fine. I don't want you to release him because he's the best guy ever, or the hottest, or the most insufferable. Although, granted, he is a few of those things. But Declan is so much *more* than that, Hades. He deserves a second chance. He's never had one, and between his brother and my parents, he's never even wanted one. With him, I learned to live. With me, he learned to trust. He's not perfect, and he's a mess, but… He's my mess." I don't realize I'm crying until snot is running down my face, so I use my sleeve to wipe it away. "And if you don't let him go and release this stupid hold the Underworld has on him, I will camp here forever and ever and make sure I drive you insane until you do."

Oops. Maybe I went a little too far. I don't like the silence at the end of my speech. Or the way Hades looks as if he's trying very hard not to laugh.

"*Now* do you understand why?"

"Oh, I do. In fact, I think what you said is so pure, it's worth it for Declan to hear it."

"So freaking *tell him*! And then let me take him home!"

He truly laughs then. "Why don't you explain it to him yourself?"

I turn and sure enough, Declan is there. Persephone smiles at me and joins her husband. I gulp, realizing he must've been there all along, a witness to everything I said. And he's panting like he's run out of breath, his form shimmering.

"You heard all that?"

A twinkle in his eyes, Declan nods. "Yeah."

"And?"

"What, and?"

I stomp my foot. "Don't you have something to tell me?"

He steps closer and cups my cheek. "You're

insufferable, princess. And I love the hell out of you. But you have to live... even if it's without me."

"What are you talking about?"

"I appreciate what you did. All of you. But we both know there's no undoing this."

Persephone clears her throat. "Actually, there is."

Declan freezes, glancing at her. "What?"

"It is true that you bled in the Underworld, but you have also bled *for* the Underworld."

Hades says, "You have taken, and given back. My duty, above all, is to protect the difference. It's quite possible you'll feel the urge to visit me once or twice a year." A glance to Persephone, a laugh. "The tie cannot be severed completely. But, for all intents and purposes, my queen is correct. As, for that matter, is your mate."

"You mean I can... leave?"

"Yes."

I force Declan to look at me. "See?"

"But... You'd be better without me, Constanza. Surely you see that?"

"No. I won't. Or maybe I would. The truth is, you may not be what I wanted, or what I expected. But I need you in my life, Declan. Same as you need me, flaws and all. And that's all that matters." I hold his hand in mine, squeezing it tight, and turn to Hades. "Now, should we involve Zeus? Or can I take Declan out of here, already?"

Hades laughs, deep and booming. "I'm sure my brother would love that. But, no. Your lover only had to ask."

"You mean this entire time..."

Gah! Gods are so damn fickle.

Declan squeezes my hand then. "Will you allow me to return to the land of the Living?"

Hades nods.

Declan turns to me. "And will you never leave my side?"

"I swear it."

Chapter 23

Sensibilitate
"There is no charm equal to <u>tenderness</u> of heart."
-Jane Austen-

Constanza

A kiss on my nape wakes me up in the best way possible. Especially when it trails down my naked back, then those lips nibble on my bottom, before repeating the path upwards.

"Wake up, princess," Declan whispers in my ear.

I stretch against him, smiling when I feel just how awake he is, and how *happy* he is that I'm joining him.

"I could get used to this."

I roll onto my back, even as Declan hovers over me. He pulls out a rose from somewhere and trails the soft petals down my chest, to my hip, then my thigh, and up again. He seems mesmerized by the path of the petals, and I grin widely.

"How about we enjoy a lazy morning?" I hitch a leg over his hips, trying to pull him closer.

He lets me... at first. We even get *really* hot and bothered, before he pulls away from me and jumps out of bed. I groan out loud, knowing what's coming next.

"After practice, and not a moment before, princess!"

By practice, he means what he and Tytus do at dawn. Which is, beat the shit out of each other in their own version of therapy. Then they go hunting–I cannot fathom how the farmers in this area don't see so many sheep missing.

As Declan saunters away from me, I stretch against his soft sheets again, then slowly get up and pull on a robe. Every morning, I go by the stables and join Fiona, the witch mated to Tytus, and we watch both brothers work out their issues. We're mainly there as mediators– but also because there's something super hot about sweaty men and swords.

A shared castle has its benefits, I must admit. None so much as seeing the two brothers tackle each other. I must say, it feels nice not to be alone.

I haven't heard from my parents and it's been a month since the Underworld debacle. But they're immortals, and I still hope they'll come around. In the meantime, I have my new life, and it's as fulfilling as I had hoped.

Fiona and I have become quick friends. And when the sun rises, we grab our cups of tea and head outside. In the fresh morning, we watch our mates spar, knowing they're safe. That we're all safe.

Declan

My brother lets me win. Again. I hold a hand out and help him to his feet, scowling the entire time. "Feeling guilty much?"

Tytus shrugs. "You won fair and square."

"Liar."

Amusement dances in his eyes. "You never used to be so humble, Declan. A while ago, you'd have boasted far and wide about beating me."

"Times change."

"Right." He laughs outright. "Or perhaps you want to be on your best behavior around your mate."

That earns him a punch in the gut and he coughs, holding up his hand. "Alright, alright. I have an idea. Let's take to the skies, like old times?"

I glance over at Constanza, perched on a boulder and chatting with Fiona. When she feels me staring, she glances at me and blows me a kiss. That odd sensation spreads in my chest again, reminding me I'm loved–cared for. I still can't get used to it. To being at peace.

One of these days, I'll have to. In the meantime, I'm thoroughly enjoying the learning curve.

I return her kiss and shout, "Be back soon, princess."

Within moments, we've both shed our human forms and taken to the skies, in full zmeu regalia. As we fly up above, I hear the girls shouting below.

"Bring dinner!"

They really do hate us conjuring and "stealing" from the families around here, I've learned.

Tytus and I share a look, and I feel that tingle of competition race up my spine.

Oh yeah. The hunt is on.

Epilogue

Făt Frumos returned home after one last trip. Before he'd even gotten to his fairytale-shaped house, the sobs within already tore at his heart. He hesitated on the threshold for long moments, then finally pushed the door open and walked in.

Ileana was by the fireplace, a white blanket wrapped around her. The flames illuminated her tear-streaked face. She didn't turn when he entered, instead only sniffled and curled up further within herself.

Făt dropped his sword by the entrance and made his way to her, kneeling on the icy stone and pulling her in his arms. She didn't resist, only buried herself in his embrace and allowed the sobs to pour out once more. His own eyes filled with tears, and he silently let them roll down one, by one, by one.

Later, much, much later, Ileana pulled away enough to look at him. The sight of his tears caused her gaze to widen, and she reached out a trembling hand to wipe them away.

"It hurt me as much as it did you." Rarely did Făt show emotion. Tonight, his voice was hoarse from it.

Ileana's expression was forlorn. "I know. I can only hope our sacrifice is worth it. That it will keep Constanza safe, even if it's with that zmeu."

"He will protect her," Făt muttered. "Or die trying. That much is clear."

Ileana nodded, then her gaze shifted to the flames. "Do you think she will ever forgive us, for appearing so... cold? So harsh, when faced with her happiness?"

Făt tightened his hold on her, pulling her closer to him. "Da, draga mea. I believe she will, because her heart is as big as her mother's."

A faint smile tugged at Ileana's lips, soon

vanishing. "Did you see her from afar, on your way to the Underworld?"

"I did," Făt admitted. "Ensured I stayed out of sight, too. But she is happy, draga mea. Rest assured."

"Good." A sigh. "Are we ready, then, for the next step?"

Făt stood and held out a hand to her. "Whenever you are."

Ileana looked at him, the man of her dreams, the consort of her heart, her other half. They had been through so much together, and their fight was not yet done. What had been unleashed, the borders that had been stretched, was only the beginning. And they both realized it.

Ileana took his hand and stood, drawing strength from Făt's determination, and her own unconditional love for her daughter. She reached towards the flames, pulling out a double-edged sword, and turned to her consort.

"Let us go, then."

The vast hall stretched before them like a mausoleum. Thick Greek columns on each side supported a domed archway. Gold littered the floor, moving and slithering through the white marble as if it was alive. The minute Făt and Ileana stormed through the golden doors, a deadly silence fell upon the gathered audience.

Their swords glinted harshly under the bright light, menacing. Before they could advance further, a bolt of lightning shot in front of them, stopping them in their tracks.

"What is the meaning of this?"

A towering giant had spoken, and he moved out of the shadows of a column to block their path. Shaggy blond hair fell to his shoulders, and his blue eyes sparkled with lightning. He was bare-chested, in jeans, and his only other adornment was a golden bracelet on his left bicep.

"I asked a question, and I demand an answer." His voice was ominous with accusation and withheld contempt.

Ileana shared a glance with her consort, then scanned the audience, looking for one face in particular. When she did not find him, disappointment coursed through her. *No matter. We can do this on our own.*

But, it seemed they did not have to. The doors opened once more behind them, and she recognized the energy of the newcomer.

The giant's eyes moved to him, narrowing. "Hades? I take it you cleaned up your Underworld without my help, then?"

A pause. Then Hades stepped to Ileana's side, glaring at the giant. "Not quite, brother. In fact, that is why we are here."

Făt, silent until then, dropped to one knee. Ileana joined him, also kneeling. Only when the tall giant gestured for them to say their piece, did she speak again.

"Mighty Zeus, we come in peace, and warning. Tartarus has been breached, and all the pantheons are in danger."

There was dead silence in the audience hall. Then a pandemonium of chaos.

Ileana bowed her head and waited for her chance to speak. To rally. To find a common ground among these gods... if they wished to survive.

ରଃ ୫୦ ୫

Curious about Hades, Zeus and the other gods alluded to?

IMMORTAL ROGUES will be the spinoff to conclude it all, coming 2021!

Different pantheons. A multitude of gods. Plenty of secrets, romance and steam... And Evil lying in wait, prepared to destroy it all. Can the world be saved?

Sign up for my newsletter to keep up to date, and follow me on BookBub and Amazon for new releases alerts!

Love mythology, romance and suspense?

This summer, fall head-first into Katya's story...
She thought the pain was normal...

My name is Katya... and I'm not crazy. Sounds kind of funny that I start the story that way, right? Trust me, it's anything but. It all started when I got these bloody migraines and began hearing voices. I was pretty sure I'd lost it.

And then the voices turn out to be two hot-as-hell guardians, here to guide me on my quest to purge the world of evil. Because apparently, that's what I was born to do. The kicker? *They're not human.*

They've stood guard since she was small, and have come to teach her otherwise...

I guess it's just as well I'm willing to play into their delusional game. Until, of course, I find out it's no delusion at all. The monsters do exist, and I'm one of them. So is my mate. And my two new buddies? Well, that's debatable.

Soon everything spins out of control and the phoenix in me rises to the surface, unbidden, unchallenged... And un-allied with either Light or Darkness.

Now the world depends on her choice... And what if she chooses wrong?

Like I said, I'm not crazy. But read if you dare, and you can judge for yourself.

Grab your exclusive sneak peek below, and pre-order your copy!

Plus, curious about the Moonlight Rogues series? It's now available exclusively on Kindle Unlimited for a limited time!
Start reading for free today!

The light shines briefly in my left eye and sure enough, the pain of a thousand knives bursts through my cranium.

"Effing hell, doc!" I yank my head away, waving uselessly to push him off, and he takes a step back. I don't even have to look to feel his frown and disapproval at my tone.

Well, too damn bad.

"I'm not sure what's going on, Katya, but I'll give you a prescription for a migraine relief pill."

"Great."

He throws me a look at the less than enthused tone of my voice. "We've been over this before. Unless you let me do some proper tests, there's no way to see what's causing these headaches of yours."

"They're not headaches," I mutter, rubbing my temples. Some of the ache dulls, but not fully. All it would take is me looking at the neon lights, and it would be back, freaking driving me insane like it has been for the last two weeks.

"No, you say they're migraines, but yet you don't have all the symptoms."

I try to glare at him, but a hiss of pain escapes me and I focus my sight on the dotted, ugly floor of the stupid walk-in clinic. "Fine. Just give me the damn prescription. It's all you do, anyway."

His voice softens. "I could do more, if you'd let me." His pen scratches the paper as it scribbles something, and the tiny noise makes me wince again. "Honestly, Katya, don't you want to get better?"

"Of course I do," I say, and hop off the stool. Nearly ripping the prescription out of his hand, I walk out.

Rude? Bite me. Try being polite – let alone conscious – when every step brings you closer to the ground and oblivion. My head feels like it's constantly bouncing around between pain and darkness, or should I say between a hammer and a thunderstorm?

The way to the pharmacy is familiar – I'm in here almost every month, usually when the pain gets too much. And every time it's the same spiel, ending with *get some tests*. As if I want to be someone's guinea pig… No, thanks.

I trudge around to the pharmacy, slap the prescription on the counter and hope to hell they haven't cut off my insurance from my workplace.

Ex-workplace, I guess.

Ex-boyfriend, too, now that I think about it. But then, finding your guy banging the CEO's secretary, then taking a snapshot to show said CEO, tends to do that. And gets you fired in the process, apparently.

Don't judge. You would have done the same.

"Here you go."

The pretty blonde behind the counter looks like a fashion model, way more dressed up than she should be, with a perfect face of makeup. I scowl my thanks and pick up the package, thanking my stars. And nope, they're not lucky.

If they were, I'd have a job, a boyfriend and a damn good action flick waiting for me at home. If they were, I'd have Perky Pharma's platinum no-hair-out-of-place look and perfectly groomed appearance.

Instead, all I have is an empty apartment, a throbbing migraine for weeks, and my usual red curls and freckly face. Even my eyes are a washed-out sea green.

Parents, you ask? Foster care, I answer.

I'm all alone in my Chinatown dingy place. But I prefer it that way. Or maybe if I keep saying it, I'll finally believe it.

Another step, and I nearly topple over. I lean against the wall, rip open the paper bag, thenpill bottle, and take two. Or, I'm about to.

"Don't!"

I jump, dropping the pills to the ground. Shit. I look around to yell at whoever startled me, but there's no one.

"Great. Now I'm hallucinating, too."

Much as it's tempting to pick up the pills from the ground, I can't lower myself to those standards. Who knows what's been on that floor? Instead, I reach inside the plastic bottle to take two others.

"Don't!"

"What the effing shit!?" I look around frantically, this time clutching the pills in my hand so I don't drop them.

"You're not hallucinating."

It's like the voice is coming out of thin air. Nope, there's no "like" about it – it *is* coming from nowhere. I gulp, pretty sure my eyes are as round as saucers about now.

"Don't take the pills."

Ah, hell no! Now I'm definitely taking them. My living situation is bad enough. I don't need to add mentally insane to the list of obstacles I have to overcome. Without hesitation, I pop two of the pills in my mouth and swallow them dry.

"What? Nothing to say?" I wait a second, then mutter, "Yeah, didn't think so." I'm well aware of how crazy this sounds, talking to myself outside a walk-in clinic. But if you think I'm delusional, you've read nothing yet.

When I say I live in a dingy place in Chinatown, I'm not joking. The apartment used to be flea and cockroach-infested, but I couldn't afford to be picky. Without a job, or much money in my bank account, not to mention a pissed-off ex-boyfriend, let's just say options were minimal. It's been three months since then, and the situation hasn't much improved.

My own stupidity is to blame for moving in with Bryan in the first place. But that's what happens when you're deprived of love in your formative years. You think you can survive without it, that you're tough as nails, then in swoops a Prince Charming that makes you lose your head.

Rather unfortunately for me, it ended in heartache. Hence the rush to search for a place, not finding anything within my means, and ending up in this bachelor studio atop a Chinese take-out place. The owner was kind enough to rent it to me on a probationary basis, at least for the first few months.

After my trip at the walk-in clinic, I stop by an ATM nearby to check my depressing account balance – nearing less than two hundred dollars, and still no job. *Guess that means it's more mac and cheese for me tonight.*

Sighing, I drag my feet to the back of the brick building, climb up the fire escape, and enter my tiny place. The inside is cozy enough – I bought everything second-hand. A green couch that's seen better days, a wall lamp, and an old-school TV. I'd never been the crazy type about electronics, even my phone was an old flip-style one.

Something Bryan always found endearing.

I wince at myself, resisting the urge to smack the back of my head. Broken-hearted doesn't suit me, and I'm not about to become the type. Even if I should have seen the signs in his deciding to work later hours, become less interested in sex, and slowly distancing himself from me. But, I guess I was too blinded by the life we had together, the illusion of a happy ending.

Resolutely, I take off my shoes and head to the corner where a stove sits, next to a fridge vibrating hard enough to make the floor shake. I take out the pack of mac and cheese from the cupboard, check inside to make sure there aren't any uninvited guests, then pour the remainder of the contents into a pot to boil.

While my breakfast, lunch and dinner cooks, I start flipping through newspapers in search of various job ads. It's hard enough to find a job in the city without a degree. Now that I've been blacklisted by a powerful CEO, it's quasi-impossible. I guess said-CEO didn't much like being made a fool of, and retaliated on the person who brought the fact to light.

Luckily, I don't give up easily.

To my right, bubbling catches my attention, informing me that my food is done. After pouring myself a bowl, I head to the couch and start munching on it. I'm hungry enough that it tastes like the best steak, and I gulp the whole thing down in seconds.

I have one more box in the cupboard, but it's supposed to last me until the end of the weekend. No way I can dig in now, no matter how bad my hunger is. Instead, I wash the bowl and place it back in the cupboard. If nothing else, I keep this place super tidy.

Then I drag myself back to the couch and drink about a gallon of water, in an effort to stop my stomach from growling. It doesn't work. My insides tighten, demanding food, demanding something I can't give them.

I'd been living the good life with Bryan, it's true. Since the moment we ran into each other at work, and he took too much interest in me, pursuing me relentlessly... I should've known he was a douchebag. But *should've* didn't stop me from making a stupid mistake.

My eyes shut, but tears still peek past. The hunger, the loneliness consumes me. I don't know who I pissed off in another life to be dealt this hand, but it sucks.

Burying my face in my elbow, I let it all out – the heartache, the helplessness, the pain. The pills seem to be finally working, because my head isn't throbbing as bad anymore. And eventually, my sobs lessen, and all that's left is anger.

Anger at this life, anger at myself for being so weak, for putting myself in this situation. *I'll get myself out of it and have the last laugh…* And then I fall asleep. If nothing else, I won't be lonely anymore for the next few hours.

The dream starts out like most times. I'm walking in a forest, inhaling fresh air the likes I never have. Butterflies fill my stomach, because I'm nearing somewhere – a meeting place. My steps falter, and I wait. It won't be long now.

A growl makes me jump, and I turn around slowly. Fur white as snow, eyes a mix of violet and grey, the wolf lifts his muzzle in the air, sniffing. Then he picks up speed, running like the wind towards me. He hurtles into me, and we roll over on the ground, me laughing and burying my face in his fur.

"I missed you, Bebo." It's not his real name, but that doesn't make this encounter any less realistic.

I've known him since I was a child, stuck in foster homes and trying to make myself small and invisible, so as to avoid the adult's rage. Bebo came to me in a dream for the first time when I was nursing a broken arm from my then foster-father. He licked the wound and stayed with me the entire night. When I woke up, I didn't feel alone anymore, but like I'd found the deepest buried treasure.

Only, of course, now I had two of them, all to myself. After I give Bebo a rubdown, and he's panting on the grass next to me, I drop my forehead to his. "Where's your master, Bebo? I could do with some human company right now."

Bebo stares at me for a long, long moment, then licks the side of my face. His raspy tongue makes me laugh, and he gets up slowly. With one last look at me, he walks back into the forest. I know I won't see him again for a bit, as they never come together. Almost like they have a pact to share me.

With baited breath, I wait. Then the forest

parts again, and he walks in. I'm pretty sure unlike Bebo, he's a fragment of my imagination, but what do I know? Dark hair, high cheekbones, Roman nose and a mouth made to kiss. Dark grey eyes smile when he sees me. He wears these shirts that are partly ripped, only adding to his appeal when those muscles get on display.

Forcing myself not to ogle too hard, I will my head to snap into focus. This is Vas, my friend. Since I turned fourteen, he's been around, growing with me – except for that time he wouldn't come, years ago... Worst year of my life. But he's been back since, looking more ruggedly handsome than any friend has a right to.

And as I get to my feet, smiling my welcome, the thought hits me that maybe, just maybe, my breakup with Bryan wasn't all his fault. Maybe I had a part to play in it too, given every night for the past year I've been opening up to Vas, telling him things, trusting him...

I shake the thought off, and instead run to Vas, throwing myself in his arms. My head reaches the crook of his neck, and I bury my nose to inhale his earthy scent. Strong and firm, his arms come around me, holding me tight.

After a moment, we break apart. "How are you?" I ask.

He pushes a lock of my hair back, angling my face so he can see me better. "I should ask you that," he says darkly. "You don't look like you've eaten or slept much."

I shrug out of his embrace, and look anywhere but in his gorgeous grey eyes. "I have, though. Promise."

Vas doesn't seem convinced. He stalks closer, tilting his head to the side. "That guy Bryan treating you right? Because if he isn't–"

Oops. I'd omitted telling Vas anything about Bryan since we broke up, becoming an expert at deflecting his questions. But now I'm a second too late in schooling my expression. Vas pounces on it, his features darkening as he bites out, "What did he do?"

I shake my head. "Nothing! It's nothing. I promise. How about you tell me of your travels? You know I love a good story."

He won't be deterred, though, I can see it in the way he's slowly closing the distance between us. "Katya…"

The warning falls on deaf ears though, and I smile a big, pleading grin. "Please?"

Vas' eyes narrow on me, his expression so close to bursting past my walls, but I resist it. After another beat, he runs a hand through his hand in frustration and holds out his arm for me.

I gladly rush back in his embrace, relishing the way he pulls me into his side as we start aimlessly strolling through the forest. It never rains, here, so the night is as quiet as ever, the moon peeking from behind dark clouds. In a soft, even tone, Vas tells me about his recent trip into some nearby mountains where he ran into a family of wolves.

His stories bring a different world to life for me, as they always do. I lose myself in the words, in the picture he creates. Of the father wolf hunting for his family, the mother wolf protecting the cubs, and his own innocent stumbling around their blissfully unaware family. He tells me how he redirected humans away from the lair, in an effort to keep the wolves' privacy, basically a Batman for the defenseless.

I'm not sure if it's real or not – how much of all of this is, anyway? – but it takes my mind away from hunger, loneliness, and despair at the world crumbling around me.

And as we walk, with each passing step, Vas lulls me deeper and deeper into the forest, and the sense of safety under his arm increases. I become aware of things I didn't, before. The scent of pine and freshness clinging to his skin, the musk of man and earth, the heat emanating into my side and warming me all the way from tip to toes...

Something else, too. Something primal. The lean muscle keeping me safe as much as captive, the deep murmur of his voice that does weird things to my stomach, *new* things.

No, not entirely true. I could lie to myself, but none of this is new. On the contrary. Since I was a teenager and he first showed up – a hot, young boy roughly my own age – I've felt this pull. Yet he's been in my dreams only, and reality demanded I find boyfriends that actually exist.

Still...

It takes me a moment to realize we've stopped walking, and even longer to catch on that Vas is no longer speaking. I can sense the intensity of his gaze on me, the expectancy in the air. I look up, and my breath catches in my throat.

His eyes have gone dark, filled with something I can't understand. And the way he's staring at me, as if he wants to eat me whole... "Vas?" I whisper.

When he doesn't answer, I bite my lip, tugging on the bottom to chew on it. A bad habit when I'm nervous, something I do unconsciously. This time, I'm aware of it, if only because of the attention Vas redirects to said lip.

The sensation in my stomach intensifies, and still we're standing, just staring at each other. Something crazy whirls inside me, almost reckless. I want to tell him, then, about Bryan. That we're no longer together, that I'm unattached and free as a bird. Free for him.

Unfortunately, I don't get a chance to. Before I can even open my mouth, something pulls at me. A pain unlike any I've sensed before, ripping my insides. My mouth opens in a scream that never escapes. Vas tries to grab hold of me, his anger gone in the wake of his panic, but none of that helps, and I lose him.

I jolt awake, disoriented. The unfinished dream with Vas, the day's burdens, and then... There's a burning in my veins, like my blood is...boiling.

Moaning in pain, I fall off the couch, stumble about the apartment like a beast in dire need of being put out. My head is killing me – again. I thought these stupid pills were supposed to help, but the throbbing has only gotten worse.

I never should've fallen asleep, I think wildly, unable to narrow down a reason. It's like everything is more vivid, and my thoughts are little butterflies I can't hang on to.

Another wave of pain rolls through me, and this time I cry out loud. No one will help me – the owner doesn't live here, I'm on my own... The idea runs through my mind that I might actually die here, all alone.

I gasp at the fresh agony, and blink – only I'm not in my apartment anymore. Rather, I'm in a park nearby, about a good ten minute walk. How could I have gotten here, when just seconds ago I felt the cheap linoleum floor under my fingertips?

Glancing around, I desperately try to seek someone out to help – but there's no one. *Shit.*

I curl onto myself this time, desperately gripping the earth as another wave, stronger than all the others, runs through me. Only instead of abating like the rest, it grows heavier, and heavier… My vision narrows…

Then, the unthinkable happens and I burst into flames.

ભ ৪ত ৪৩

Release date: July 21, 2020
Pre-order now!

Author's Note & Acknowledgements

When I decided to not exit the universe of *Moonlight Rogues...* Who am I kidding, I didn't decide. My characters decided for me. So let me start again.

When Tytus and Declan became more than just side pieces in a wolf shifter series, and demanded their own stories, I knew I was in for a hellish few months. And I was right! As an only child, writing about sibling rivalries was hard, but I hope to have done them justice. If nothing else, the main thing I wanted to communicate was that no one is perfect, and having a sibling isn't always a walk in the park.

As always I want to thank my husband and family and puppies for their patience with me, the never-ending care and love. They fill my days with joy, and that allows me to fill these pages with my own brand of it :)

Huge thanks to the team behind this, from the beta to the edits to the proofreads, you guys are awesome! Extra thanks to Eldon at Luna Imprints for the awesome job he did on formatting!

I'm always amazed by the cover work, and credit for all that goes to Ammonia Book Covers! (Seriously, **all** the credit; I fail at simple color coordination!)

Last, to my readers… I know 2020 started off weird, and got even weirder. We live in a world right now that has us stuck within four walls, unable to do many of the things we rely on to fill our lives. I know I miss hiking, and seeing friends and family. My mom lives 5 hours away from me, and the distance has been even harder this year. But, in all darkness there is light, and we will get through this!!! In the meantime, I hope Declan's story allowed you to escape, even if only for a little while :)

About the Author

Alexa Whitewolf is a fiction writer, newspaper columnist of daily issues and author of the critically acclaimed *Moonlight Rogues* shifter series.

Alexa has been a lifelong writer and first began creating other worlds and characters at the ripe age of 12. Growing up in the Transylvania region surrounded by epic mountains and a never ending stream of legends and stories was bound to create an overactive imagination. This shines through Ms. Whitewolf's writing by creating worlds filled with unique folklore, life wisdom and plenty of furry creatures.

An avid traveler, Alexa writes under a penname and spends her days between an office job and writing in Canada's capital, when she's not flying somewhere with lush landscapes and plenty of hiking trails.

Her series focus on strong heroines, kind yet sexy men, fights of good and evil and the never-ending learning curve of humanity's strong – and weak – points. Romanian folklore is intertwined with her writing, more notably in her shifter romance series, the *Moonlight Rogues*. Her other series draw on world mythology, such as the Avalon myth and Arthurian legend (*The Avalon Chronicles*) and Ancient Egypt (*The Sage's Legacy*).

You can follow her blog at www.alexawhitewolf.com/blog or on social media. Her column in Observatorul also tackles various issues, including health, technology, and a writer's life.

If you want up to date releases, make sure you sign up for her newsletter. For new releases notifications, you can also follow her on Amazon and BookBub.

Igniting the Ice
Exclusive inside look in the series

Demoni Sancti series
Blazing Ashes (Standalone)
Fallen
Broken
Unshackled
Risen
Ascended
Exclusive inside look in the series

Standalone novels
Blood Ties, Love Binds
Unconditional Love

More novels **coming soon**